EXPOSED

Books by Susan Vaught

Stormwitch
Trigger
My Big Fat Manifesto
Exposed

The Oathbreaker saga
with J B Redmond

Part One: Assassin's Apprentice
Part Two: A Prince Among Killers

EXPOSED

Susan Vaught

BLOOMSBURY

NEW YORK BERLIN LONDON

For Victoria, who imagined this first

Copyright © 2008 by Susan Vaught
First published by Bloomsbury Books for Young Readers in 2008
Paperback edition published in March 2010

Published by Bloomsbury Books for Young Readers
175 Fifth Avenue, New York, New York 10010

The Library of Congress has cataloged the hardcover edition as follows:
Vaught, Susan.
Exposed / by Susan Vaught.—1st U.S. ed.
p.   cm.
Summary: Chan Shealy, a sixteen-year-old baton-twirler and straight-A student, becomes involved with an
Internet predator, despite strict parental rules and her own belief that she knows how to keep herself safe online.
ISBN-13: 978-1-59990-161-9 · ISBN-10: 1-59990-161-7 (hardcover)
[1. Online sexual predators—Fiction. 2. Sexual abuse victims—Fiction. 3. Sisters—Fiction.
4. Family life—Fiction. 5. Schools—Fiction.] I. Title.
PZ7.V4673Ex2008   [Fic]—dc22   2008007008

ISBN-13: 978-1-59990-460-3 (paperback)

Typeset by Westchester Book Composition
Printed in the U.S.A. by Worldcolor Fairfield, Pennsylvania
1 3 5 7 9 10 8 6 4 2

All papers used by Bloomsbury U.S.A. are natural, recyclable products
made from wood grown in well-managed forests. The manufacturing processes
conform to the environmental regulations of the country of origin.

EXPOSED

I'm nobody! Who are you?
Are you nobody, too?
Then there's a pair of us—don't tell!
They'd banish us, you know.

How dreary to be somebody!
How public, like a frog
To tell your name the livelong day
To an admiring bog!

Emily Dickinson

WISHING

If this were my dream, someone
Would come to me now,
While moonlight hangs
On my lashes
Like tears.

If this were my dream, darkness
Would drift from me now,
While I run fast
Listening to
Nothing.

If this were my dream, lonely
Would end for me now,
While I sit quiet
Face on knees
Eyes closed.

Chan Shealy

MONDAY, OCTOBER 13

"It's all a total fantasy," Devin Macy says as we shove our way down the crowded school hallway, making the long trek to the gym after last bell.

Devin's my best friend, and that's what she thinks about Internet relationships. She's not much on fantasy—or relationships. Not because she's not beautiful. She's completely gorgeous, like supermodel unbelievably pretty, but she's way Baptist. Which is fine. But kind of strict about stuff like fantasies and serious boyfriends.

I'm not sure I believe in real-life boyfriends, not since the whole Adam-P nightmare last year. Adam Pierpont's a quarterback, not a Baptist. He's not my friend at all anymore; he wouldn't know a fantasy if it busted him in the nose, and he might not even be human.

I squeeze my stack of books against my chest to keep them from flying everywhere and get close enough to Devin to say, "I don't want to get into anything real with a guy."

She manages to laugh at me even though fifteen people bang against us with backpacks or books in a span of less than five seconds.

"Not exactly," I add. "Well, sort of. Maybe?"

Devin laughs again and doesn't even bother looking at me as we leave one building and jam our way into the next one.

"Okay, not a flesh-and-blood boyfriend, but is it a huge crime to want a nice guy in my life without all the complications?" I elbow past a couple of sophomores near a water fountain. "Somebody I can be close to. Somebody I can talk to who'll say sweet stuff to me and be there when I need him and tell me everything about his life and his mind and his heart."

I can't help a big, huge sigh, but I so shouldn't be thinking about any of this right now. And I definitely shouldn't be thinking about it here at school in the hallway before practice, right beside Devin, who has asked me everything about why I'm thinking about finding a guy online—including whether or not I'm planning to sign up with an online dating service.

I'm not.

I promise.

Really!

Though that *would* be an idea. . . .

"I'd like it if you had a special guy again." Devin sounds a little faraway and distracted, even though she's having to talk really loud when our heads aren't right together. "It'd be nice to see you happy that way."

Her expression says the rest—that we both know I'm never going to find a boyfriend here at West Estoria High School. Even if I did find someone I liked, he wouldn't have anything to do with me. Not after the Adam-P mess.

Thinking about all of that makes us both go quiet as we walk.

Devin whips through guys like disposable tissues, so it's not like she doesn't want a guy, too, in spite of her religious beliefs. She's looking for that feeling just as hard as I am, only she doesn't have my problem or my reputation, so she has more options.

It's been a *year* for me.

It would be so nice to have somebody again. A guy I can ask anything, tell anything to, do anything with, and not have to worry, ever. Except about Mom (uptight, even though she's a Democrat). And Dad (not uptight, even when he should be). And my little sister, Lauren, bursting in on my private conversations because she can't sleep. (If Lauren were black, I'd think she was secretly Devin's sister and not mine. She's high maintenance and gorgeous, too, even though she's only eight.)

Thinking about trying online dating and maybe getting caught by somebody in my family makes my heart beat fast.

What will *he* be like when I find him?

Imagining *him* makes me tingly, and I never get to feel that way except when I'm planning how I'll talk to *him* or living in that place in my head where only *he'll* be able to take me.

So, some of it will be fantasy, yeah. But some of it will be real, too.

And we won't get serious for a long time, and it won't really be *serious* even if we do, at least not in my opinion.

I shake my head and try to focus on here, now, on real life and the next hallway and Devin. There must be two hundred things I need to be doing instead of daydreaming about online guys. Like plotting a new strategy to help my dad lose weight or figuring a better way to help my little sister get over freaking out all the time. Oh, and finding an aspirin before twirling practice because we've got to dance today, and dancing makes my back hurt, never mind my brain.

I just wish any of that seemed important.

People are still bashing against us as we make it to the last building before the gym. It's god-awful hot, and the air smells like sweat and mold.

Devin stays close, briefly changing subjects, chattering about the English paper we just got assigned and all the outlines and rough drafts we have to turn in before the final product, how we're dividing up the workload, how we're going to get our *other* work done—and I couldn't care less about that, either.

It's *him* in my head.

All *him*.

Whatever *he'll* be, whoever *he'll* be.

I know it might be a totally screwy idea, but the weird thing is, I'm not sure that bothers me. It's not like I'll ever see my soon-to-be dream guy in person no matter how bad I end up wanting to. So, I could fall in love with him, no strings, no complications, no problems. Unless I get caught, of course.

"Skank!" yells a girl I used to like. Ellis Brennan. Blond. Senior majorette. Thinks she's better than the rest of the universe.

She's banging Adam now, so I should feel sorry for her.

Ellis and her friends act like I stink as they mince past without touching me, like I'm poisonous. Add that to the couldn't-care-less list, along with the half of the school that thinks Ellis is exactly right about me.

Devin ignores the witch-monster and her minions because she's good at that, and we've both had a year of practice.

"So are you going to try this tonight?" Devin asks as we finally get out of the main school building and reach the gym door. "Finding a guy online?"

Her question welds me to the door handle, fingers on the warm metal. Two seconds flat and I'm already there in my head, *tonight*.

"It might not be such an awful idea." Devin's worry

and excitement cuts beneath the class-change clatter. "The pickings around here are way slim. Totally slim." She clutches her books and bounces up on her toes like a little kid, stretching her long, dancer legs as she waits for me to open the door. "So, how are you going to do it? If you've been thinking about it all this time, you've got to have a plan."

"No plan." I'm smiling like a total freak and sort of lying, and not getting the door open no matter how hard I try. "I'll just put myself out there and hunt around a little."

Devin grins until she's all teeth. "I'll bust you when you start scribbling love poems all over your class work."

"Yeah, well, at least I don't draw hearts. With flowers. *Shaded* flowers."

She blows me off with, "You'll have to give me all the details every step of the way, or I tell the Bear something awful, like you ate six cupcakes last night."

The Bear is Alexa Baratynsky, our twirling coach. Russian. Short. Wicked. Does *not* approve of cupcakes.

I yank at the door, and it bangs open against the outside wall. "I did not eat six cupcakes!" I grab it before it can swing back and smash me in the face. "Only two. Well, maybe three. And a half."

Devin's laughing. At almost six feet tall and totally slender and graceful, she has to be the most perfect majorette ever, no matter how many cupcakes she can stuff down her throat in one sitting. She'd never tell the Bear about our food binges, either. That would be like blasphemy or sacrilege, or one of those other heinous-betrayal words.

"Brat!" I shout over the roar of people jamming the gym hallway as we head toward the locker room.

"I want all the dirt!" she yells back. "When are you going to start? *Tell me.*"

If I could steal a magic lamp and rub out a genie, my three wishes would be *sooo* simple—after I tried the whole infinite-wishes trick and endowed myself with wealth, brilliance, and the ability to write poetry like Emily Dickinson, of course.

Wish one: let me look like Devin and dance like her, too.

Wish two: make my dad healthy, my mom patient and understanding, and my little sister all relaxed and happy.

Wish three: find a really cute, really sweet, totally perfect guy to talk to online so I can have all the fun and absolutely *none* of the real-life hassle.

"When are you going to start?" Devin repeats, twice as loud to make sure I answer her.

"Okay, okay." I lean toward her as we stop outside the locker room door and whisper the magic word.

Tonight.

MONDAY, OCTOBER 13, LATER

In the locker room, Devin pulls back and gives me the high eyebrows. Her dark eyes glisten with surprise.

"Jason?" she asks. "Cody? Oh, come on, get real. Those names aren't sexy."

I jump and look around at the other majorettes, like anyone at West Estoria would be listening to anything *The Skank* and her friend say anyway—but the others are too far away to hear.

"Ssshhhh." I snatch my practice clothes from the locker. "Please!"

"Cody." Devin shakes her head. "I'd look for an Emil, or Armando, or I don't know, Pierre. Something... hot."

"Okay, we totally have different ideas about hot guy names," I mutter as I pull on my sweatpants.

She keeps this up the whole time we dress out for practice, asking me a million questions about names and height and weight and exactly, exactly, exactly what kind of guy I'll try to e-mail, and where I'm going to look on-line to find one.

It goes on all the way through weigh-in.

Of *course* weighing students isn't "legal" by school rules, but *you* go to the principal, tell on the Bear, and wreck the entire state-championship twirling program. And I'm one pound over, like always, but it's not official until Thursday.

The start of dance practice is actually a relief.

For ten minutes. Maybe nine.

Music floods the gym, echoes off the walls, and we're moving, and Devin can't ask me any more questions about my plans, and I'm trying hard not to dance my heart right out on the wooden floor.

"Pay attention to the rhythm," the Bear bellows as she marches toward the freshman end of our dance line. "Feel it." The Bear claps the next four beats. Her Russian accent gets worse as she gets madder. "Live the mu-sick!"

Her voice blasts through the gym, jamming my brain, blocking the tune we're supposed to follow.

Beside me, Devin keeps a perfect body line and perfect rhythm.

I imitate her as best I can.

I'm sweating. No, I'm way past sweating. Did somebody set the thermostat on fifth ring of HELL?

But smile plastered in place, I keep dancing because it's that or get eaten by the Bear. I've never figured out why majorettes have to learn to dance anyway. Every

Monday and Wednesday I have to get tortured, but Tuesday, Thursday, and Friday we march and twirl without dancing—so much better.

Any second now, I'll drop dead of heatstroke and beat my namesake Chandra Atwood's record for dying young. Chandra Atwood was Mom's best friend in college. She passed away from breast cancer. Very sad. Mom's still not over it. I never knew her, but I got her name—and I've tried to like it, seriously. I just . . . don't.

Hmm.

I wonder if I could talk the genie into another wish.

A new name would be way good.

I blow out a breath, wiggle my shoulders, and ignore the sharp pains in my side and ankle—never mind the river of sweat splattering from my forehead to the gym floor.

Even following Devin move for move, I manage to step forward instead of back.

Crap!

"Mu-sick!" the Bear screeches. "Count it, Shealy! Concentrate!"

Concentration. So not my strength. Can you tell?

I swear it's hotter each time I breathe. My heart might explode. The clock says it's after five. Not that the Bear cares about things like schedules and rides and homework waiting to be done. She has girls to mold, dreams to shape, and all that other stuff she repeats ten times every practice.

"You are like the but-ter-flies," she yells, fluttering her hands in front of her face. Her voice booms off the folded bleachers and basketball goals. "You are *fantasies* of grrrrace and co-vordination!"

Still beside me, and still not even out of breath from an entire hour of jazz dance, Devin whispers, "You must *look* the part." Devin dips low, adding deep shoulder action to her shimmy. "You must *plaaay* the part."

"You must look the part," the Bear echoes, still down at the freshman end of the line. "You must *plaaay* the part."

I shimmy harder than ever. The Bear claps again and barks, "Four, five, six, se-ven, eight!"

We all step out, then slide—the move's called a shim sham. Right, left, right, right, left, right, left, left . . .

Wrong step!

But the Bear's busy again, back turned, hollering at a freshman. Ellis Brennan takes the opportunity to flip me off.

Devin whip-kicks Ellis without breaking rhythm, and catches the blond witch-monster upside one delicate pink ankle.

Have I mentioned Devin is the *best* best friend ever?

Ellis swears and hops sideways, but she magically falls back into line, and here comes the Bear to the center of the gym, glaring at all of us. My heart's bouncing, bouncing against my ribs. I'm wanting to hug Devin so bad for kicking Ellis, but we all keep dancing like nothing happened.

At least the Bear's sweating, too. Her silver and black hair's pulled so tight against her head that her eyes slant, and her blue silk warm-ups are stuck to her skinny arms and legs.

"Eight," she says loudly, keeping her fierce stare on Ellis, Devin, and me, and back to Ellis again. Then: "One!"

Another move, this one called a jazz box. Forward, left, back, across. I don't trip.

The Bear's dark eyes narrow. "Chan Shealy, your feet—like concrete. Pick them up!"

She pops a quick, fluid jazz box at the next change in music. I try to follow without a mistake and do a fair job. I think.

Parents slip into the gym through the door on the other end of the line, no doubt hoping to cue the Bear that Monday practice should be over and dinner's getting later.

There's Devin's dad in his pin-striped lawyer suit. He pauses by the end of the bleachers. Glances at his watch.

And there's Mom coming in right behind him. French braid, totally un-lawyer jeans. Her sweatshirt says *Republicans Suck*.

I wince as the Bear waves for us to stop, then shuts off her boom box. Maybe Mr. Macy won't turn around—though he's pretty relaxed about stuff like Mom's slogans.

For a Republican.

Not only did Mom name me after a dead person, she has to wear sweatshirts like that one almost every day. In West Estoria, other people's moms work at banks or bake cookies or rescue animals or run marathons. My mom talks about living on a commune during her college days, carrying protest signs at strikes and demonstrations, and organizing local campaigns for the Democrats.

She even has a bumper sticker on her hybrid that says *Voldemort Votes Republican.*

Devin elbows me. "Stretch."

Oh, yeah. I lean down until my palms touch the damp gym floor.

Too late.

Scrawny blue-clad legs stop dead center in my field of vision.

I stand, trying not to breathe too hard.

The Bear steps closer, so only Devin and I can see what she's doing. She gets hold of my belly, pinches a roll between two of her bird-claw fingers, and murmurs, "Are ve following our food plan, Chan?"

"Yes, ma'am. Holding my weight."

I am so totally lying.

Devin gives me a look as she rises from her stretch.

The Bear grunts and turns me loose, but only long enough to grab a handful of my frizzy red ponytail. "You should straighten this mess before Regionals. Such a pretty auburn. At least comb it now and again, hmmm?"

This time I keep my mouth shut.

The Bear flips my hair and stalks off to torment Ellis, who's still limping and whining about Devin tripping her.

"Maintaaaain," Devin whispers as I jerk my ponytail back into place.

We go back to stretching, along with everybody else. The ten of us who twirl for West Estoria High School, ve are *fantasies* of grrrrace and co-vordination.

Translation: we have to stay within two pounds of our ideal weight, or the Bear will move up a girl from the junior varsity section to take our place. Right now we have four seniors, two juniors—me and Devin—two sophomores, and two freshmen in the varsity section. But that could change in a hurry.

I rise from my stretch, push up to my toes, and lift my hands over my head. I need to be serious and keep my mind on what's important. And I need to run through my competition routine like a thousand more times at home. Regionals hit on the third Saturday in November, about a month away, and I want to rule Trick Twirling. As in, beat Ellis if it's the last thing I ever, ever do.

But first I've got to lose that extra pound before weigh-in.

I can shed a pound in three days. No dinner and a couple of long walks and maybe a run or two should do it, even if I do find another cupcake stash or stuff my face on the chocolate éclair ice cream Mom "hides" in the basement freezer so Dad won't find it. On the biggest shelf. Right up front. *With* the spoon lying on top of the carton.

The Bear finally releases us from warm-down with a dramatic wave of both hands.

"Bye," I say to Devin.

Devin doesn't answer right away. She's too busy eyeing Mom's sweatshirt, looking horrified. After a few seconds, she shields her eyes like Mom's clothes are radioactive.

"Might come over later, to start that lit project," she mumbles kind of loud, where parents might notice and get to feel like they're eavesdropping. "You'll have to help me start the research note cards. I still think Emily Dickinson's boring."

"You have no appreciation for poetry," I shoot back as I pack my batons in their case, knowing she just wants to be there the first night I go hunting for an online hunk.

Devin slips closer to me, and for once in her life, speaks quietly, where only I can hear her. "I'm really coming over, okay?"

I'm quiet when I answer, and a little weirded out by the sudden change in her atmosphere. "Of course it's okay."

Her eyes dart from her dad to my mom, to the Bear and back to me. "I'm—I think I'm worried about this whole online thing, Chan."

My stomach sinks a little. I hope she doesn't start a

freak-out worthy of my little sister, or get going with the you-really-shouldn't's—because if she does, I probably won't, and I really, really want to.

My cheeks are turning red. I can feel them.

Devin stares at her feet for a second. "Don't leave me out, okay? If I'm there at least the first time, maybe it'll be safer. Or something."

I rub my palms against my hot cheeks, then pick up my baton case and strangle the strap. "This is really nothing. Just a thing. Something fun. After Adam-P and this whole last year, I need some fun. I *deserve* some fun, right?"

Devin gives our parents another quick glance to be sure we're not getting the evil eye from either direction. "Yeah, I know. And I'll help, okay?"

I ease up on my baton case strap and dig out a smile for the best best friend ever. "Sure. Absolutely. Okay."

MONDAY, OCTOBER 13, LOTS LATER

Mom and I roll up to the house and bang through the back door into the kitchen—and the first things I smell are oil and butter and syrup.

We both stop, side by side.

All my muscles get tense at the same time.

Mom sniffs and narrows her eyes.

As we both gaze around the big room with the island in the center, voices chatter from the television in the living room. Here in the kitchen the stove lights aren't on. The griddle's not glowing. There's no pan anywhere, the table in the breakfast nook is totally clean, and I don't see any dishes in the sink.

But the entire space definitely smells like pancakes, enough to make me want to run back out the door to Waffle House and eat my way right straight to a junior-varsity bust-down from the Bear.

When Mom glances in my direction, I know she's

thinking the same thing I am about smelling pancakes, and my stomach tightens.

Dad.

He must have made himself a major snack after he sent Brenda, Lauren's babysitter, home.

This is going to be bad.

My eyes drift toward the door separating the kitchen from the living room, and I know my father's on the other side of that door, probably in his recliner, watching one of his favorite shows.

I want to hug him and slap him all at the same time.

Not this again. *Pancakes and butter and syrup? Of all the things . . .*

"I'll handle it," Mom says in her too-quiet voice.

I jump from the sound of it. "Everything we've read says confronting him will just make him eat more."

Mom clenches both her hands into fists. "I can't just do *nothing*, Chan. He's already had one heart attack. He needs to take responsibility for himself."

My brain flashes back to two years ago, sitting beside my father in Cardiac Intensive Care, holding his big hand, kissing his big fingers, and begging him to wake up and live, and I want to sob and start begging Mom to just leave him alone. "It's my fault. I'm so sorry practice ran over. If we'd gotten home earlier—"

"That doesn't matter." Mom glares toward the closed door like she has X-ray vision and she's lasering Dad through the wood. "Or at least it shouldn't. He could have made himself a salad or cooked us all something better. Something reasonable. Like I said—responsibility. What time is Devin coming over?"

"I'm not sure—maybe in an hour?" I risk taking hold of her elbow, but she's so pissed with Dad she pulls away from me. "Please don't yell at him, Mom. Please?"

"Fix yourself and Lauren a sandwich while I go to the bathroom—and I'm not going to yell." Mom's already walking away from me, fists still clenched, but at least she's heading for the hallway and her bedroom instead of the living room door. "I never yell."

The entire time I'm making turkey sandwiches for me and my sister, I listen for Mom to come back out of the bedroom. Thank God she doesn't—so I at least get to say hello to my father before the trouble starts.

I carry the plate of sandwiches into the living room and find Dad just where I figure I will, in his big brown leather recliner, watching a sitcom on our giant television.

"Hey, doodlebug," he says, and I manage not to groan at the nickname.

He's wearing a white sweatshirt with the sleeves cut out and a pair of stretchy pants that outline his paunch. Somehow his belly seems bigger when he's all leaned back, but I make myself look at his sweet face with all those sweet freckles, and the way he grins when he waves at me, and his bright red hair, and I smile at him even though I know he's so busted for sneaking food the doctor told him he shouldn't eat.

My hair's red, too, just like his—and I've got freckles, but not so many.

As I put the plate of sandwiches down near the stairs and walk back to give Dad a kiss, I notice how he fills the entire chair, and then some.

My chest aches a little more with each step.

I'm such an ass, worrying about losing one teeny pound to keep twirling. My father needs to lose one hundred times that much just to be healthy again.

Was he this large last year?

I mean, he's been trying to eat better and exercise and lose weight. I know he's been trying to take responsibility like Mom wants.

Hasn't he?

Leave it alone. It's not your business.

"Love you," I say as I bend down and give his freckled cheek a big kiss.

He pats the side of my head as I stand. "Love you, too. Was the Bear polar or grizzly today?"

"More like . . . Kodiak. Yeah. Definitely." I try to give him a real smile. "I think she's growing a big hump between her shoulders and everything. Maybe she'll move to Canada and live with the rest of her kind?"

His eyebrows arch. "One day she'll make it to panda. You'll see."

"Oh, yeah, sure. Right." Now the smile is real. I glance at the ceiling. "Have you been hallucinating pigs with wings?"

He laughs, and I can't help warning him. Just can't. "I made dinner for Lauren, but Mom—I think Mom wants to . . . uh, talk. You know. About the pancakes."

Dad's cheeks turn red and he meets my gaze. He looks so sad my insides twist and I want to give him another kiss, but I know it won't help.

"Okay." He sighs. His expression goes a little vacant. "Thanks for taking care of Lauren."

When I hear the faint click of my parents' bedroom door opening from down the hall, I zip to the plate of sandwiches, grab it, and shoot upstairs.

.   .   .

Almost an hour later, Lauren and I are in my room and through with our sandwiches, and I'm relieved that I haven't heard any loud voices downstairs.

I snap a picture of my little sister with my laptop's built-in camera to make her happy, but it doesn't.

"Cut it out." Lauren stops beside the desk and covers her face with her hands. No bruises or blood blisters on *those* fingers. Lauren's not at that level of twirling yet. She's still all kid nail polish (black, because she's so uptight and weird no matter how hard I try to help) and bubblegum-machine rings (silver, shaped like skulls and stuff).

"One day you'll have to give up on nail polish and jewelry." I almost snap another picture but don't because I don't want to upset her. She takes really good pictures because she's so skinny, just like my mom. I'm glad she didn't get Dad's fat gene like I did. "The sport of twirling really wrecks fingernails."

Lauren jerks her face out of her hands and glares at me. "Baton's not a *sport*, stupid."

"Twirling," I say in my chill-Lauren-out voice. "That's what you're supposed to call it. Twirling. Not baton. And if twirling's not a sport, what would you call it?"

"It's . . . It's . . ." Lauren sighs with way too much drama. She actually has on black eyeshadow. "It's what a princess would do."

I want to laugh so bad, but I know that'll make her go off, so I suck in a breath and hold it. Until I feel my brain expanding. When I can handle speaking without giggling, I say, "A princess on steroids, maybe."

Zombie-princess-with-no-steroids shoots me a nasty look. "I'm telling Mom you talked about steroids. Steroids are drugs, right?"

"You know that's not how I meant it." I wish she weren't so touchy.

She heads over to my closet and yanks open the white folding doors. Her hands fly to her hips like always, and she mutters something about finding something fit for a vampire princess.

"Try the blue one." I point to one of my older school uniforms. "It'll look good with your eyes."

Her black tap shoes drum against the wood floor while she tries to make up her mind.

Cute.

At least nobody's yelling from downstairs and Lauren's calm for now. Hunting through my stuff's keeping her sort of happy. I always feel like I'm winning when she's not fake-crying or worrying about something or having a sort-of-real, sort-of-drama panic attack because she's not absolutely perfect at everything she does. I'm good at twirling and decent at school, but my little sister's "gifted." I'm kind of glad I'm not, because being gifted is way hard on Lauren—or at least it seems like it is.

Lauren finally selects the leotard I suggested, the one from four years ago. It's blue for the Blue Dolphins—my middle school. I've been twirling forever.

Lauren jumps in my closet and slams the door, and I know it's so nobody can see her through either bedroom window. She can't stand the windows in my room because they go from the floor to the ceiling, and I've got shutters instead of curtains. She thinks people can see through shutters, even though they're closed. She got wild last week about curtains, too, but Mom settled that problem by adding blackout shades in Lauren's room.

My room looks like a page out of *Designer House*. Antique white dressers and chests that match my sleigh bed, matching lamps and rockers, and the best red print sheets and spread to coordinate with my area rug. Lauren's room? Think medieval dungeon with black lights and neon posters and the windows virtually taped shut.

Yes, my little sister's in therapy, but I don't think it's doing much good.

"It's a phase," Mom insisted when she hung the shades and I griped about the cave radiating darkness since Lauren painted it black two months earlier. "You were scared of stuff when you were little."

I was five. *Lauren* is eight.

Lauren pops out of the closet wearing the long-sleeved blue uniform with the glittering dolphin on the front. My finger's still on the keyboard like I'm going to snap another picture, and she screams and hides her face.

Devin picks that second to pop through my door, wave a shut-up hand at Lauren, and croon, "The mo-oahns ah meek-ah thahn they wehrrrre, the nuts ah gettin' broo-oowaahn, the berry's cheek is plump-ah, and the roo-oose is out of tahw-ahn."

Translation: *The morns are meeker than they were, the nuts are getting brown, the berry's cheek is plumper, and the rose is out of town.*

That's Emily Dickinson, the poet. My idol. Uh, minus Devin's crappy fake Massachusetts accent.

I punch up my screen saver, which announces that my laptop is "Chan's Baby" in fluffy purple letters, and spin the machine around to show Devin the new script I'm using.

28

"Ooooooh," Devin says, admiring the size and color. "Prodigious!"

"Oooooooohhh," Lauren echoes. "Progy-dose." Her black-lined eyes go all fake-wide.

Devin ignores her.

"Think you can head to your own room now?" I smile at Lauren to encourage her. "You can take two leotards with you."

Devin brushes her fingers against the chrome edge of the computer's screen. "Love the purple letters. Too bad the Bear won't let the majorette section get a little class." She smooths her sleek black hair. "I would *shine* with a purple streak right down the side."

"No vay!" I flutter my hands in front of my face like a wounded insect. "You are like the but-ter-flies. You are *fantasies* of grrrrace and co-vordination!"

Devin shakes her finger at Lauren as Lauren stomps out of the room with two black sequined leotards draped over her arm.

"You must *look* the part," we chorus. "You must *plaaay* the part."

Lauren slams the door behind her, bringing an instant "Knock it off!" from Mom downstairs.

The sound of Mom's voice jams a silence into my room.

Devin's eyes get wide. She sits down on my bed, where she can stare at me more effectively. If her look packed any more heat, my face might flame and crack.

For a few seconds, I wonder what she's so intense about, and then I remember.

Internet hunk search.

My insides go all squishy and I glance at the bedroom door. With the late practice and all the Dad-stuff tonight, I almost forgot about my online plans.

My fun.

I *need* the fun.

"Let's do this," Devin says, but loud tap dancing breaks out in the hallway.

We both flinch.

"You need to get a life, little girl," Devin hollers through the door at Lauren. "Or at least some real batons."

"Devin," I say to hush her up.

"I *have* real batons," Lauren yells back, starting to sound panicky and upset—pretty much fake, from what I can tell. "And this year, I'm getting my own costume."

Devin leans forward on the bed and shouts, "Leotard!"

"Devin." I hold up both hands. "Let her go, okay?"

She shakes her head and frowns as she sits back. "You know all that hysterics crap is total drama. You spoil that little emo, Chan. Seriously."

"Um . . . emo? Is that good or bad?"

Devin snorts. "It ain't wonderful. Emo's like—like all fake-goth and pretend-intense and dark and—Lauren. And you spoil her."

"Spoiling is necessary to keep the peace." I inch forward in the rolling chair, holding the computer. "Besides, I got some really cute pictures of her. She looks just like us back when—"

"You're a butthead!" Lauren yells at Devin, now sounding lots more pissed than upset.

"I said knock it off!" Mom screeches from downstairs. "Lauren, thirty minutes until bedtime!"

Lauren answers with huffy, smacking steps to her room.

"Back to the computer." Devin points at my bouncing, fluffy screensaver. "I think you should start on BlahFest, looking at some profiles. At least it's kind of moderated."

I open the BlahFest home page I've been building since school started. Lots of sparkling letters flash my name, alternating with a baton, my favorite links, a picture of our new uniform, and a picture of this year's majorette section. As soon as it loads, I log into BlahFest's GoTeen.SafeChat, the only online community our folks let us use (that they know about), because it's monitored (supposedly) and they don't let the perverts in (yeah, right). It's supposed to be students only. You don't have to list much info to build a profile, and there's a hookup section where people can find "e-pals."

I'm already listed there, profile only, no e-mail address. Have been for about a week. I highlight my profile, but I don't have any hits or messages.

"It's *not* a dating site," I say as Devin's glare gets worse. "Just 'e-pals.' That's all."

"AmherstViolet?" Devin reads aloud, along with the number the site generated to go with it, since the basic name was taken. "Three-three-seven. Since when are you AmherstViolet? I thought you were—"

Without looking up, I interrupt with, "Amherst is for where Emily lived and violet's my favorite shade of purple next to amethyst, and I couldn't think of anything to go with amethyst. I changed to this one because Ellis found out my last one and I got sick of her IM-ing me to tell me I should die or get tuberculosis and move to the desert."

Devin's mouth twitches.

"I mean, I kept blocking her, but she just kept using new profile names."

Devin doesn't argue with me, but I knew she wouldn't, not if I brought up Ellis and her cyber-bullying. Ellis is such a cretin. Like I would *ever* want Adam-P back? What planet did she fall off?

Devin's expression turns to a mixture of concern and admiration. "And you got this new identity past your parents?"

"They don't know about it." I tap the PROFILE button and enter my e-mail address.

"Are you crazy?" Devin tries to grab the computer, but I keep it in my lap and roll the chair back. "Chan. Take that e-mail off right now."

"How am I ever going to get to talk to somebody if I don't give them a real e-mail address?" I make myself hold Devin's gaze even though she's really skewering me with those dark eyes, and I'm sure she's winding up with about two hundred oh-no-you-shouldn'ts. "Come on. Who wants to leave a message on the board for everybody to see?"

She blows air out of her mouth but keeps quiet as I check the screen.

The profile won't let me enter the e-mail address without more information, so I quote my absolute total favorite Emily poem as I type *I'mnobodywhoareyou?* into the blank for *Gender*. That's PIR—Parental Internet Rule—1, never put any identifying information on the Net without parental approval. That one, at least, I follow, so I make up a postal code, then type *280 Main Street* for my country—Emily Dickinson's house number in Amherst, Massachusetts. I think her house is a museum now, but I'm not sure.

I show Devin all of that. "Safe enough?"

She grunts, but doesn't argue.

I press SAVE on that stuff, and the BlahFest pulls up an interest-match section.

"Your folks will just catch you and make you turn it private." Devin sounds hopeful that this will actually happen, which makes me frown at her.

"I turned off cookies, downloaded some scrubber programs, and I always erase my history every day—so they have to find it first. And I'll play stupid and say it was a mistake. Besides, with this laptop, they can't watch me all the time, right?"

Devin doesn't respond, but her disapproval is obvious.

PIR 2—no public profiles—is the *biggest* pain in my butt. No public information, period, without parental approval. Which sucks, because when I'm using my main profile, the one everybody knows, I have a hard time adding new friends to my hotlist, even when I see a really hunky guy's picture.

I finish filling in *twirling* and *poetry* under the *Interests* section as Devin bites at her thumbnail, then says, "My dad got all up in my e-mail last night, and read my chat logs, too. I mean, I turn seventeen in less than fourteen months, and he's still that deep in my business?"

PIR 3—the last and biggest of all, and Devin's folks follow it, too. Everything we do on the Internet gets supervised or reviewed—if our parents know about it.

"I want a Berry3000." Devin worries her nail again as she stares at my computer screen. "Handheld, wireless, and totally private."

"And the monthly plan costs a fortune," I add, which makes her sigh. "If you're annoyed with your dad and planning on a Berry3000, why are you so worried about me on dating sites, or putting my e-mail here?"

"Private e-mail with people you *know* is a lot different than what you're doing," Devin points out.

I keep my eyes on the screen and add a webcam icon to my profile, then open my camera and set it to stream at high resolution. I save my new BlahFest e-pal profile, then click PUBLIC. "Three, two, one. We're live!"

Devin takes another sharp breath.

I know she doesn't usually break rules like this, but if I'm going to meet cool guys, I know I've got to attach something interesting to my e-mail address and profile.

For a few seconds Devin sits on the edge of my bed, breathing hard, enjoying the thrill of being live on the Internet—against all our parents' rules and wishes.

My heart beats a little faster as I wait for her to scream, or yell at me, or make me shut off the camera.

Instead, she leans forward and kisses the tiny camera lens in the front of the laptop. I jerk the screen toward me and wipe off the lipstick.

She springs up, kicks those long legs, and pretends to twirl.

I use the button icons to adjust the angle and width of the lens until it picks up the whole space between my desk, bed, and rockers. Then I run to the closet, grab my case, throw it on the bed, unzip it, toss Devin a baton, and keep one for myself.

We move through our steps with no misses, marching with the military strut the Bear likes us to use for band routines, only really quiet so Mom won't hear us and start yelling about twirling in the house. Devin hums last year's band routine and steps us through the lobs and rolls, then a vertical twirl and a horizontal twirl. We only pretend to do the big tosses and ham it up major on the dance steps, but when we get to the exchange, I start the pass too soon, and Devin's arm crashes into mine.

Both batons slam to the floor. Devin's bounces, tip first, and bangs three times.

"Crap!" I grab for the one closest to me.

Devin snatches the other one off the floor.

By the time Mom storms into my bedroom (with Lauren right behind her, of course), we've stuffed the batons back in the case, tossed the case in the closet, jerked the door shut, crashed back into our chairs, and almost stopped laughing.

Mom's cheeks are bright red and her eyes squint like they do when she's trying really hard not to lose her temper. She points her finger and counts all the lamps in my room to make sure they're still in one piece. Lauren steps up beside Mom, points her finger, and counts lamps, too.

When Mom speaks, her voice is icy-nice. "I know you ladies weren't twirling in the house after I remodeled our *entire* garage just for indoor practice."

Neither one of us says a word. I risk a glance at Lauren, and go for shifting attention away from Devin, me, and the baton-sounds Mom heard. "Are you through with my leotards? You know the rules—if you change back to regular clothes, they go back in my closet so they're clean and nice when you want them next time."

Lauren huffs and starts to throw a fit, but Mom reaches down and squeezes her shoulder. "Go get the uniforms."

Like a cartoon character, Lauren jerks herself free, smooths her hair, and stomps out to fetch them.

Mom watches her go and shakes her head. "Dad and I really need to talk about that new play she's doing. Lauren's dramatic tendencies do *not* need more encouragement."

She starts to leave, seems to remember why she came, and turns back to us, pointing her finger at our faces. "If the batons come out in the house again, I don't care how old you are. I'll use them to tan your hides. Got me?"

"Yes ma'am," we say at the same time.

Devin lets out a breath as Mom shuts the door. So do I.

But when I turn back to the computer, there's my new e-pal profile, blaring out, bigger than life.

"Oh, no." I grab both sides of the screen, then throw Devin a desperate look. "Did she see it? Did she see us in the streaming video window—or the AmherstViolet337 name?"

Devin shrugs and glances back at the door as if waiting for Mom to come charging back in and start yelling.

At that exact second, a new message pops into my in-box, and not one of the generic porn-and-perv spams I usually get when I start a new profile.

This one's from KnightHawk859 with a subject line of: "Dear Goddess of Twirling."

Devin and I stare at the message, then at the door.

No Mom.

My finger slides across the laptop's touchpad.

"Girl, you better delete that," Devin says in a low, tense voice. "It's probably some freak."

"Yeah, but he thinks I'm a goddess."

She shakes her head and gives me the shut-up hand. "See, now you're trippin'. He thinks *I'm* a goddess, not you."

I highlight the message from KnightHawk859 and click OPEN.

MONDAY, OCTOBER 13, WAY, WAY LATER

Devin's halfway through a sentence about how I'm an idiot for clicking on the message and how Knight-Hawk859 is probably some gutter-kissing lowlife when the message opens.

KnightHawk's face fills my screen.

The sight of him makes Devin suck in her breath and shut her mouth so fast her teeth click together.

So . . . do . . . mine.

My entire world spins down to stillness. In the distance, I hear the murmur of Lauren's television. Something clatters downstairs. Neither sound seems real or connected to the universe.

In my room, the only noises are the soft rattle of the central heat and air fan and Devin's breathing.

KnightHawk has thick black hair trimmed even with his jaw, and he has big brown eyes. The kind of eyes I could stare into for hours. His upturned mouth makes a perfect heart, and his chin has the cutest dimple dead center. I want to push my thumb into the spot and watch him grin. KnightHawk's head rests against his hand, and tattoos peek above his black shirtsleeve.

Does the boy *ever* have some muscles, too.

His note says: *Great stream, Red. You should pop a video to the Band Section.*

"OhmyGodhewaswatching," Devin blurts. Then slower, "He saw us. Me. On that video."

I'm too busy staring at the e-mail to say anything.

It's signed *Paul, 1st Trumpet, Jazz Band*, with a link to his profile at BlahFest. Under that is a P.S. reading *I'm nobody, too.*

"Now that has to be a coincidence," I mutter, running my finger over the line of type.

But how incredible is it that he's finishing a line from the poem I quoted in my profile?

No guy really knows an Emily poem well enough to do that, right?

No straight guy, anyway.

Devin's probably missing that reference, because the only Emily poems she knows are the two I gave her to learn so we won't flunk the classroom part of presenting our paper.

After a few seconds of shameless staring, she says, "Daaaaaay-um, Chan. Click that boy's profile."

I don't waste any time following the link.

A private profile unfolds on the screen, tagged *Paul Hawkmore*. He lists himself as eighteen years old and a senior at Underwood High School in Burbank, Michigan.

That's pretty good.

Michigan's what, seven hours from West Estoria? Maybe eight.

Paul's other info is definitely phony—all sixes on the numbers, and his street is Louis Armstrong Way. Guess he has PIRs, too, even if he's eighteen like he claims.

Under *Interests*, he's listed *horns*, *jazz*, and *redheads*.

Devin punches my shoulder.

I ignore her.

My fingers move fast as I click on Paul Hawkmore's message, hit REPLY, and write:

Thks.

You have a video at BlahFest Band?

I sign it, *Chan, Majorette*, with a P.S. of *Then there's a pair of us—don't tell!*

"Don't put your real name." Devin knocks my hand sideways before I can hit ENTER.

"Ow!" I move my hand back and push hers out of the way. "You did agree this Internet guy thing's not a bad idea, and I'm only using my first name like he did."

"His first name could be Merwood or Spitball for all you know. Merwood Spitball. That sounds about perfect."

"You're as bad as Mom." I hit ENTER.

It's not like we haven't dodged Parental Internet Rules before, especially with chat and stuff. With the laptop, I've been dodging them a lot more lately, within reason. I'm sixteen, for God's sake. I know how to protect myself from freaks and perverts.

Devin snorts after the message sends. "Bet his name *is* Merwood, and that's a picture of his older cousin or something. Paul Hawkmore's probably five foot nothing and eighty pounds soaking wet."

"You're just jealous because he likes redheads." I sit back in my chair, surprised by the sharpness in my voice. "I think that's his picture. It *is* possible a good-looking guy would like me, you know."

Instead of you. It's not always you, even though you're perfect.

Devin stares at me. "Duh? You dated Adam Pierpont all last year. He's a god."

"A god who likes to boink cheerleaders." I turn back to the computer and try not to feel sick to my stomach. "A god who wrecked my entire life."

I so need to be over all that, but it's hard with the daily reminders I get.

Irritated with Devin, but more with myself, I turn my eyes toward the bottle of pills on my bedside table. Antiviral "suppressive therapy." One per day, forever, to reduce my number of herpes outbreaks. I'll be dealing with herpes the rest of my life, courtesy of the best-looking guy in my class and the biggest pom-pom whore in school.

And me, not making Adam use protection because I was on the pill.

Did I actually give that cheating, lying moron a book of poetry because I loved him sooo much?

Barf.

I'm such an idiot.

So much for pretend-friends I thought were real friends.

So much for boyfriends and dates and self-respect.

Oh, yeah. And parental trust. That's still pretty empty, too, even a month into the new school year. If I did produce an actual as opposed to cyberspace boy-friend any time soon, both my parents would probably die of sudden strokes.

The silence in the room gets heavy, and my stomach twists.

After a minute or so, Devin says, "I'm sorry I brought up Adam-P. I thought you were past all that."

Sure. Like that'll ever happen.

Out loud, to Devin, who never quits defending me when the skank-whispers start or the Ellis witch-monster rears its evil blond head, I say, "I'm over it. More or less. It just hits me sometimes, you know?"

"Yeah." Devin's eyes look unfocused. She doesn't like to think about negative things very much. "We, uh . . . I guess we should . . . Do you want to look at some other profiles before we make notes on our paper so you can get that outline done? The outline's due first, right?"

I glance at the mailbox again.

Still nothing.

"I don't want to look at any more profiles tonight," I tell Devin, knowing it's probably better if we just move on to other things.

Paul—or whatever his name really is—might have gotten busy, or maybe his parents made him knock it off for the night. Mom would be making me shut down if I was using the computer downstairs, or if Devin weren't here to work on our assignment.

I hit REFRESH one more time, but my BlahFest mailbox still doesn't have a new message. "Okay." I click over to a search engine page. "Shoot. What should we look up first?"

For a few seconds, Devin doesn't say anything.

I glance toward her as Mom and Lauren break into a typical bedtime why-can't-I-stay-up-because-you're-eight argument out in the hallway, near my door.

Devin rolls her eyes and raises her voice over the chaos. "Before I came over, I did a few searches. Got a lot about Emily's poetry, but we need more about her life. Ms. Haggerty wants *an exploration of her inner being*. Or some crap. You heard her."

My turn for the eye-rolling.

Woo-hoo.

We get to write a paper exploring the inner being of a reclusive hermit who never went farther than her garden after she dropped out of college. Emily Dickinson's poetry wrenches my soul, but her life—a little on the tame side.

"Do you think Emily was queer with her brother's wife?" Devin shuffles the stack of note cards she brought—the ones I can't believe she already made, but Devin is all about A's. "Sue Gilbert. Yeah. I found some articles that say they were, you know, philandering with each other—but other sites swear Emily was in love with a bunch of different guys but too shy to say anything."

I stare at the search engine page and chew my lip, resisting an urge to zip back to BlahFest and check my messages. "Emily and Sue Gilbert Dickinson wrote lots of letters to each other, and they were sort of passionate in that old-fashioned way. But I think it was normal for women to talk like that back then."

"Lots of letters?" Devin scoots closer to me, on the very edge of the bed, ripping my brain away from the blank search engine screen for five seconds. "So, you've read some?"

My cheeks warm up a little. "Okay, I'm a total Emily geek. I've read a few—some of her poetry came out of those letters."

Devin snickers. "How many did she write? I mean, they lived next door to each other for like thirty years. No real need to epistolize on a daily basis."

Epistolize.

Devin and her ten-dollar words.

She studies vocabulary like a fiend to keep her English grade up—and it usually works, too. Her motto's simple.

If you can't dazzle them with brilliance, baffle 'em with bovine excrement.

"Emily and Sue *epistolized* more than two hundred and fifty times," I explain, "but I don't think the letters are all online." I type in a search to show her, cue it up, and wait a second for her to scan the headers. "Sue Gilbert's family burned her epistles, so all we have are Emily's letters. Sue might not have answered her the same way."

"What way?" Devin reaches over and flips on my desk lamp, brightening the room and her smooth, perfect face. Her eyes sparkle as she asks, "Are the letters sexy?"

"Well, sort of. Not really. It's all 1800s language. Pounding hearts and fainting bosoms and all that." I pick up my Emily compendium from the corner of the desk, flip to one of the poems taken from Emily's letters to Sue, and read: "Her breast is fit for pearls, But I was not a 'Diver—' Her brow is fit for thrones, But I have not a crest."

Devin stares at me blankly as I put the book down.

"See what I mean?" I gesture to the thick volume of more than seventeen hundred poems. "They're like that, the poems from her Sue letters."

"'Her breast is fit for pearls'?" Devin shakes her head. "That's got to be more than friends. I'd never write a poem about putting pearls on *your* titties. No offense."

I rest my hand on the book's worn cover. "I don't

think it's about putting pearls on titties. I think Emily's trying to say Sue should be wearing pearls, that she's fit for expensive things, deserves the best—that she's classy."

"Whatever you say." Devin turns over a note card and writes down what I said. "Give me a calculus equation any day."

"Forget that." No way will I ever take calculus. Math class has got to be one of Dante's Nine Circles of Hell. "Just let me handle the poetry interpretation, okay?"

"We so need to put this maybe-lesbian stuff in our paper. That had to be what Haggerty wants us to explore. Haggerty likes controversial."

"I don't know." I rub my stomach, which is starting to hurt a little bit. "Using that stuff seems disrespectful. Emily Dickinson was so private."

Like me, before my sex life became last year's big news.

"Time for her to be exposed." Devin grins. "Hey! We could write this like a feature exposé. The Wild Dyke of Amherst. That would totally get us an A from Haggerty."

"Maybe." I try to muster a big smile. "Let's get all the note cards done first, okay? If Haggerty likes the Sue Gilbert angle, she'll say so when she reviews the outline."

Devin nods and scribbles some more, and makes me click an Emily-Sue-letters site so she can take more notes. Completely immersed, like when she twirls.

Devin lives for those twirling moments. All out, kicks

high, arms straight, eyes and smile shining. She probably can't imagine somebody like Emily, who wouldn't love all the gaping mouths and camera flashes.

As for me, without twirling, I'd just be *that girl with—you know <insert giggle and knowing look>*. Or on a good day, *spawn of that liberal-freak-woman who works for the Democrats*, or *daughter of <gesture to show Dad's size> that poor man*.

Winning competitions erases every wrong thing in my life, every wrong thing about my body, my family— just, everything. When I win, I *know* I'm good. And I plan to be great on November 20, when I strike my first pose at Regionals.

Sometimes, though, the lights and cameras make me queasy.

I'm nobody, just like Emily, with all my secrets and private things crammed inside some drawer I never let anyone open. Not by *my* choice, anyway.

We work another half an hour before Devin's dad shows up to take her home.

Of course we stall a few minutes, make some extra notes, and then Mom bangs on the door and Devin has to go. Mom insists on walking her downstairs and out to the car, and tells me to shut down for the night and go to bed.

She eyes the laptop as she pulls my bedroom door closed. "We might need some time rules for that machine," she says. "You're staying on it a lot lately."

I snap the top shut to make her happy—but the

second her footsteps move down the hallway, I open the top and wait for the computer to come out of hibernation.

It gives me a logo picture, then a wait-bar, and I want to scream.

I have what, two minutes before Devin gets out the door and Mom comes back?

"Sometime tonight, pleeease." I force my fingers to stay off the touchpad as the machine finishes waking up again.

The minute I can, I click the icon for my BlahFest homepage and go straight to my mailbox.

One message.

My pulse starts thumping, thumping as I click it.

Probably just spam.

But it's not.

It's from KnightHawk859.

At first, my heart plummets because the message is so short, until I read what it says:

Have to QFT. Sorry, Red. POS.

2morrow, 11P.

Under that's a link that I recognize as a BlahFest private chat room. Embedded in the link was the name he gave the room—*paulandred.*

This time he didn't sign his name, which I totally understand because of his message. QFT meant he had to quit f'ing talking because of POS—parent over shoulder. So he probably couldn't sign his name without getting chewed out for breaking rules.

The P.S. says *They'd banish us, you know.*

My mouth opens.

He *does* know the Emily poem I quoted in my profile.

Okay, this guy is totally better than any of the guys at West Estoria High.

For a few seconds, I let myself imagine him gazing at me with those dark, dark eyes and that silk-soft black hair curling around his handsome face as he recites one of Emily's love poems, just for me.

My heart completely races.

An older guy—a handsome older guy who plays in a jazz band and knows poetry—yeah.

Now *this* is what I was talking about.

This is exactly what I wanted.

Now he wants a private, unsupervised chat—totally against my PIRs.

At 11:00 p.m., an hour after my lights-out, computer-off time.

How can I pull that off?

Downstairs, I hear the front door close.

In a big hurry, I hit REPLY, type *B-there*, hit SEND, and close the laptop's lid.

Before Mom makes it to my room, I shove myself out of my chair, strip off my clothes and hurl them in the closet, and grab a sleep shirt from my drawer.

Another few seconds, and I've got my notepad to write a few wind-down poems.

As Mom opens my door, I'm heading toward the bed.

"Everything okay, Chan?" Mom asks. "The paper going well?"

"Sure," I say without sounding out of breath. "Everything's just fine."

"And your other homework?"

"Done."

She gives me the funny-Mom eye, but surrenders with, "Okay, then. Don't write too long."

"I won't."

But of course, I do.

It's all I have to bring to-day,
This and my heart beside,
This and my heart, and all the fields,
And all the meadows wide.

Be sure you count, should I forget,—
Some one the sun could tell,—
This, and my heart, and all the bees
Which in the clover dwell.

Emily Dickinson

FOR ADAM, EVEN THOUGH I'M OVER HIM

Silent dawn
Holds me
Like an angry lover,
Feeding rage and passion
Into my pacing thoughts.

Dark mountains
Hold their thunder
But when it storms in the flatlands,
Lightning surrounds you.

I keep throwing the pieces around me,
Picking them up and rearranging them,
Trying to make the picture
Turn out
Differently.

Chan Shealy

TUESDAY, OCTOBER 14

KnightHawk.

What a great nickname. How did Paul think of that?

Thick black hair . . . those eyes.

Wonder what his tattoos are. I couldn't see them clearly.

It would be a bad idea to fidget, so I force myself to be very, very still. My physics teacher assumes fidgeting equals a desire to answer questions like *How many angels can really dance on the head of a pin—if the angels have a width and depth of exactly one micrometer? Or If a tree falls in the forest and rolls down a hill, how do you calculate the coefficient of friction?*

I grip the sides of my desk and glare at the back of Ellis's blond head, two rows up and one to the right, and wish I could flip a paper wad into all that golden perfection without getting forced to recite the metric prefixes. Since we both sit close to the front of the tiny box of a classroom, I leave that in the fantasy category. Along with Paul.

Well, I'm trying to quit thinking about him, but it's hard.

I keep imagining his smile, his dimple—and those muscles.

The bell rings.

Ellis springs out of her seat, glances in my direction, and gives me a *very* nasty smile.

I hold back for a second, to let the witch-monster clear the room. No way I'm getting close to her, not after *that* smile. But a minute or so later, I've got my books in my bag and I'm off and running after waving at a couple of seniors who aren't assheads like Ellis. I mean, not *everybody* believes Adam-P's lies.

But a lot of people do.

They will, at least until some other girl catches cooties from him. And if there is any justice in the universe, or anything like God or karma or whatever, Ellis will come down with the worst case of itching, burning sores ever known to humankind.

I zip out of the building—and water slaps against the side of my head. A whole wave of it. In my eyes. In my hair. It's all I can do not to drop my bag. I spin to my right just in time to see Ellis drop an empty water bottle into the recycle bin. Her friends are laughing so hard they can't even get breaths.

"Oops," Ellis says, all sweetness and sunshine. "It just . . . slipped out of my hand."

Can't win. There's no way. If I go after her, I'll get suspended. She'll say she threw the water in self-defense, and her trained monkey-herd will back her up.

I turn my back to her so I can't see her smirk, smear the water out of my eyes with my palms, smooth my hair as best I can, and walk away. My whole body feels like it's sparking, I'm so mad. And wet. When I shake my head, I shower droplets like a dog that ran through a fire hydrant. I probably look that bad, too.

Imagining ten different ways to dump buckets of stagnant putrid pond water on Ellis to get even, I round the corner, heading for fifth period. Even if I'm half-drowned, it's time for in-class band practice, which majorettes have to attend before sixth period twirling—and oh, God.

All of a sudden, I'm face to face with . . . him.

Just . . . great.

Adam-P's standing in front of my locker.

I stop so fast somebody bangs into me from behind.

Water drips from my ears to my shoulders, then splatters on my shirt.

My heart does something between a dive and the splits, and I can't breathe. Everything feels hot and still and sticky even though it's October and cool today and I'm drenched and people are whizzing past me on both sides.

My eyes dart around, searching the hall, which seems like one big blur.

Please, fate, please, universe, let Devin be late to practice. Let her float around a corner with that big smile and way-deadly whip kick.

But she's not here, and I know she won't be. I always get to the band room after her. Devin can't save me from—from whatever Adam-P wants.

What's he doing in this hall, anyway? He's a senior and most of his friends revolve around the new lockers, the *good* lockers, up in the main hall. They don't come slumming with us "underclass trolls."

Adam-P's keeping his head down, gaze cutting back and forth toward everyone else in the hall like he wishes nobody would notice him.

Yeah. As if.

He sees me. His blue eyes grab me even though he's standing kinda far away, and I'm not moving on purpose, but people are shoving me forward to get me out of their way.

Closer now.

He glances at my wet head, my damp face, then gives me a nod like, *hey.*

Adam always looked at me like that when we were going out. It made him twice as—I don't know—Adam-P or something.

Why am I remembering what it felt like to kiss him? How it felt when he touched me, and we—you know.

I wish I could drop dead on the spot so I'd never have to remember that again, or see him again, or hate myself *this* much. I'm scared and sick and excited all at the same time. My stomach doesn't know whether to grow butterflies or spit flames up my throat.

What does he want?

He comes toward me, and I realize he's got something in his hand.

A book.

And now my heart's dropping and splitting all over again, because I can see it's my book—well, one I gave him. Emily Dickinson, *Poems of Love*.

God, I am a total idiot.

When he reaches me, Adam-P holds out the paperback with the sweet gray cover I inscribed just for him.

I make myself keep my head up. Try to find my voice, or get ready to throw my bag smack into his handsome face. Because, oh, yes, absolutely, every hour since we broke up and had the whole in-the-halls-screaming scene about who gave what to whom and who was a slut (him, him, *him*), I've been planning for this moment.

My chance to shout the dozens of things I forgot that day.

The thousands of insults I didn't think of until later. Like, constantly, since the moment we had that last fight.

And now he's here, and the noise in the hallway turns into background static, and the air smells like fourteen different kinds of perfume and cologne, and I'm not seeing anybody but Adam-P in his slacks and black *WEHS* letter jacket.

"You're, um, soaked," he manages.

I don't answer.

He clears his throat, then shoves the love poems I gave him closer to me and mumbles, "Ellis found this. I didn't want her to tear it up."

Adam-P hesitates as he puts the book in my outstretched hand. (Is that hand part of my body?)

"Chan." He clears his throat again. And looks at me with those blue eyes I want so, so, so badly to hate and scream at and *why* can't I say anything?

I have a flash of what he used to call me.

Cutie. And sometimes, *China Doll.*

My stomach spawns fire-breathing butterflies. I know my face has to be a shade of red not found on any color chart.

"Hey—oh, no way." One of the sophomore majorettes, Carny Zin, seems to materialize at my right elbow. She's one of the few people other than Devin who'll stand up to Ellis and Adam-P, only usually not to their faces. This is surprising. This is good, right?

Because Carny's glaring at Adam-P right now, through twisty brown curls that hang in her face. "What do *you* want?" she asks. "You lost or something, sleeze-bag?"

She puts a scrawny arm around my waist, and Adam-P steps back, and all of a sudden, I'm furious, but I don't know who I want to throw my stupid book of love poems at, him or Carny.

I don't have to decide, because Adam-P turns around and walks away without another glance or word.

As loud as I can, I yell, "Asshole!"

He doesn't slow down.

Everyone left in the hallway stops and shuts up, though, and Carny snatches the love poem book right out of my hands. Double time, she drags me and the book and my bag down the hall before any teacher can stomp out in the hallway and give me detention for the rest of my natural life.

We make it to the band room in one piece, but of course Ellis is there, and the sight of her laughing with all her snot friends makes me want to grow fangs and claws and commit bloody, disgusting murder on the white tile floor. If it's really murder when the victim's not truly a human being, but a witch-monster.

Instead, I throw myself into a chair, fold my arms, and sit there. Just . . . sit there, listening to my hair dry. Even as the music starts, and Devin's trying to get my attention. I can't speak. I can't listen. I can't march. I can't do anything but sit—and tuck that poetry book Carny hands me into my bag, so it's not technically in the same room with Ellis.

Who laughs at me three times, and gets in three *skank* coughs between routines.

The band director doesn't make any attempt to get me out of my chair. I'm pretty sure he'll tell the Bear, though, and I'll probably get a *lot* of laps to run.

By the time we make the slow walk to the practice field to march, Carny's filled Devin in on the latest Chan–Adam-P hallway scene, and Devin's right beside me, doing her best to make me smile. "He's not worth it, baby. Keep your head up. He's an apogenous, bovaristic, coprolalial, dasypygal—"

"Okay, okay, okay." I wave both hands to stop her before she can get all the way through her all-time favorite bunch of long words, the Abecedarian Insult—but my mind reels through it anyway.

Apogenous, bovaristic, coprolalial, dasypygal . . .

It's from the *Superior Person's Book of Words*, by Peter Bowler.

Translation: impotent, conceited, obscene, hairy-buttocked . . .

Second translation: Adam-P. No, wait. Ellis. Both of them.

Devin gives my shoulder a squeeze as we make it to the field. "I'll stop if you'll march and smile so the Bear doesn't *kill* you."

I march and smile.

Well? What would *you* do?

But when marching's over, I go to the stinky single-stall field bathroom to lose Devin for a few minutes and hang back from everyone else. Partly because I'm still thinking about the extremely low form of animal life, and partly because I can't stand weighing in in front of people, and it's mid-week check time.

When I'm sure everybody's ahead of me, but well before the football team and Adam-P come charging out to take over the grass, I make my way across the field and the parking lot, back to the gym where we have twirling practice.

Weighing in before weigh-in sucks, but not knowing where I stand sucks even worse. So, like everybody else, I do it. The Bear always leaves the smaller digital scale out before, during, and after practice, but she puts it up between times, so it won't get broken.

I know this seems harsh, my girls, she explained when she made us start weighing in last year. *But you vill never make it on a college level if you don't accept this pressure now and find vays to cope.*

She's right. I know she is. All the best schools have height-weight requirements, and stocky majorettes never do as well as Devin-majorettes, even if they twirl better.

I tap the scale to make it reset. The scale's display moves to zero. I suck in a breath of sock-tennis-shoe-sweat-steam air, let it out in a rush, and step on the little white platform.

Numbers whirl upward. High. Higher. Too high.

No way.

Lightning crashes through my brain. I close my eyes and open them, but the truth stares back at me in square red numbers.

Another pound up?

No Cheetos, no dinner, no breakfast, a salad for

lunch (no dressing), a run this morning—and I'm up *another* pound?

Doesn't this just frost the perfect frigging cupcake of a day?

The locker room's empty since Devin and the other girls have already dressed out and hit the track for a warm-up jog. Nobody's here to laugh at me, so I get off the scale, zero it again, and get back on.

Nothing changes.

If my tear ducts hadn't been . . . I don't know . . . broken since last year, I'd burst out crying. My eyes actually hurt like they want to have tears, but nothing happens.

I can't cry.

Two pounds over limit, and two days before the Bear bumps me to the JV squad and I miss Regionals and my chance to beat Ellis. I'll die if she does that. But she will.

"Bad?" asks a quiet voice from behind me.

I spin around, grab my chest, and glare at Devin. "You scared the crap out of me. Don't do that!"

"Sorry." Devin tugs at her purple warm-up jacket. "I came back to check because I was worried." She glances at the scale, her dark eyes wide and sympathetic. "Did the number come down?"

For a few more seconds, all I can do is look at Devin.

She's probably dropping pounds just standing there—but that's not her fault, right? She doesn't have Dad's genes. I got those. Me and only me.

"It's up a pound."

Devin's face freezes, part sad, part shock. "Chan, what did you do?"

"Nothing!" I rub my eyes, wishing, wishing, wishing I *could* cry. "I'm starving to death, and I'm gaining! How is that even possible?"

Devin runs to me and hugs me. "Don't starve. Don't freak out. Just—just keep eating less. You *have* to lose before Thursday. If the Bear boots you before Regionals . . ."

"I know, I know." I hug her back.

"Maybe you should spend less time on the computer?" she whispers in my ear.

With a start, I realize I haven't thought about Paul for at least ten minutes, or the illegal chat we've got planned tonight. I pull away from Devin and shake my head.

Crap. Why didn't I throw *that* little fact at Adam-P—that I'm not all alone anymore?

Get away from me, you lying freak. I've got a new guy now. One that can kick your sorry ass all over West Estoria High School.

Okay, so I don't exactly have Paul. I don't even really know Paul yet, and he's not my boyfriend . . . but that would have been way fun.

Devin's chattering about Pilates and yoga and elliptical trainers and saunas at her mother's health club that would sweat the pounds right out of me.

"It'll be okay," she assures me as I grab my practice clothes. "We're going to figure out how to keep you where you need to be, okay? We're taking Regionals, every category—and after that, Nationals, this year *and* next year. Besides, this freaking out every week makes me agitated."

The whole time I'm changing into my West Estoria sweats, I want to scream. Devin keeps listing exercise regimens and diets she'll help me follow, like I haven't tried all of those, like I haven't tried everything from cabbage soup to grapefruit fasts. She thinks I'm eating too much, or not moving my ass enough, or else I wouldn't be pounding up.

Spend less time on the computer.

Devin thinks this is my fault, that I just need to try harder.

The Bear probably thinks that, too. And Mom and Lauren and everyone else.

And I don't eat that much. I really, really don't. Since yesterday at dinner, I've had one salad, for cripe's sake. A *salad*.

Who else but me can gain weight eating lettuce?

Majorette practice drags by, from my warm-up jog to our stretches to our twirling.

I only drop two tosses, though, and don't break any of my blisters from last twirling practice. Mom shows up five minutes late to pick me up, breathing hard and saying something about the "latest polls had to be posted, sorry."

The slogan on her shirt says, *If you can read this, you're too smart to vote Republican.*

My stomach growls as we leave the gym, and I want to scream at Mom to get me a hamburger. A big double cheeseburger with fries and a milk shake, too. "Do you *always* have to wear shirts that slam other political parties?"

Mom glances down at her chest as she gets in her car. After about two seconds, she says, "Yep!"

I sigh and buckle up. "Some people actually think Republicans are good at running the country and stuff."

"Then they should read all of my shirts—and get brain transplants." Mom sounds way too perky for my need-a-cheeseburger-now mood.

I really, really want a cheeseburger, and I really, really don't want to talk about politics anymore. So instead of screeching at Mom to let me make up my own mind about government—or forcing her to stuff me with junk food—I do something much worse. When we're halfway to the Civic Center to pick up Lauren from her gymnastics class, I ask Mom about seeing a nutritionist.

"What?" She hits the brakes hard at a yellow light, and I'm scared to death the car might snap in half from the g-force. "Who put that idea in your head?"

"Mom, I'm almost seventeen. Believe it or not, I can have my own ideas." I close my eyes and press my palms against them to stay calm. If I was going to have this conversation, I should have done it from the backseat.

A foot from my left elbow, Mom's energy's way too intense.

"But why would you think you need to see a nutritionist, Chan?" She flashes me a what's-wrong-with-you look. "You're within the weight range for your height. Normal. Absolutely healthy."

She doesn't say *Nothing like your father*, but I feel it.

She keeps up the look and adds a concerned frown. "Are you having body image issues? Are you thinking about purging—you know, vomiting? Oh, God. You're not doing that, are you?"

"No!" I rub my hand across my throat. "I don't want to talk like a million-year-old smoker, thanks."

I'm not bulimic. For real. Tried it once. Puking just wasn't for me. Besides, I gained weight while vomiting. Big surprise.

"Do you think you're fat, honey?"

Like your father?

"No." I squirm in my seat, then realize I might as well scream *I'm lying* and sit still. I suck at lying to Mom, among other things—at least outright lying. "I don't think I'm fat. I mean, I don't think I have a bad problem like Dad, but I don't think I'm normal, either. My body, I mean. I think I'm made like Dad even if I haven't gotten really big yet, that I gain weight really fast, even though I'm not eating much. If I don't learn how to eat—for me, for my body and genes—I'll be dieting my whole life."

I'm sick of dieting. That much, I don't say out loud. I also keep *It's easier for everyone else* to myself, but it is. Everything's easier for Devin and the other majorettes and probably witch-monster Ellis, too.

Whenever I say "diet" or compare myself to other people, Mom goes into near-hysterics over me getting anorexic or bulimic. She even programmed those two words into the security program on the downstairs desktop so I couldn't go find pro-ana or pro-mia Web sites, in case *somebody put that idea in my head.*

"I don't have an eating disorder," I assure her for the zillionth time before she can ask me about all that mess yet again. *I'm probably the only person in the history of humanity who actually* tried *to have an eating disorder and failed.* "I just really need some help, that's all. From an expert."

Mom lets off the brake when the light changes. She doesn't say anything for a mile or so, and I actually get hopeful that she's hearing me, that she's listening—but as we turn into the Civic Center, she says, "Nutrition is pretty basic, Chan, and your problem is nowhere near as bad as your father's. I've got some books, and I know some Web sites. Let's start there and . . ."

And, and, and . . . the same old thing.

Eat less. Eat better. Exercise more.

Do all stick-skinny-eat-anything-they-want people think the same thing?

It's so simple. It's so easy.

A salad. I gained a pound from a salad, and I have weigh-in in less than forty-eight hours.

Easy, my ass.

My stomach growls, and it's all I can do not to start yelling at Mom about her stupid political shirt, just so I'll have something to yell about.

TUESDAY, OCTOBER 14, LATER

"Devin, *please* don't break up with Eric." I stare at my ceiling so I can't see *Poems of Love* lying on the corner of my desk and start thinking about Adam-P again. The cordless feels slippery in my tight grip. "Eric is nice."

"Nice is boring." Devin's voice sounds tense and distracted, and my heart sinks.

Devin never stays with a guy longer than a few weeks, sometimes only a few days. In between hookups, she gripes about being lonely and how nobody really likes her for herself—other than me, of course.

The patterns in my ceiling spackle look like angels or whipped cream or maybe ocean foam. "Nice is hard to come by. You really should give him a chance."

She blows air so loud I move the phone away from my ear. By the time I put it back, she's going on about twirling practice and the Emily paper all at the same time, and I know Eric's history. Which is too bad. He's her best pick in a year.

Talking to Devin about her seriously bad disposable boyfriend habit is a lot like talking to my dad about how much he eats. Saying it out loud just makes everything worse.

Devin talks and talks and talks, but her words fade into the background as I remember how Dad looked when Mom and I got home.

No food smells in the house tonight, but he was sweating, and that made my neck go tight, because when Dad had his heart attack, he was sweating major. Like, enough water pouring off his forehead to need towels.

Maybe I can get him to walk with me tomorrow.

"Are you paying attention?" Devin's irritated tone slices through the fog in my head.

My fingers tighten on the cordless. "Um, yeah. Sure. You were talking about Sean."

"Have you ever noticed how dark his eyes are?" And she's off again, and we talk—or she does—until her dad makes her go do homework.

I'm supposed to talk to Paul, and I haven't let myself think about it for a minute or two, but now I can't *stop* thinking about it. By the time everybody goes to bed, I'm nearly sick. My heart's beating so fast I'm afraid I'll die as I open my closet and arrange everything on the floor. Pillows. A small stack of clothes. A few shoes. As soon as I've hollowed out the perfect cave, I carry the computer inside and pull the door almost closed behind me.

It's so dark in the little space.

I sit cross-legged under my twirling uniforms and dresses and blouses and pants, and I sneak a peek around the closet door into my room.

Everything's just as dark, maybe darker, since there's no light from the computer screen out there. It's quiet, too, with Mom and Dad and Lauren asleep for the night.

I glance down at the computer—and hear a creak in the hallway.

On reflex, I slam the laptop's lid.

The pop of the latch sounds like a cannon shot in the silence.

Panic floods my nerves, my face, my skin. I get hot and cold and short of breath all at the same second—but I don't hear anything else. Nothing but my gasping. The thudding rush of blood in my ears.

Nobody's there.

My parents aren't awake. Lauren's not busting into my room.

I'm still alone.

And I'm an idiot.

Biting my bottom lip hard enough to make my eyes water, I manage to slow down my breathing and get a grip on myself.

I fumble with the laptop, get it open, and bump the power button to bring it out of hibernation.

Since I still have a few minutes, I check my e-mail

and find five or six more posts that came through my new BlahFest profile. I even follow a few links, look at a few guys—and one girl.

Interesting—but not like KnightHawk859.

I'd still rather talk to Paul—though I do save a couple of the posts in case things don't work out with him.

When I check the clock, it's 11:00 p.m.

I type in the chat address. Get in the room. It's empty, except for me. So I suck in a breath and wait.

What if he doesn't come?

What if he does come, but we don't have anything to talk about? The whole thing might be a flop anyway, us just sitting and staring at a blank screen not knowing what to say. That would suck.

11:01.

11:02.

Even though the computer clock doesn't tick out loud, I imagine the sound.

11:03.

I flex my fingers, which are sore from twirling practice out in the garage-gym Mom and Dad had fixed up for me. I worked for four straight hours after I got home, going over and over my competition routine, until Mom made me go take a shower.

11:04.

Maybe I should open another window and surf—but what if I screw up the chat screen?

11:05.

I am a *total* freaking idiot. Why am I doing this?

An almost-muted bell chirps, and the screen flashes: *KnightHawk859 has entered the chat room.* Just as fast, the *Paul is typing* icon blinks.

"Sorry." Paul's first word shoots through in tall, pulsing red. "I got busted for not putting out the trash." That came through in normal type. "Had to do it before I could log on."

Relief hits me like a warm, tingly wave. "My parents make me do trash, too," I type back as fast as I can. "I get grounded if I forget."

"I live half my life grounded," Paul writes. "Or at least restricted, where I have to stay right under Dad's nose. Nothing I do is ever good enough, you know?"

He's not using abbreviations, which makes me happy. I know most of them, like *u* for *you* and *c* for *see*, but after a point, those things make my eyes cross—and make me feel like I'm talking to cartoons and not people. I tell him that.

He answers with a smiley. "I'm glad. I like to keep it real. Wait a sec. Got something for you."

He sends me a couple of pictures, then types Emily Dickinson's entire "I'm Nobody" poem, followed by, "You like that one, right?"

I tap LOAD two or three times, because one of the pictures won't cooperate. It sets off my virus filter, and I have to disable the stupid thing to view the shots of Paul goofing around with his horn.

God, he's more gorgeous than I remembered.

Just *look* at that thick, curly black hair.

My heart starts beating fast all over again, this time in a good way.

And he's waiting.

Oh, crap. I'm supposed to be typing.

"I like all of Emily's poems," I write back as fast as my fingers will move. My eyes flick to the small opening I've left so I can see out into the room—straight to the leg of my desk. I know my Emily compendium's open on top. And right beside that, *Poems of Love.*

Don't go there. Just type, idiot.

"I like Emily so much I think I'll steal her name."

Paul sends me a confused smiley with red cheeks. It blinks wide, blank eyes. "Why don't you like *Chan* for a name? Is it short for something?"

"Chan is *so* stupid." I dread typing the rest, but since he asked, I write, "It's short for Chandra. Go ahead. Laugh."

"????" comes through ahead of a pair of confused smileys. "Your name is just fine. Interesting and intriguing."

"Call me Red, okay?" I smile as I type, like he can see me, even though neither of us has our streaming video turned on. Nerves, I guess. I really don't feel like broadcasting myself to anyone right this second. "I like *Red* from you."

"Done. I hate my name, too. Always wanted *Ben* or *Dirk* or *Stone* or something with a little more . . . I don't know. Muscle, or something."

I glance at his chat nickname. "What about Hawk?"

"Can't." \<sigh\> "My older brother uses that one. I've tried a few, but nothing sticks. Guess I just look like a *Paul*."

"So *Paul* who likes to keep it real, you saw me and my friend Devin at the same time, and you wrote to me instead of her. Are you blind, or do you just like redheads that much?"

"Redheads have a lot of spirit. I bet you're a spitfire, Red. Are you?"

Keep it real.

"Sometimes I am." I frown. "Sometimes I just wish I was. You?"

"Some stuff makes me mad, but mostly, I let everything slide because I don't want to be like my dad."

My turn for question marks and "Why? Is he a temper freak?"

"Total bastard, more like. Stick up his ass *all* the time, you know?"

"Yeah. My mom's uptight. She treats me like I'm seven and too stupid to know what's good for me."

"Are they idiots? Your parents." Paul types the question really fast. I like how well he types and keeps up with me.

I gaze at the words as the light of the laptop's screen cocoons me inside my closet. "Idiots? No. Well, maybe. My mom's a Democrat and she wears these freaky shirts that everyone laughs at," I whisper as I type. "And my dad's . . . different. Sweet. Almost too sweet."

"My dad's obsessed with the trash and me keeping my room clean," Paul types. "What's your mom uptight about?"

I imagine him asking the question out loud, like he's sitting on the other side of the closet, just inside the shadows. He probably has a deep, mellow voice, like all jazz trumpet players should have. Kind of a husky, sexy whisper.

It's kind of amazing, how un-nervous I feel talking—well, typing—to him. I already feel like I know him a little, like maybe I've known him for days or weeks instead of a few computer minutes. I provide him with a list of Mom's obsessions, from politics to grades to shaping my future, all the way to her worrying about Lauren and me getting eating disorders.

"How old is Lauren?"

"She's eight. And she can be real high-drama. You should see *her* profile at BlahFest. She listed herself as *MajorBabe* until Mom made her change it to *PrettyLittle-Girl*. You'd think she was the next Hollywood bombshell-in-the-making—when she's not busy freaking out over more stuff than I could type in one night."

"Two little brothers, pains in my ass." He sends a smiley with crazy, rolling eyes. "They have obnoxious BlahFest profiles, too. One of them calls himself *Hercules*. Yeah, right." Then: "You don't really have an eating disorder, do you?"

"No." I almost laugh out loud, but hold it back. "But I suck at getting in shape."

"Your coach a hard-ass like my pops?"

"Absolutely. The Bear bites."

"Had a wrestling coach like that." Paul cues a blue frowny-face. "He was a bastard about us making weight early in the week instead of just at match time. I had to learn a lot about fitness and strength and weight training."

I fidget, not sure what to type, but Paul adds: "Maybe I can help you with the training stuff? I don't mind."

My jaw goes loose, and my stomach flutters.

That's . . . sweet.

And all of a sudden, I want to tell him about Mom and Devin and the whole skinny-people-think-it's-easy problem. Somehow, I think Paul would get it. In fact, I know he would, but I don't really want to go there. I mean, what if he starts seeing me as all fat and freckled and just . . . not good enough?

But he's asking my height, and how much weight I want to lose—jeez. At least he's not asking me what I do weigh, because if he does, I'm not answering.

"Don't bother," I tell him. "It's hopeless. I gain weight eating lettuce."

"Only if you overtrain," he types back.

My eyebrows shoot up. "What do you mean?"

"It's when you exercise too hard and don't take in

enough calories. It puts your body into storage—you know, slows down your metabolism so you don't lose anything. Sometimes you even gain at first." The icon for *Paul is typing* blinks, so I know he's not finished.

Overtraining?

That's why I gain weight on lettuce?

I'm exercising *too much*?

"It's a balancing act," Paul writes. "You have to take in fewer calories than you burn up, but more exercise isn't necessarily better—and you have to rest in between hard training sessions, or you'll just get hurt and stuff."

I tell him how much I exercise every day with the Bear's practices, but he says my body's probably used to that level of exertion.

Before midnight, he's laid out a training schedule for me, and helped me figure out a calorie count, and given me some Web sites to help me pick foods to get what I need without going over. He sends the training schedule in a file that I save to my desktop.

"I'll send you some free weights, okay?" The words fly across the screen and I imagine him telling me those words in that laid-back, low musician's voice he probably has. "Just the basics for now, 2s, 5s, and 8s. It'll be enough for a start."

"Those cost money," I hack back, doing my best to keep my spelling straight even though my stomach's roaring and my eyelids are drooping.

"I've got money," Paul answers immediately. "My dad is loaded. It's no sweat. Should I send them to your house?"

"God, no, my mother and father would have a total stroke!" I hesitate, then glance back over the training program he gave me. I really need those weights, but I'm flat busted. And Mom getting me weights when she just knows I'll use them to be anorexic or bulimic somehow—that so isn't going to happen.

Dad might get them for me, but who knows when he'll have time—and if he could get it past Mom?

Devin.

I could have him send the weights to Devin's—but no, no. Wait. Her folks'll stroke just as fast as Mom and Dad.

"Why don't you get a P.O. box?" Paul types back. "Well, a personal mailbox, I mean. At one of those mailbox places?"

I grin. "Don't you have to be eighteen? I'm still underage, remember?"

Paul punches up a wicked winking smiley face. "You could get an I.D."

He explains how easy that is, setting up a fake I.D. He says all I need is a headshot to pull it off.

I click open my photos and send him one, the best one I have, and he writes, "Perfect." Then: "Give me your address. I'll send it when I get it finished."

My fingers starts moving to say, "Okay," and type in the street and number, but I jerk my hands off the keyboard before I send the response.

On the laptop's screen, in the little blue chat box, my address seems to stare back at me.

PIRs scroll through my head.

Never put your real name on the Net. Never put your address on the Net. Never put your telephone number on the Net. No public profiles. Everything you do should be—and will be—supervised.

I've broken some of those rules without feeling guilty or weird, like talking to Paul in the middle of the night in my closet, and letting him know part of my name.

But handing out my street address?

That makes my insides lurch.

I delete the address and write, "Sorry. Can't give you my 411."

For a few seconds, nothing happens. I bite my lip and ping Paul to make sure he's still in chat. According to the signal drifting through the ether, he is, but . . . the icon that tells me whether or not he's typing doesn't light up.

He's not answering.

It gets hard to swallow.

Is he really getting mad over me not giving him my address? Because if he is, then Devin's right and he's probably just some pervert after all, and I'm definitely the biggest idiot on the planet.

He starts typing.

I let out a huge breath, then take another one and hold it.

What if he's telling me to kiss off?

Words flash onto the chat screen.

"I understand. You need to get to know me better." He ends the sentence with a smiley slapping its head like "Duh."

Before I really start breathing normally, he adds, "Can you get the free weights?"

I type back, "Maybe," and realize my hands are shaking with relief. He's not mad, and he's not acting like a pervert. "It'll take me a few weeks to get the money or convince Mom, but I can at least get the first pair and add as I go."

Another long few seconds pass, nearly a minute, then Paul comes back with: "Had an idea. Open a new window."

All the pervert fears come creeping back, but I can imagine him grinning and what that grin would do to his already way-handsome face. The thought of it gives me new rounds of shivers and flutters.

When I open the new window, I type, "Okay."

"Go to *portalpay.com*. Use *redgetsfit* as a username and *amherstemily* as your password."

Confused, I do what he says. Portalpay's an online banking site lots of people use to keep accounts to buy things online if they're paranoid about putting credit card or bank info on merchant sites.

When I open the *redgetsfit* account like he instructed, I find a new account label with a time stamp of like three minutes ago, and a balance of $150.00 transferred from a blinded account.

Oh, no way. One hundred and fifty bucks?

"It'll clear by tomorrow, and you can order the weights and a bench," Paul types. "Your delivery address will be stored wherever you buy the stuff, so I won't see it. Fair enough?"

My eyes stay fixed on the money in that new account as I fumble on the keyboard. "Paul, I can't take money from you—especially not that much!"

I can't believe he opened me an account that fast—and that he has that much cash hanging around in his own account to transfer over without a second thought. His dad must be super-loaded, like he told me. What would *that* be like, to have hundreds of dollars to blow whenever you want, on whatever you want to buy?

And he wants to buy weights for me.

"This is pocket change for my dad. Trust me." Paul gives me a winking smiley. "If it doesn't feel right to take it as a gift, you can send the weights and bench to me later, once you move up to better equipment. But, Red, I do have a price."

Oh.

My fingers come away from the keyboard, and I feel a little dizzy.

One hundred and fifty dollars. All mine for the clicking. And now the price.

So, he's a pervert after all?

What if this is something way gross or out of the question?

I press my hands against the sides of my head to keep it from falling off my neck.

"Two things, okay?" he types.

I don't answer because I know my fingers won't move.

Paul is typing.

"The first thing is, my dad's got bucks because he's somebody. Like, somebody other people might know. You know?"

My eyes get wider. "Somebody famous?"

"Yeah. But I can't give any of that out, okay? And you can't ask me about it or tell anybody. Nobody. About my dad, or the money and stuff. We have to be a secret. Deal?"

I answer with "Sure."

Easy enough, but I'm way curious now, and thinking of ways to Google famous guys with sons named Paul. Actors. Musicians. Politicians. Or he could be a mobster or something. Like in the television shows. . . .

Paul is typing.

Part two of the deal.

Is this the perv part? Is this what's going to freak me out and make all of this not real and not fun and just something nasty and stupid?

I squirm against the closet wall and wait, and wait. The words seem to take *forever* to pop up.

"Once you get all set up, you'll have to stream me a few minutes of your workout." Paul adds a smiley. "Bet you look twice as hot pressing weights on a bench."

I do laugh out loud, then swear and clap my hand over my big mouth.

Crap.

Did my parents hear that?

And this boy is out of his mind.

For real.

Thank God I don't hear any noises outside my room.

When I think I can safely let go of my mouth, I risk it and type, "You're going to get me caught if you keep cracking me up."

"Can't have that. So . . . will you do it? Buy the weights, I mean. And keep my secret—and pay my price?"

"Yes." My hands are shaking all over again, but it's not hard to agree. "I'll do it."

Heat covers my whole body. If Paul could see me through the computer screen, he'd get a good look at a totally pink girl with even brighter pink cheeks. My toes curl and my heart squeezes and beats funny. It's so warm and so, so nice. The last time that happened was when Adam-P first asked me out last year.

My eyes shoot to the crack I left so I can see into the room, and to the leg of my desk, and I think about *Poems of Love*. Adam-P's handsome, grinning face pops into my head. Then it morphs into embarrassed-sad-Adam-P, when he was apologizing for having herpes and me needing to get tested. Then it turns into angry-yelling-Adam-P when I got in his face about the cheerleader, after everybody told me who gave him that "gift that keeps on giving" *while we were still dating*, thank you very much.

How do you even know for sure you got it from me, bitch? He was so horrible that day.

Because I've never been with anybody but you! Me, I had been furious . . . and pathetic.

Then the smirk, and the way Adam-P rolled those blue eyes—eyes I thought were just so cute when he was saying sweet stuff to me—lies. I'll never forget what he said next.

Yeah, Chan. Sure. Whatever you say.

Bastard.

I clench my fist and slowly come back to realizing where I am, what I'm supposed to be doing—and who I'm talking to. Not Adam-P. Not the bastard. Not anyone bad at all.

"Hello?" Paul's typed a few times. Then, "You still awake?"

"Sorry. Spaced out for a second." I shake my head and try to slam the door on all things Adam-P. "Thank you so much. You don't know how much you're helping me."

Paul blows that off and gives me a few links where

I can order the weights and bench. I'll have to think up some story for Mom about how I saved money, but that's doable.

"I'd love your help with training, but do you really think I can do this?"

"Absolutely, Red. I can tell. You can do *anything*." He calls up another smiley face. This one has a pounding heart, and I stare at it.

Paul likes me.

And he'll help me. He's already helped me, giving me the bucks to buy my weights and the links to get them ordered. Besides that, hundreds of miles away, on the other side of a keyboard, he won't be a temptation in ways he shouldn't be. After Adam-P, and what with fighting those stupid sores every month or two, I don't want to have sex with anybody—or even the pressure of maybe possibly getting asked about sex.

Or the off-chance freak occurrence that I'd actually *want* to do it.

Maybe not until I'm in college. Or thirty.

I just don't want to go through that again. And with school and twirling, I don't have time. An Internet relationship will work just fine for now.

I click open the word processor and glance at the training program once more. I'll have even less time if I stick to Paul's plan, but I think I can do it. At least there's hope, right?

And even better, if I get going and lose weight, maybe

I can help Dad do the same thing. That would be way past perfect. Dad and me, joining the ranks of the stick-thins-who-can-eat-anything.

"When can you talk again?" Paul's font is bright purple, no doubt to get my attention. "Please say tomorrow night."

I grin at the shining laptop screen. "Same time, same place," I type.

He signs off with "CYL," for "See You Later," and "P.S., Because I could not stop for death . . ."

More Emily.

I smile all over again, sign off with a hug symbol, and "P.S., He kindly stopped for me."

Then I sit there like the big idiot I am, with my fingers on my monitor, wishing I could part space and time and give Paul a kiss on the cheek.

Just a quick pop-kiss.

But he'd know I meant it to be more.

THURSDAY, OCTOBER 16

I didn't make it.

I bite my lower lip. I knew I couldn't, knew I probably wouldn't, but the reality feels like forty extra pounds on my head instead of one extra pound . . . probably on my butt.

JV, here I come.

Devin will die. I'll die. I'm so dead. I'm so done.

I twist in my yellow plastic chair as the Bear squints at the papers I gave her. She tips her head back and scours each line and paragraph, peering underneath the lenses of her thick gold-rimmed glasses. Every few seconds, she sniffs as if to say, *This is such the bull droppings, Chan Shealy.*

Above us, fluorescent lights buzz and fritz. Shadows pitch across the Bear and her desk, then vanish when the blue-white glare blazes strong again. Outside the Bear's windowless cube of an office, out in the main gym, Devin and the other girls have already started warm-up. The *thump-thump-thump* of dance music invades the space, bounces up the yellow concrete walls, and ricochets over shelves of trophies and plaques and the dusty row of photos of the Bear standing on medal platforms, waving to crowds at gymnastic competitions.

Ve had no choice in Russia, she had explained once, late at night when we were locked into the gym during a band retreat. *Children vith talent trained and performed. It vas expected.*

When we asked what would have happened if she had refused to be a gymnast, she just stared at us and never answered.

Devin thought the Bear had downed a bit too much vodka from the little silver flask she usually kept tucked in her purse, especially on retreat nights.

Me, I thought I was glad I hadn't grown up in Russia and gotten snatched away to live in some isolated gym the whole time I was little. I wouldn't have known what to do without my parents and my house, without my stuff and my computer. How did people live before computers, anyway? It must have been so boring, not to know people from other places and be able to e-mail and send messages and chat.

Paul's image floats through my mind.

Computers.

More opportunities. Better choices. And personal trainers who look like wicked Greek gods.

I almost have my weights-and-weight-bench cover story ready for Mom. And Dad, if he notices.

The Bear smacks her hand on the top page of my training plan.

I jump—and slam back to the reality of her office, her frown, and the fact I didn't make weight.

Thump, thump, thump. The beat from the music imitates my heart, only slower.

"Who gave you this?" Her eyes look ginormous behind her magnifying lenses. "Did you hire a trainer?"

Thump, thump, THUMP, thump . . .

"Hire? Uh, yes. Sort of." I clench my fists and try to keep my breathing even. "It's . . . on the Internet, you know?"

The Bear stares at me so long I scoot back in the chair and brace for the tirade. The icy look in her giant eyes makes me shiver inside. A stupid five-year-old part of my brain screams, *She knows, she knows, somehow she knows all about Paul and our chat. She'll tell Mom.* But an older, less lame part of my brain insists, *That's totally ridiculous.*

And from outside, in the gym, where everybody probably thinks I'm dead or on the first bus to Fat Camp—*thump, thump, thump, THUMP.*

God, could somebody shut off the music? I can't take it.

Any second now, the Bear will just laugh at me and pop me back to the JV squad, and tell me good luck earning my way back up to varsity.

Thump. Thump . . .

She lets out a long breath and nods. Her fingers tap the papers as she speaks. "This is the first sign of you taking responsibility for *you*. Good. I am impressed."

Responsibility—me—whoa.

Okay . . . she's . . . impressed.

Color me stunned.

But *responsibility*. There's that Mom-word again, the one she's always using to beat Dad to death. And me, too, when she's mad over something I've done—or not done. Responsibility, responsibility, responsibility. I go to school and practice and work my ass off at *everything* I do. How much more *responsible* can I be?

The music outside the office fades, and the question marks floating through my brain must be showing on my face, because the Bear says, "You have so very much talent in many things."

What?

"Twirling, poetry, the language—vhatever you decide to pursue. But no belief. No confidence. And no—vhat is the right term. Ownership?"

More question marks float through my brain.

"You look for fast vays. Easy vays." The Bear waves both hands, a lot like she does when she imitates butterflies in our practices. "Fast and easy earns you nothing but debts you can't afford to pay. Your father, he knows, poor man. There is no fast, easy vay to fight how your body's built. Maybe vith a plan, ve see some real progress, yes?"

My mouth drops open. All I can do is nod like a stupid bobble-head doll.

The Bear exhales out her long nose. "I vill give you another chance. Thursday two veeks from now, you veigh vith everyone else."

I leap out of my chair and almost vault over the desk to hug her. At the last second, I manage to hold myself back. "Thank you. You're—I'm—just thanks, Coach. I'll—"

She cuts me off with a wave, then gestures toward the door.

Her meaning's clear.

Practice, Chan Shealy. You are already late.

"And I should not see that number on the scale too far down, either," she says loudly as I open the door.

I stop and look back.

Behind her desk, in the corner of that dark, dusty little office, the Bear reminds me of a mysterious wise woman hiding out in a faraway cave. Once upon a time, when she was younger, she might have been beautiful in that Devin-perfect way—only lots shorter, like some sort of Russian pixie.

She taps her copy of my training plan again. "Following this. Moderation. Do ve understand each other?"

"Yes, ma'am." I play bobble-head doll again, then run into the gym before she can change her mind.

As I scramble onto the floor to take my place, Ellis tries to trip me, but she misses.

"Don't be a bitch," Carny says, her high-pitched voice shrill over the music.

Ellis wheels on the sophomore before I can step between them. "Back off, you little twit." Her icicle blue eyes stab in my direction, and that fast, we're in two lines, with Ellis, the other three seniors, and one sophomore under the basketball goal and Devin, Carny, me, and the two freshman twirlers (kind of hiding behind us) standing at the baseline.

Everybody's got fists clenched.

Nobody has batons.

Probably a good thing.

I wonder what it would cost to pay a hacker to splice Ellis's grades, wreck her college applications, and transfer her folks to some corporation in Bora-Bora.

As calmly as I can, I match Ellis's equally cold stare. "I'm still varsity."

Devin snorts with relief. Carny grins. The freshmen cower, but they're still on our side.

Ellis smiles, way nasty. "She's a skank *and* a liar. I saw the scales."

Devin leans forward, but I grab her slapping hand and keep my eyes locked on Ellis. "For God's sake, I *don't* want Adam-P back. You have to know that by now."

This catches Ellis off guard. I can tell from the twitching in her witch-monster mask and the way those cold blue eyes get a little wide. Her minions stir beside her, but nobody says anything.

Maybe it's that little success, the fact I'm right about why she's such a total jerk to me. Maybe it's the rush of gaining the advantage, no matter how slim. Or maybe I'm as big an ass as Ellis, because what I say next just flows out of my mouth, perfect and smooth.

"But if I change my mind, I can take him."

Ellis throws herself at me, flailing both arms and shouting at the same time.

Heart banging, I jump to my left. Slam into Carny. Pain flares up my shoulder as Ellis's grabbing hands miss my throat by inches.

Carny hits the floor. My brain sees it in slow motion. Ellis stumbles and thumps to the floor beside her, landing on her palms and knees.

I'm breathing hard, like I'm running.

Freshmen scatter and scream.

Devin groans. Wades in. I turn toward her as she snatches two big handfuls of senior hair and the girls start hollering. The other seniors stand very still, arms hanging, mouths open. Shocked by Ellis? By me?

Thump, thump, thump. My chest might explode. I want to yell, make a noise, a whoop, some kind of battle cry, but when my mouth opens, nothing happens.

Ellis staggers to her feet and rounds on me. Her perfume smells like rotten lilacs.

I've got both fists ready, and I swing at her and miss, and the Bear's there like she popped out of thin air.

Blood roars against my eardrums, but I hear the

Bear's bellow over all that racket. Russian. No idea what she's saying, but my heart keeps thumping and my breath catches and I don't move at all.

Neither does Ellis. She's about a foot from me when she stops. Her blue eyes go wide as the Bear yells again, still in Russian.

Devin lets go of senior hair, Carny cowers on the floor, and God only knows where the freshmen are.

The Bear's furious glare might kill a healthy plant at twenty paces. It's directed first at me, then at Ellis. My heart slows down a little bit, and the noise in my ears eases a fraction. Devin looks like she wants to hurl.

Then the Bear claps her hands, and Carny jumps up, and freshmen reappear, and seniors stop restraightening their hair, and everybody scurries into line, Ellis and Devin and me included.

We stand, shoulders back, chests out, hands behind our backs.

Now my heart's drumming for a whole new reason. Everybody's breathing hard. I want to smash my head through the bleachers.

Was I out of my mind, baiting Ellis?

Do I need medication?

Fighting? In the *gym*?

The Bear will kill us all. She'll move the whole JV squad up *today*.

For now, she storms up and down the line, lecturing us—I know that's what she's doing, even if I don't understand a word of it, except one that sounds like *dura*, which I think means *idiot*.

You're an idiot, Chan.

I'm really, really a total idiot.

What if Devin gets busted down because of me?

The Bear stops in front of me. Her dark eyes are bloodshot and narrow and for one long, awful second, I'm afraid she's actually going to bite me.

She gets close to my face.

Closer.

I feel her breath on my cheek. Smell the pimento cheese on her breath.

My stomach churns.

I can't keep looking at her, even though I know I should, and my face is so hot, and my insides feel just as hot, and the Bear, through her teeth, growls, "Laps."

Laps.

My brain hears the word, but doesn't register it.

"It's my fault," I say in a rush. "Don't make—"

"Laps!" the Bear yells so loud my whole head rings. "Field! Now! Laps!"

And we're running out of the gym, running as fast as we can, to the track around the football field, where I know Adam-P's practicing with the two other Adams (Adam-L and Adam-B) and the rest of his team.

When I slow down, Devin shoves me from behind.

"You've got to run," she wheezes as she passes me. "Move!"

I move.

We all move.

For a very, very, very long time.

All of practice, we run. If we slow down, the Bear's on us, in our face, screeching in Russian.

I also don't know why I worried about seeing Adam-P. The football field and everyone on it's just a blur as we speed by, running for our lives. Maybe Ellis is worried. Maybe she hates that Adam-P's seeing her all scared and sweaty. I sort of care, but I don't. Not really—about him seeing her, or me, or any of it.

I *don't* want him back.

I've got Paul now, and Paul can't see me sweat unless I turn on the computer. For a while I run with my eyes closed, not even caring if I fall flat on the black, rubbery track surface. That's how it felt to talk to Paul the last two nights. Running with my eyes closed. Dangerous, but safe, too. Thrilling, but scary. Something that takes me totally away from the real world.

"Faster!" the Bear thunders from what seems like miles away, and I open my eyes. I'm in front of everybody, and I'm running harder than I've ever run before.

It feels . . . great. Like I'm flying.

Until later, when we're crawling back toward the gym, and I want to throw up everything I've eaten for the last two weeks, and my ribs are coming apart, and I feel like somebody crammed torches down both my shins.

Devin's limping and leaning on Carny and calling me

names. She's calling Ellis names, too, and anybody else who gets too close to her. Otherwise, nobody's much talking to either of us, Ellis or me.

We fall through the door and collapse on the bleachers beside our twirling bags. I make sure to drag my bag toward the door and sit far away from everyone, except Devin. She might call me names—but I know she loves me.

The Bear marches straight to her office and slams the door so hard I'm surprised the wood doesn't split. She's not going to say anything to the parents. That's up to us.

Friggin' wonderful.

Maybe I should go run with my eyes closed again. In traffic.

Any second now, Mom'll pop through the door in the shirt she had on this morning—*I Think, Therefore I'm a Democrat.* And I'll have to explain before other parents call her.

Devin leans toward me and nudges my shoulder. "Hey, butthead. I'm gonna hate you until tomorrow, 'kay?"

The look I give her says *You totally have my permission.*

She scoots closer. Drops her voice to conspiracy level. "Now confess. Where did you get that training program you showed me earlier?"

I shrug and try to look relaxed, try to *feel* relaxed, since I haven't done anything wrong. My throat's dry when I swallow. "I got it online—but the Bear thinks it'll work."

I'm still sweating so hard I'm sure I look guilty of murder or something. Parents are showing up. Ellis, Carny, and the freshmen stand and get ready to leave.

When I dare to glance at Devin, her bland expression sharpens. Then she frowns. "You got it from *him*, didn't you? You *have* been talking to him!"

More people are leaving, so I watch them instead of Devin for a few seconds.

She punches me in the shoulder.

I manage what I hope is an innocent look. "Him who?"

"Chan." Devin's frown turns almost as scary as the Bear's.

I should feel touched that she cares, or nervous, or something, but really, I don't feel anything but hot and exhausted, and a little like I've got the flu. I don't want to tell her. I don't want to talk about Paul with Devin again, because she might not understand, and her not understanding would just . . . drag everything down and make it feel bad. I don't want to feel bad. I don't want to feel anything but that rush of running with my eyes closed.

"Devin," Mr. Macy calls from the gym door, saving my ass. "Let's go, honey. Chan, do you need a ride?"

"No, thanks." I do my best to smile at him.

Devin studies me without moving. She looks miserable and concerned and interested all at the same time.

"Okay, yes, I've been talking to him," I whisper as the rest of the parents edge into the gym, and girls stagger off the bleachers. "But he's nice and sweet and totally un-pervy so far. Please don't worry so much."

"Chan," she says again, flat and definitely worried now. Her fingers tighten on the strap of her baton case.

"It's fine for now, Devin." My voice sounds hoarse. "I'm going slow. I'm being careful."

Devin jerks her twirling bag off the bleacher steps. "Don't forget the outline for the Emily paper. It's due Monday."

God, is she pissed about *this* instead of my psycho behavior with Ellis and all the running?

I want to groan really loud, and really long.

Why did I say anything at all?

A few steps later, she's gone.

The gym door bangs shut behind her, then opens, and a man pokes his head inside. I catch the flash of red hair, and my spirits jump. "Dad!"

A blast of energy.

I'm up.

I'm running again, carrying my baton case, eyes open. I pop through the door into the entrance hallway, drop the case on the floor, and throw myself into Dad's embrace.

His big arms smash me to his chest, and I do my best to give him a hug even though I can't reach around him. His brown suit smells like spicy aftershave.

When I finally pull back, he's smiling. "Glad to see you, too. Been working hard?"

"Practice sucked," I whisper, then let him hug me again.

This time when he lets me go, his green eyes flick toward the gym door. "Most of the parents already gone?"

He sounds casual, but I know what he means.

Tears push against my eyes as I take his hand and start walking toward the parking lot. I feel more like an ass than ever in my life. "I'm not eight anymore. I don't care what people think. Seriously."

He doesn't say anything back.

It hurts my heart, how I was so awful to him when I was younger.

Don't pick me up. . . .

I don't want you to pick me up. . . .

You're so big, the other kids laugh at me. . . .

God, I suck.

Total little bitch. That was me, pre–Dad's heart attack. When the other kids called him *fatso* and *whale* and other crap, I hung my head and whined. Post–heart attack, I started punching out big-mouths, or cracking their knees with a good, fast kick. Shut them up pretty fast, too.

Twirlers have muscles.

When we get to his SUV, he opens the door for me, and I climb inside.

Definitely more roomy and comfy than the covered

roller skate Mom pretends is a car. *Gas hog. Politically insensitive. Draft SUV drivers. . . .* Mom's sentiments on the subject haven't changed since Dad bought it, but he drives it anyway and just smiles at her. On some points other than pancakes, they "agree to disagree."

"I need your help with something," I tell him as we head out of the parking lot. "Two things, really."

"If these things involve extending curfews or stretching lights-out time, can't help you."

"Nothing like that. It's just, well, the first thing is, I got in a little trouble in practice, and I know you're going to hear about it." I risk a quick glance at Dad as I finish the sentence.

He surprises me by looking more worried than pissed off. "What happened?" His big hands tighten around the steering wheel like he's choking the life out of the leather. "Was it that—that little punk you dated last year?"

"Oh. No. Not Adam-P." My throat feels tight when I swallow. "It was his new girlfriend, Ellis. You know, the senior? We sort of had—uh, a, well, kind of a fight."

Dad's face goes all red and stormy.

"She called me a name and I said something nasty back and she tried to yank out my hair—but the Bear made us run laps," I add in one big rush. "Like, all of practice."

Dad shakes his head and glares at the road. "I thought

the teasing was over. If it's still going on, I'm contacting the principal, and we're going to—"

"NO. I mean, Dad, it's not like that. I can handle it." My gaze shifts from Dad to the back of my hands. "The Bear *did* handle it. It was . . . it was girl stuff, that's all."

Everything inside me winds up like a rubber band twisting and twisting and twisting. "That's not the big thing I need help with. I mean, I guess punish me and stuff if you need to, but what I really need your help with is talking to Mom about another . . . um, thing."

Dad's face gets redder and he snorts like a bull.

This time when I swallow, the muscles don't work right and I almost choke before I get out, "I had some money. And the Bear thought I needed to tone up, so I got a training plan. And . . . I ordered some weights."

"From the Internet?" His voice is loud enough that I flinch. "How?"

"I used a Portalpay account." A hedge, but not a lie. "It's completely safe, Dad, I swear. Passwords and everything."

Absolutely nothing from Dad.

Not for a second.

Five seconds.

Ten.

Longer.

He's still red like a cherry and breathing hard and

strangling the steering wheel. And now he's frowning, too, big-time.

My heart drops. "I just didn't want to ask Mom to buy them for me. You know how she gets when I try to talk to her about exercise and stuff."

This makes Dad frown worse, and I hate that. He doesn't look at me. In fact, he seems frozen to the SUV steering wheel as he drives—but his face slowly changes from bright red to white again. Then pale. Finally, about a block from the house, he says, "Yeah, I know how your mom gets. I'll help you talk to her, but I'm not making any promises. She'll be pissed, Chan. About the fight—and the weights."

"I tried to talk to her about the exercise thing!" I'm yelling all of a sudden, even though it makes my sore ribs hurt. "I asked to see a nutritionist, and she said no and freaked on the eating disorder thing again. So I did it on my own. I *had* to. If I don't work at it—" I break off as my brain tilts sideways and closes my mouth just in time.

I so need to explain this to Dad, but at the same time, I don't. I can't. What I really need to do is shut up. We can't talk about this.

What *is wrong with you?* The voice in my head sounds like Devin tonight. I suppose I deserve that.

"I know, Chan." Dad's sigh cuts across the whole SUV. "You don't have to say it." He pulls into our driveway, stops, and shuts off the engine. Before I open my door, he reaches across the seat and touches my cheek. "I don't want you to get as big as me, not now and not ever. So, come on. Let's talk to your mother."

"Dad, it's not—" I start, not wanting him to think I'm calling him fat or thinking of him as fat, but then I don't know what to say, so I stop. And come up with "Thanks."

I smile at him. My face hurts, and I feel like running in traffic again.

What *is wrong with you?* the Devin-voice repeats.

Nothing, I snap back.

But I wish I knew.

THURSDAY, OCTOBER 16, LOTS LATER

"The conversation with Mom sucked," I explain to Paul in chat that night, after telling him about the Bear's approval of my training plan—but not the part about the fight in the gym. "The whole time Mom was talking, Lauren kept interrupting with opinions. She yelled at Mom for being mad at me, then yelled at me for upsetting Mom. The kid's got issues, seriously. I didn't get grounded—but I only got in three hours of competition practice."

"I'd rather be shot than lectured." Paul's words blink through the blue chat box, pushing shadows around my closet. I shove a few pillows back and forth on the floor. The door's cracked so I can keep watch for parents and my neurotic little sister, and cool air stirs against my face every time I move.

"I HATE LECTURES," I type in bright purple letters. "Mom finally calmed down later and admitted maybe, just maybe I have a brain and know what I'm doing. I get so tired of her thinking I'm six. Or stupid. Or both."

Paul answers with: "My dad treats me like I'm twelve half the time. Five the rest. I think it's a parent disease. They don't get it that we're growing up. First time I had a girlfriend, I thought both my parents would spaz and die."

I laugh, but not too loud. "I wasn't even allowed on alone-dates until I turned fifteen. Devin still isn't allowed one-on-one dates. It's ridiculous."

"Did you wait?" Paul's question comes through in black-and-white. "I mean, did you really wait? Or did you sneak out on dates before you turned fifteen?"

I remember my first few dates with Adam-P, how wonderful they seemed, and go cold inside.

Why can't I stop thinking about that piece of dirt? I hate it, hate it, hate it. Sometimes just the image of Adam-P's face in my head makes me hurt.

Don't think about the book of love poems he gave back. Don't think about the book—

But that's all I'm thinking about, and I'm feeling stupider than ever.

I bite my lip hard enough to send currents of pain to both ears. "Sneaked out," I make myself type, even though my lip's hurting and I'm shivering and my stomach's getting all knotted. "Guy was a jerk, though."

The pain gradually stops, my stomach relaxes—then growls. Thanks to Paul's training plan, I'm not starving myself with a lettuce diet, but I still don't get to eat what I want, like Cheetos. Or the leftover chicken in the fridge. Do I get extra calories for staying up past midnight? Overtime calories. Yeah. That has a nice ring.

"So, were you and Jerk-Guy tight?" Paul asks, and I imagine he sounds jealous. Maybe a little possessive. My toes curl, and I get a bit of that running-with-my-eyes-closed feeling.

"We were tight for a while," I type, not wanting to spend one more second on Adam-P or any of that mess, not when I'm starting to feel better—not when I'm starting to feel like *this*. "He's over now."

Seconds go by, then more seconds.

What . . . does Paul not believe me about Adam-P being history?

I type it again, in all caps. "HE'S OVER." Then I add, "Has been for a while, too."

Paul is typing blinks, relieving my insta-anxiety a little bit.

"Do you have a new off-computer boyfriend?"

Oh. So not happening. "If I did, I wouldn't be talking to you." I cue up a winking smiley. "I'm not that kind of girl."

Paul is typing. . . .

"Do you want me to be your boyfriend?"

My heart stops. I swear it does. And I stop breathing and typing and moving at all.

What am I supposed to say?

My heart starts a loud, hard pounding.

Yes, and I'll look desperate and pathetic. *No*—now, that would be a total lie, and it might hurt his feelings. My toes won't stop curling over the fact he even asked that question. It takes me a few seconds—forever and a few seconds—to give him the only answer I could possibly give and survive to type another line.

"Maybe." I hunt up the perfect smiley, too. A sly-looking little vixen smiley with a red rose in her teeth.

Paul is typing. . . .

I close my eyes. Open them. Could Paul type a little faster, please?

His answer starts with a blushing smiley. "Maybe is definitely better than no. Say yes, Red. I won't tell anybody. You don't have to either, at least not until you're ready."

Oh, God.

When I don't type anything back, he adds, "If I turn into Jerk-Guy, you can always delete me and never type another word. I'm safe. Calorie-free. Give me a try."

Double oh-God.

The boy thinks he has to make a case?

My toes curl so hard I almost get cramps in my feet.

"Red says yes," I type back in a hurry, with a few more vixen smileys.

Then I hit SEND and wonder what I'm supposed to do next.

I have a boyfriend online. And it's Paul. And he's so totally a Greek god.

My toes actually start to hurt, so I stretch them out and wiggle them.

"Turn on your camera," Paul types. "Please? I want to see your face. I want to see if you're smiling."

I flush and smile even bigger and click on the camera. A few seconds later, I have it set, and my face pops up in the stream box next to my chat icon.

My hair looks *awful.*

I smooth it down in a big hurry, then wish I still had on makeup. And why did I wear a cartoon pajama shirt tonight of all nights?

"There you are," Paul says. I can almost hear his voice flowing out of the typed words, smooth like silk, hot like jazz, as if he had spoken them aloud. "You're so cute. I like looking at you."

Okay, now I'm pink. Great.

"I like it when you blush," he writes, and of course, I blush harder. My heart's pounding so hard I can barely breathe, and for some stupid reason, I want to cry.

Instead, I type, "Okay, your turn. I want to see if you're smiling, too."

A second later, Paul's stream box flickers, and a picture comes through—of his great big grin. I can't see anything but his lips and teeth and tongue as he mouths, *I like you.*

I mouth back, *I like you, too.*

Paul's camera pans outward. The lighting in his room sucks, and I can barely see the outline of his face when he moves back from the lens.

"Show me your right hand," he says.

After giving him an okay-I-thought-you-weren't-weird look, I hold my hand up to the camera. Then he asks for my wrist and my elbow.

I give him a quick view of those, then write back, "What are you doing?"

"I want to get to know you. All of you. An inch at a time." His grin fills the stream box again. "So far I like what I see."

Even the totally idiot grin and the bright pink cheeks?

"Show me your eyes," I say.

Paul leans forward and gazes directly into the camera. His brown eyes, lit by the glow from his computer screen, are just to die for. They seem different from his picture, a little more crinkly on the sides, but that just makes him look softer and sweeter. Even better.

He shows me his tattoos next. One's a sad-faced clown crying the single teardrop I had seen above his sleeve before, and the other's an upside-down pyramid he says was drawn to look like the one at the Louvre in Paris, France.

"Art's my other big thing. If I can't play my horn, I want to draw."

If Paul weren't watching, I'd put my hand on my chest to squeeze the fluttering muscles. A musician *and* an artist. Too perfect.

"I want to see you better." I smile into the camera. "Turn on a light or something?"

"My dad can see if I do," he writes back. "Sorry. We'll day-chat soon, right?"

"I don't know if I can do that. My mom might slip a cog."

"Go here," he types, and sends me a link. "These look like screen savers, only you can click them on fast by hitting control-enter twice. They hide everything, and erase your tracks, and you can password them."

Like Mom wouldn't beat the password out of me with my own batons, but okay. Whatever. I'll try them.

I click over to the site, scroll through puppy, bird, and cartoon options, and finally start a download of some bouncing kittens.

Then I switch back to the chat screen and type, "Got one. But this doesn't mean Mom won't catch me, drive out to where you live, and give you a twelve-page questionnaire to make sure you don't have any secrets."

"We all have secrets, Red. Don't you have a few?" Paul flashes his crying clown tattoo in front of the lens, then leans in to show me his eye and give me a big wink.

I look away from the computer and stare at the closet wall.

All the excitement floods out of me, but I don't want

to lose it. I want it back right now, so I glance at the computer screen to try.

One word jumps across my consciousness again and again.

Secrets.

Each time I read it, it feels like a punch, right in my belly.

My thighs start to itch and burn even though I'm not having an outbreak now, and all of a sudden, I don't want Paul , or anybody, to see me, not ever.

How do you even know for sure you got it from me, bitch. . . .

Yeah, Chan. Sure. Whatever you say. . . .

My throat closes and all of a sudden, I can't even stand the idea of being on camera at all. In a big hurry, I click it off. My pale face and freckles vanish from the stream box.

I try to breathe without my chest hurting, and I force myself to type a one-word answer to what Paul asked about me having a few secrets.

"Yes."

"I didn't mean to upset you," he types back right away.

Breathing better now, I write, "I'm not upset."

"Bull. I'm supposed to be your boyfriend now." His shadowy image moves around a little, like he's the one getting upset. "Don't blow me off. You're upset. I can tell even without the camera."

I hate Adam-P. I wish I could slap his smirky face.

I wish I *had* given him some disease he'd never get over. Jerk. Asshole. Bastard!

Stuff rattles in my mind. I feel kind of guilty like I do when I hurt Dad's feelings—like when he told me he knew I didn't want to get as big as he was. He was right, but what good did it do to talk about it? So, I'm afraid of getting big like him. So, Mom's afraid of it, too, even though she'll never say so. I know that's a big part of why Mom totally doesn't want to talk about weight or exercise or anything like that. Sometimes, talking about secrets or problems—even obvious, titanic ones sitting in the living room—just doesn't help anything.

I need to say something, type something, before Paul gets any more upset.

But what?

"I just had . . . a really bad year last year, that's all. A bunch of stuff happened I don't want to talk about. When you said that about secrets, I thought about it and it bothered me. Not your fault."

He sits still for a while.

Having the camera on helps. At least I can see him there, and I know he hasn't just switched off his computer and headed to bed because I got too weird. He hits a key on the keyboard and turns his head, like maybe he's listening for his parents.

My muscles tense on his behalf. I don't want him to get in trouble on my account. I'm about to tell him that when he leans forward and writes, "After you know me better, maybe you'll feel okay telling me. I know I'll feel okay listening."

That's . . . *really* sweet.

I tell him so, followed by: "Sorry I got freaky."

"No problem." He leans back, turns his head, then bends forward and types again. I have a good view of his left shoulder and the sleeve of the white T-shirt he's wearing. His arms look muscular. "If you want my forgiveness, you'll have to show me your toes."

I blink and write, "What?"

"Toes." He dips close to the lens and flashes that grin. "As in, turn on the camera and let me see your toes."

My toes curl like they know Paul's talking about them. I type, "No way. You're nuts. Or you've got some kind of foot paraphilia."

Now that's a major Devin-word. She got it last year when her dad helped put away a guy who kept swiping people's shoes and holding chicks down to sniff their feet. Paraphilia. After hearing about all that, the word lives vividly in my mind, and probably will forever.

"What the hell does *paraphilia* mean?" Paul shakes his shadowy head. "Never mind. Don't answer that, because I'm ready to pay you twenty bucks for your toes. I'm serious. Show 'em. Show 'em!"

"Absolutely out of your mind." I send him a bunch of goofy, crazy smileys.

Okay, so he's obviously trying to make me feel better, but it's working.

"Try me." A flash of the upside-down pyramid tattoo to the camera. "Show me your toes, then check your Portal account. Twenty bucks for toes!"

By the time I get the camera back on, I'm laughing so hard I have trouble positioning the computer. It takes some doing, but I manage to bend my ankle and get my feet up to the camera lens and wiggle all ten of my toes at him.

Paul's right in the middle of typing something back when I hear noises out in the hall.

My heart thumps to a stop again, but this time not in a good way. I type *POS* as fast as I can, then: "Later tomorrow night because we have a game—probably 12," hit ENTER, then slam my laptop shut.

The noises get louder. Definitely somebody walking. Definitely coming closer.

I put the laptop on the floor near my backpack, slip out of my closet, and push the door partway closed, then fast-tiptoe to my bed.

Whoever's walking stops at my door.

I yank back my covers and throw myself into my bed.

My breath comes sharp and short, and I want to grab my stomach and chest at the same time. If it's Mom, I'm so dead. Mom always knows when I'm faking sleep. Dad—well, fifty-fifty. At least I'll have a shot if it's Dad.

I pull up the covers, try to force my eyes shut, and try to make myself quit gasping.

The handle rattles, and I hear the door swing open.

My eyes are still partway open, but my vision hasn't

adjusted to the darkness. I can't see if I'm doomed or not until I hear Lauren say, "Chan?"

All my energy flows out in one big wave. I almost laugh, then I almost cry. Lauren's voice sounds sleepy, not completely awake. Probably had a bad dream. Lauren has lots of bad dreams, or at least she says she does, every time she wakes up and comes to my room. Usually with lots of tears and sniffling and other theatrical stuff.

I reach for the Lauren-shadow beside my bed and touch her hair. "What do you need?"

Lauren gives a huge, loud sniff and puts her hand over mine. "I dreamed about bad men," she says with a movie-diva flair. "I thought I saw a kidnapper outside my window."

Yeah. Through the shutters and blackout shades, never mind Mom's prickly bushes and the house alarm. Is this kid *always* rehearsing? Or did she see this on a movie?

Not that it matters.

I learned a long time ago that it's pointless to fight with Lauren about stuff that might be real in her head, even if it's not real in the world as I know it. Besides, if I act like I don't believe her, she'll cry really loud and wake up Mom and Dad.

I scoot over in the bed and give her shoulder a tug. "Come on. I've got to get some sleep before morning. You need some, too, or you'll snooze all the way through school."

Lauren sniffs again, then a third time before she runs her hand over her forehead like some nutty chick from an afternoon melodrama.

Somehow, I manage not to groan.

Lauren finishes her dramatic rendition of *Poor Little Had-a-Nightmare Child*, climbs into bed beside me, and settles in quick, drop-kicking my leg a couple of times in the process.

In the interest of remaining Mom-and-Dad-less for the rest of the night, I ignore the pain and start telling her a story about princesses and swans and beautiful ponds and gardens, one of my favorites from when I was a little kid. A few minutes later, when she's ripping snores in my ear and half shoving me out of my own bed, I wonder if I'm out of my mind. And I wonder about Paul, and whether or not he's disappointed I had to go so fast.

I hope he got my last send, about parents over my shoulder.

We'll have to make one up, Paul and me, for this situation. *SOS*. Sibling over shoulder. Almost as bad as parents, but twice as likely to pee on your sheets.

Paul has little brothers. He'll get it. I'll talk to him tomorrow. At least I hope I will.

Maybe that kitten screen-hider thing will work and I can risk talking to Paul for a few minutes before everyone goes to bed. CONTROL-ENTER twice. I can hit that pretty fast, right?

My eyelids drift shut.

I hadn't realized how sleepy I was getting when I was in the closet, before Lauren scared me to death. Two late-night chats in a row . . . but I'd make up for it on the weekend, when I wasn't practicing or talking to Devin or working on the Emily paper outline.

Oh, crap. The paper. I didn't do a thing on it tonight.

Lauren jerks and lands another major kick to my thigh.

My eyes pop open and I rub my leg.

That one might leave a bruise.

I sigh.

In the little sister lottery, I think I came up short.

At least I'm doing better in the hot-online-guy department.

When Lauren nails me with another bruise-worthy kick, I get up, grab my poetry notebook, and dig my flashlight out of my bedside table drawer. I don't worry so much about Mom catching me up in the middle of the night writing at my desk, since Lauren's invaded my bed. Besides, Mom's never gotten too upset about my poetry, or snatched it away from me or anything—though she did offer to take me to a shrink once after reading one called "Blood and Tears."

I love writing after dark. I really love writing late, late, late, when everyone's out of my face. Everything always seems easier in the middle of the night, when I'm the only person awake in the world.

For a second, I stop writing and think about Paul.

He got my message.

I'm sure he did.

Will he show up in chat to find me late tomorrow night, after the game?

The poetry-feeling gets hold of me, and somehow it seems like everything's going to be all right. That I'll get everything I want, and more.

So, yeah, Paul probably got that last message I sent. And he understands.

But . . . will he show up tomorrow night?

Yes, I scribble in the margin of my paper. *He'll be there. I know he'll come.*

The soul selects her own society,
Then shuts the door;
On her divine majority
Obtrude no more.

Unmoved, she notes the chariot's pausing
At her low gate;
Unmoved, an emperor is kneeling
Upon her mat.

I've known her from an ample nation
Choose one;
Then close the valves of her attention
Like stone.

Emily Dickinson

REALITY

Endless, ceaseless, faithless
There is no depth to the water
Splashed across the bathroom floor,
The water that won't wash you away.

Broken, shattered, twisted,
There is no hope in the acrid fire
Eating away the letters and notes,
The fire that won't burn you away.

You, you're alive but you died.
I don't want to see you.
I don't want to touch you.
I don't want to feel you
All around me.

I don't want to remember your eyes.
The joy, running to you in the autumn air,
Dry leaves swirling as you let me in,
As you throw your arms around me.

Do you know how much I miss you?

You walked away.
You left me
With the scars of your actions,
And I shower and burn and try again
Not to stare at the line in my life,
The line that cuts down the center
Of before and after You.

Chan Shealy

FRIDAY, OCTOBER 17

"Maybe you just need to try something new—something fresh." Stroke, the new drummer who transferred to WEHS from Northside, keeps trying to grab Devin's arm as we head to the gym parking lot to do our game walk-through. He's tall with really long arms, and his fingers brush her elbow. "Give me a chance. Come on, baby."

Devin stops so fast I almost trip when I put on my own brakes.

She props both hands on her hips and winks at Stroke, but her voice comes out low and quiet. "You call me baby again and we'll see who cries."

Devin's smile makes *me* step away from her.

"Besides," she says, "I'm taken."

Stroke puts a little distance between himself and Devin. "I just heard you don't waste time on local losers. So if there's a tryout list, put me on it." He shrugs, keeping up an I'm-so-handsome grin. "I'm no local—and no loser, either."

As he struts off, I glance at Devin, then groan at the smile on her face. "You are *so* not considering that guy. He's all mouth."

She's still watching Stroke fade into the gathering crowd of band members ahead of us. "He's cute. And good with those sticks."

"But you just said yes to Tevo, and Tevo's nice, and—"

"You have raccoon eyes." Devin's tone dares me to say anything else. "Better use heavy cover-up this afternoon, or the Bear's gonna let you have it."

Look the part. Play the part. Yeah. Right. Okay.

I'm already feeling sorry for Tevo, Devin's boyfriend du jour, as I do my practice and take position to rehearse lead-out. Not much I can do, though, so I leave it alone.

Thankfully, the Bear spends most of warm-up hollering at freshmen, not examining my eyes. I don't drop a toss, and I keep rhythm pretty well, even though Devin gives me a few worried glances. When we get back to the lockers to change, she asks me how much sleep I've gotten.

"Not much." I extend one of my bruised legs. "Lauren's having more nightmares and she got in my bed last night. It wouldn't be so bad if I could tie her feet down so she couldn't kick me."

Devin rolls her eyes. "Your mom needs to get that child some pharmacological intervention. This whole scared-all-the-time thing's just not normal."

"She was in my practice garage as long as I was last night." I keep my gaze on the lockers as I slip my dance shoes out of my bag. "If I hear 'My Favorite Things' one more time, I really might vomit raindrops on roses."

"Whiskers on kit-tens," Devin sings as she smooths her hair, and I scream loud enough to shut her up.

It's not like I don't want to tell Devin about the chats with Paul, but . . . actually, I don't. Well, I do, but . . . not. It feels complicated.

As we pull out our leotards, we ignore Ellis the witch-monster and her whole entourage, and they ignore us right back. No time for crap. Not right before the game, anyway. If I give her a black eye, it'll just make us all look bad.

Devin and I lotion up and powder up, then pull on our tights and strapless bras. Devin does my hair and I do hers, complete with the light purple glitter spray we special-ordered to match the leotard. Devin also does my eyes, because I always get the liner too thick. I take her advice and use cover-up to conceal the dark circles earned from my late-night chats and Lauren's I-had-a-nightmare kicks. Like always, my heart starts to race when we pull on our leotards and do the final inspection, first in the mirror and then for each other.

Almost time.

Nearby, Ellis and her minions finish their fancy dos and makeup, and Carny and the freshmen and other sophomores are already dressed and doing little twirls and tosses, muted, since we're still inside. Right outside the gym door, the clang and whistle and whine of instruments warming up mingle with the increasingly louder crowd murmur. And the popcorn-hamburger-hot-dog smell filling up the airspace definitely makes my stomach growl.

The Bear steps into the locker room wearing her best purple and gold warm-ups, with the team logo embroidered on the cuffs, thighs, and back. "Are ve ready?" she asks in her room-grabbing voice as she takes baton cases from the sophomores who have to carry the flags.

"Yes, Coach!" we yell back, just like the football team does with their coach.

A rare smile graces her sharp face. "Then line up. Ve march!"

She bangs open the door to the parking lot with a flourish, and a blast of cool air makes me shiver. The sophomores head out first, holding their folded flags. The freshmen go next, then Devin and me, and the seniors and the Bear bring up the rear.

The band members see us coming, stop warming up, and snap into line as the band director barks at the jazz section.

One step. Two step. Position by putting my left hand on the shoulder of the girl in front, then moving that hand to Devin's shoulder. Let it fall back to my side. Lined up. The drum starts, a rim tap, marking time, and we march in place, batons at rest in the crooks of our right arms. Steam rises from each of us as we breathe, little feathers of white in the night.

The Bear nods to the flag-bearers, and we march across the parking lot, past the practice field, through the gate, and onto the track surrounding the football field.

Legs high. Shoulders back. Chin up. Shoulders *back*.

On either side of the field, bleachers stuffed with people stretch toward the night sky. Lights blaze as we march onto the grass. The announcer's saying something, but I never can understand him. All I can hear is the rim tap of the drum, the sound of feet striking grass, my breathing, and Devin's breathing beside me.

I march past the flag-bearers to my position at the thirty yard line, stop, and mutter, "Luck and legs," to Devin as she heads for her spot five yards farther down.

"Luck and legs" replaced "Break a leg" last year, after one of the seniors really did break her ankle.

"One, two, three, four!" the drum major bellows, and the band hits the school song.

Blinking against the lights, heart slamming, I swing into action with them, two batons whirling so fast the people in the stands see a silver-white blur.

First toss. Dance step, dance step, second toss. Clean. Clean catch. Somebody swears—a freshman. Dropped baton, but she grabs it and pastes her smile back on and twirls harder.

Boy will she ever hear about swearing from the Bear.

Look the part. *Play* the part. If you screw it all up, just snatch the stick off the ground and keep going.

I'm going.

Am I ever going.

High kick. Just right. Perfect. Yes. Yes! I toss high, freakishly high, and watch the silver and white blur shoot up, then sink straight back to my hand. Bam! Another clean catch. The skin around my perpetual twirling calluses burns. I suck in a huge breath and hope my smile glitters like my hair.

Batons high in the crooks of our arms, we transition to marching as the band shifts to the fight song of the university in the next town. It's fast and bouncy. Illusion, illusion, then marching again . . . and . . . present for the National Anthem.

The Bear paces by on the track.

I thrust my chin up and straighten my back before she even glances in my direction.

It's cold enough for me to see my breath, so maybe my face isn't wet from sweat. I want my hair glitter to gleam all the way to the stands, but definitely *not* my face.

The choir director warbles, "And the hooooo-oooome of thuuuuuuuuh brrrrr-aaaaaaaaave."

We run into two straight lines. On cue from the drum major, we separate into a band-twirler-flag-corps corridor, and the Bear and the band director wheel the big paper tiger into place at the head of the lines. Seconds later, with loud roars and lots of mouthing, the football team explodes through the paper tiger.

I do not trip Adam-P, even when he throws me a weird look on his way to the sideline.

You get what you give, I think at his retreating back, and imagine him upside down with some 300-pound linebacker smashing his head into the grass.

"Break," the Bear calls, and we scatter-drill off the field like a barely controlled riot, running back to the track, then charging into the reserved section of the stands, where we're supposed to watch the game and cheer at appropriate times.

Devin and I flop into our seats, where the Bear distributed our baton cases, and we put away our batons for the moment. My heart beats hard from the pregame well into the first quarter, and I jump and yell the first time Adam-P gets sacked.

Devin drags me back into my seat. "You are so gonna get Bear-bit if you don't knock that off." She smacks me in the shoulder. "Want a hot dog? Tevo's got first quarter break."

Tevo, the nice, nice guy with the misfortune of being Devin's latest selection, looms beside us, resting his tuba on his hip.

He has to be eight feet tall, I swear.

I hold back a sigh and say, "No hot dog."

Then I glance around Tevo in hopes of catching the next pile-drive on Adam. "But thanks."

"A hot dog won't hurt," Devin insists. "Just one."

"No, thanks, really." My stomach rumbles and clenches.

"Well, okay. Save your calories for the Eatery, I guess." Devin's breath-cloud surrounds her like a halo as she jumps up, gives Tevo a quick kiss on the cheek, and sends him off toward concessions.

I stop watching the game since our side has to punt, and there's no chance of serious pain for Adam-P until the next series. My eyes follow Tevo as he trundles down the steps to do Devin's bidding.

Having an in-person boyfriend has its good points, I guess.

Would Paul fetch hot dogs for me if he lived here and came to the game with me? But then, he might not even like football games.

If he did, though, and if I could drug my parents and leave them in the trunk or something, he'd hold my hand, or keep his arm around my shoulders. When I get cold, he'd give me his jacket. It would be so nice to feel his warm body next to mine on the bleacher seat, to put my head on his shoulder and let him kiss my hair and hug me closer.

An empty-blah sort of feeling tries to poke its way into my body, as though I'm getting all hollow and un-real and flat like a cartoon character under a giant piano. Before it can get worse, I switch to thinking about stuffing my face at the Eatery.

Oh, crap....

How could I have forgotten about the Eatery last night, when I told Paul what time I'd show for chat?

After the games, the band always goes out for pizza, but I so totally don't need pizza. And if I go to the Eatery, I won't get to talk to Paul, probably at all. The way I had to leave chat so fast last night, he might even think I'm blowing him off.

But if I *don't* go to the Eatery, I'll have to hear it from Devin, and probably my parents, too, wondering what's wrong with me.

Are you sick?

Don't you feel well?

Chan, are you restricting your food?

Honey, a little pizza won't hurt.

I can just see Mom confiscating the laptop to make sure I'm not reading about anorexia or bulimia.

Somebody edges onto the bleacher beside me, and when I look over to gripe at whoever just stuck an elbow in my ear, I find myself nose to nose with the Bear in her gold and purple warm-ups.

"I—oh," is all that comes out in an icy swirl of breath.

Devin scoots away from me in a big hurry. So does everybody else.

The Bear's dark eyes narrow as she gazes into mine. Her black hair's pulled back like always, but a few strands blow in the cool evening breeze. She studies me for endless, endless seconds. Meanwhile, Tevo shows up with a chili dog that Devin sends him off to eat rather than down it in front of the Bear.

Finally, the Bear says, "You looked very good in pre-game, Chan Shealy. If you toss like that at Regionals . . ." She raises a hand and snaps it closed into a fist. "Advanced Trick vill be yours, easily."

I squirm in my seat. "Um, thanks. I—yeah. Thanks."

She keeps staring at me. "Your training, you'll work hard, yes?"

"Yes." I force a smile, like I do right before marching out on the field.

She pinches my right forearm really hard. "Solid. Don't let it get bigger." She nods toward Lauren and my parents, who are sitting two sections away. "You don't need two seats like Poppa. Train vith heart, and you never vill."

The crowd groans as the other team scores. I want so badly to look down at Adam-P and laugh, but no way.

The Bear, reading my mind as usual, says, "This thing with you and that quarterback boy, it needs to end, yes?"

I think about arguing with her, telling her it was over a long time ago, but I'm not stupid. I keep my mouth firmly shut and try to look like I'm happy she's paying attention to me.

"Holding on to things—even vhen you have every right—can take your life avay from you. You understand?"

The Bear straightens my hair, then straightens the sleeve of my leotard. "Your father, that quarterback-boy and his cheer-shouter, vorry, vorry, vorry." She reaches up and rubs the concealer out from under my raccoon eyes. "Think about your priorities. Let these old bothers go. Sleep better. Sleep more, yes? I vant you sharp for Regionals."

Can a hole please open in these concrete bleachers so I can fall straight to hell?

Anything would be better than sitting with the Bear when she's in this kind of mood. Besides, Adam-P's back to getting the snot kicked out of him and I'm missing it all. As far as I'm concerned, relishing his weekly gridiron abuse *is* part of letting go. I feel a little more free each time he eats grass and limps off the field.

The Bear gets up to leave, and all the majorettes are either hiding or pretending to be in deep conversation, so she won't sit down with them next. Devin won't even come near me for the next five minutes, until I give her the you're-so-not-being-a-best-friend look.

"Well?" She shrugs as she flops down beside me. "I didn't even get one stupid bite of my chili dog. Ooooooh."

That last was for a big sack on Adam-P. I smile, she hits me, and so it goes, until we have to line up for half-time.

We lead the band and flag corps onto the field, do a butt-busting routine to "Beast of Burden" and "Miss You" by the Stones, and finish with "Jumpin' Jack Flash."

I have one bad miss on a toss-pass, but it's Devin's fault. Which doesn't take the sting out of the lump over my right eye, but at least I don't have to feel bad about screwing up the exchange.

After we march off, Devin and I stay on the track with the freshman, twirling and tossing and talking about competitions, and even doing a little of our competition routines. The score's 48–0, and even the parents are talking to each other and cramming down hot dogs instead of watching the slaughter.

When the massacre ends, I'm the first one back in the dressing room to scrub off the glitter and makeup and get my jeans on. Devin's not far behind me, and of course her first question is, "Whatcha having at Eatery? I think I want waffles."

I fasten my jeans, then turn my attention to lacing my shoes. "Um, I think—tonight, just once, well—I think I just want to go home and try to get some sleep."

When I chance a glance at Devin, she's got her eyebrows raised. "No way. You can't go home. Chan, what—did the Bear freak you out that bad? She's probably halfway home by now. She won't bother you again."

I stand and shake my head, then tell my best friend an outright lie. "I'm just tired. I really want to go to bed. Just this once, okay? You party for both of us."

Her eyebrows lower, then she gets a suspicious look. "This doesn't have anything to do with Internet Paul, does it?"

My lips tremble when I smile, but I pull it off as best I can, then lie a second time. "No. Seriously. I'm sleeee-eeepy."

"Well, okay." Devin pouts. "But I'll miss you!" She gives me a quick hug.

I try to smile again, feeling a little sick, and don't quite make it.

Devin doesn't seem to notice. Another hug, then she dashes off to find a ride. I gather my things and hunt down my parents before they leave because they assume I'm going to the restaurant with everyone else.

They seem a little surprised to see me, and Lauren complains because she won't be getting her compensation visit to Fruity's Ice Cream. Still, it doesn't go too badly, and most important, I get home before the time I told Paul I'd be in chat.

Priorities.

Letting go of old bothers.

Later that night, as I curl up and wait for Paul in chat, I feel like I'm really finally and totally moving on from Adam-P. Maybe I can watch him get sacked next game and actually feel a little sorry for him.

SUNDAY, OCTOBER 19

Paul and I chat late Friday *and* Saturday night—but we avoid the whole no-secrets step in our relationship. He doesn't laugh about the bash-lump over my eye, and the idiot really did put money in that Portal account for me showing off my toes before I had to leave so quickly last time, thanks to Lauren.

I tell him he's a nutcase.

He agrees.

On Sunday, after two hours in the garage working on my twirling program, I finally risk day-chatting a couple of times, hitting a double CONTROL-ENTER to use my bouncing kitten screen-conceal program every time somebody comes too close to my door.

"I understand you might have to go fast," he says. "If we don't have another time set, I'll just e-mail you, or check now and then, okay?"

I swivel in my desk chair and grin at the screen.

"Okay. Deal." After a few seconds, I type, "So, it's still daylight. Can I finally get a good look at your face?"

The *Paul is typing* icon stays dead still and quiet.

I glance down at my clothes. Jeans, decent black sweater, and my hair's not as bad as usual, so I write, "Here. I'll go first."

After switching on some lamps, I click open my webcam and let Paul see me in the full light of day.

He still doesn't say anything, and his webcam icon doesn't so much as flicker.

"I've seen your photos," I type. "I know what you look like in stills. I just want to see *you*, you know? While we talk. I want to see you smile and stuff. I don't care if you've got scars or zits or anything. I mean it. I hope you trust me."

My breath gets short and jerky when Paul still doesn't type.

Way back in my head, worry lights flash off and on.

What's the big deal about this? I'm about to ask him when he finally starts typing.

I sit back and realize I'm clenching my fists and my jaw.

What pops onto my screen is: "We all have secrets, remember?"

Okay.

That doesn't sound good.

What if his actual name really is Merwood Spitball like Devin said?

Or—oh, gross. What if he's some sixty-year-old naked perv after all?

Or maybe he's a convict in a prison somewhere.

How stupid have I been?

But that really can't be possible. I've seen his photos. I've been talking to him for hours and hours. I've sort of seen him on camera, even though his face was mostly in the shadows. I *know* him. I know Paul.

Don't I?

Wait a minute.

What if it's not his dad who's famous. What if it's *him*?

I mean, I don't recognize him from his stills, but they never really were face-on, mostly from beside and behind, except for that first picture he sent—the one Devin saw.

If that's it, then it really isn't a big deal, except he'll be taking a risk, trusting me with more of his identity.

But then, my secret—oh, crap.

Hi, I'm really some big rock star or actor. What's your big secret, Chan?

Me? Oh, nothing. I just have herpes.

This could be so totally bad. Why did I push things?

Worry jiggles around inside me until I feel like maybe I should just lie down. Like maybe I should just go to bed and give up on ever having a normal relationship. I shake my head to keep my eyes open.

My fingers and hands weigh like lead, but I write,

"Yeah. We all have secrets. I know. We don't have to do this, Paul. Really. Just never mind. We'll wait until you're ready."

Until I'm more ready. And that'll be, let's see . . . never?

"Now's probably good, before we go any further." Paul sends a serious-looking smiley. "I get to find out if you mean what you say, Red. If I really can trust you. Because when I show you my face, I'll show you a great big secret."

"Don't. Just don't, okay?" I'm typing so fast I trip over the letters and goop *okay* into *sodfj*. Really fast I write, "Not *sodfj*. That was supposed to be *okay*."

"Give me a sec," he answers, then types some more.

For-friggin'-ever. Minutes. More minutes. I turn the screen saver off and on as Mom and Lauren go by outside, and Dad calls upstairs to Mom twice.

It takes Paul almost a full minute to type out what he wants to say. He keeps starting and stopping. I figure he's writing and deleting, writing and deleting. And he looks at his door a bunch of times.

Finally, his response pops into the chat box.

"You know how you need time before you're ready to pay up and give me my little show, Red? Well, I thought I needed more time before I told you more secrets."

"Why?"

"I've been afraid."

I blink at that answer. "Of what?"

Long pause. More looking at the door. More starting

and stopping. The shadowy darkness around him drives me nuts. I want to see him. *Need* to see him. Then: "I'm afraid if you know my secrets, the bad things about me, you might not talk to me anymore."

Tears jump to my eyes, but of course they won't come out. "Like that would ever happen," I type and whisper at the same time. "I have bad things about me, too."

"It could happen," Paul responds, then adds, "What bad things?"

"It couldn't happen." I shake my head. "You can't lose me."

"Red, don't say that. I'm good at losing people."

The tears ease away without a single one finding my cheeks.

Good at losing people.

That's *my* line, isn't it? Being good at losing people, being good at screwing up. But he typed it first.

"You won't lose me, Paul. I'm the KnightHawk's lady."

"Swear?"

Well, that's an easy promise to make. I lean back against my chair and type, "Of course I swear. You're not losing me, Paul."

A few seconds tick by.

Paul glances at his bedroom door.

Then he answers with a blushing smiley.

"Okay, this is killing me," I type. "If you're going to show me your face on camera, get it over with. I'm freaking out. What's the big deal?"

Paul is typing.

"Well, I hope it isn't a big deal. That's just it. I don't know for sure."

"SHOW ME."

"You first. Tell me something. Tell me a big secret, the biggest. Let's get everything out in the open, and then we'll both know if we ever want to talk again. Though I'm pretty sure I'll want to talk to you."

Hot and cold sensations travel all over my body, and I shudder. My fingers barely work as I type, "You want my biggest secret? You're nuts."

"Okay, maybe not the biggest. Just one in the top five. At least the top ten. Unless you've got a really bad one that's as bad as mine."

Oh, God.

I can't move.

Yeah, we should dump all this stuff on the table and decide whether or not we need to keep talking—but no way his secret is as bad as mine. I can make something up, maybe—but what?

"Just pick anything," he writes. "I'll listen."

Breathing too fast, I type, "My dad is very, very overweight. Like, giant. A couple of years ago, he had a heart attack and it totally freaked me out." I hesitate, because it's the next part I hate admitting.

"Before Dad had his heart attack, I was ashamed of how he looked. I wouldn't let him come pick me up from practice and stuff."

"Ouch," Paul writes back.

I chew my bottom lip and type, "Do you like me any less now?"

Paul is typing.

"Of course not. I wish people wouldn't judge me for stuff I did when I was lots younger and lots more stupid." The icon lets me know he's still writing. "My secret is bigger than that, though."

I tell him how I feel about having red hair and freckles, and how I sometimes get jealous of Lauren's singing and Devin's looks. I even dump about staying irritated with Mom and hating math really bad.

"Do you really have no bad secrets?" Paul types.

"Oh, I've got a bad one. Trust me. It's . . . awful." I'm blinking fast again.

Did I really send that?

I can't believe I sent that!

"Then tell me what it is," Paul writes, "and I'll tell you my secret, and we'll be even."

"I can't, Paul. I just can't." I can't even breathe right.

"Let's do this, Red," he types. "I'm liking you too much not to know, and not to tell you my bad thing."

I get that weighing sensation in my head again, where I can see the logic on one hand, but on the other hand, I'm totally freaking out. In my very few seconds of calm thought here and there across the next minute, I realize he really does have a major point.

I mean, if I tell him and he blows me off, I can just

block him from my profile and forget about it. It'll hurt bad once, and then that'll be it. If I don't tell him and keep liking him more, and tell him later and *then* he blows me off—

"Okay," I write before I can change my mind. "Here it is. Last year this guy, the first guy—the only guy—I was ever with gave me herpes. Then he told the whole school I gave it to him, and everybody felt sorry for him. He wrecked my life. That's my bad thing."

Paul starts typing right away and I don't know whether to feel relieved or scream. Screaming would feel so good, but then I'll have to deal with Lauren and Mom and Dad.

No screaming.

"That just sucks, what that guy did to you," scrolls up on the screen. "If you tell me his name, I'll find him and pound his ass into the dirt. I'm serious, Red. Tell me the bastard's name."

I stare at what Paul wrote, not quite able to believe it. He . . . wants to pulverize Adam-P? Like my dad and Devin and, well, like me?

"Thanks, but I don't want you to go to jail," I type back even though my hands feel a little numb.

Paul is typing.

"GOD that had to be hard for you to tell me. It's totally okay, Red, I promise. I'm not some baby who doesn't understand about safe sex. If we ever get that far, we'll both just be careful, okay?"

All the blood in my head moves down, past my ears and face and lower, until I have nothing but limp, cool relief inside me. He asks me about how I treat it, and I tell him about the daily pill thing. Then he asks me stuff nobody ever thinks to ask, or maybe it's stuff nobody feels comfortable enough to even consider—like how often I have to deal with outbreaks, and what triggers them. Stuff I've sort of wanted to talk about, but never do, except to my doctor.

"Sometimes," I tell him, "like if I get sick or stressed, an outbreak starts, and I'm supposed to take a double dose for five days or so. At first, I had one outbreak after another, but it's finally settled down now. I've been okay for about four months."

"That's good. I hate to think about you being in pain, Red."

I start to write something back to Paul about how amazing he is, but he finishes what he's typing first.

"You make me feel like a total coward for being so scared to tell you my secret. Obviously, I should have trusted you."

Then his webcam blinks.

Seconds later, there he is, gazing right at me, full in the light, no shadows at all. Not one single bit of darkness to hide his face.

Right away, I see the secret.

And I have no idea what to say, or what to do.

I just sit there staring at him, at those big brown eyes,

at his thick wavy hair, at his perfect mouth and the dimple in his chin, and the tattoos on his muscle-bound arms.

It's Paul, all right, just like in the pictures, just like I've imagined every time I've gazed at his streaming image inside all those dark, fuzzy shadows.

But . . .

My concrete hands lift and I barely manage to hack out, "So how old are you, really?"

In the camera box, Paul's head droops down, defeated, like I slapped him in the face. My chest gets tight, and I want to grab him and shake him and tell him I didn't mean it in a bad way. I just need to know. Have to know. So I type, "I told you the worst thing in the world about me. So just tell me how old you are, okay? And stop worrying."

After a few seconds, he writes, "I'm twenty-three, and my dad's not really famous or anything. But I don't feel like I'm twenty-three—and I'm sorry I sort of lied about my dad so you wouldn't tell anybody."

"That's not bad," I say out loud. That's not so bad. Twenty-three isn't bad.

He looks young, but up close like this, I can see he's not eighteen like his profile claims.

He's five years older than he said he was. Seven years older than me.

Just seven years.

An older guy likes me? I mean, he's like college-guy old.

Should I yell at him or smile?

A college guy likes me.

"Why didn't you just tell me from the beginning?"

"I was afraid you'd think I was a perv!" He gazes into the camera and shrugs before typing, "Besides, that question leads to more secrets. Some more bad stuff about me. I guess you might as well know it all, since you told me all the dirt on yourself."

My bottom lip hurts, and I realize I'm biting it.

I so don't know if I'm ready for the "all" he's talking about.

Too bad if I'm not.

Paul is typing.

The whole time he hacks at his keyboard, I sink lower in my chair, bite my lip, and try to keep breathing. The noises outside my door fade back, and I don't bother with the kitten screen concealer. I don't really think I could move that fast if I tried.

"I had some problems back in high school," pops up from Paul, with a blue frowny face. "Drinking and weed and stuff. My dad sent me away for a while. I missed my junior and senior year in that youth camp, and the next year, too—it was like almost four years all together. When I got out, I felt like I had just lost those years. I didn't feel any older. Just kind of lost. Does that make sense?"

He stares into the camera, and his wide, deep eyes make me want to hug him. He looks *so* sad and, like he said, lost.

My hands finally move, and I type, "Yeah, it makes sense." And then: "What do you really do all day?"

He lowers his head again and answers with, "I go to some meetings so I won't get mixed up with alcohol and drugs again, and I'm doing some college courses online. I don't feel like getting out much, and my dad treats me like I'm still fifteen. Plus, all my old friends still live around here. It's embarrassing, and they don't understand. They think I'm stupid."

"You're not stupid." Those words come easier, like I'm slowly thawing out of frozen-numb.

Twenty-three really isn't *bad.*

It's not bad to me, anyway. My parents—and Devin—will probably blow three major arteries and drop dead at the thought, but I'm sixteen. When I'm eighteen, he'll be twenty-five. When I'm twenty, he'll be twenty-seven. Seven years really isn't that much of an age difference.

And he knows my big secret, and because he's older and mature, he's still right here, typing away.

"Are you mad, Red? Do you want to stop this? Because if you do, I totally get it, and I wouldn't blame you." Paul gazes into the camera when he finishes, and this time he looks sad and nervous and completely hug-able.

"I'm not mad," I write back. "And I don't want to stop talking to you. Next time, though, you have to just trust me, and tell me stuff if I ask."

He gives me a little grin.

Somebody knocks on my door.

I jump and stare at the knob. When I look back at the computer screen, Paul has switched off his camera and vanished out of chat. I punch up the kittens in a hurry, unlock my door, and back away.

"Come in," I say as I sit back down, only I cough more than anything, because my throat's so dry.

Dad's nervous, smiling, rosy face eases around the edge of the door. "Paper going okay?"

"What?" My brain fritzes and sparks like a power cord on overload.

Dad steps into my room and gestures to the laptop. "Emily. The paper. Your mom said you were working on one of the steps of that big project you and Devin have to turn in before your competition."

My mouth drops into an O shape, and I nod. Clear my throat. Try to focus. "It's okay so far, I guess."

Dad looks down at his hands, then back up to me. "Interested in a break?"

That clears out a few of the sparks and smolders left in my head. "Sure. Ice cream?"

"I was thinking about a walk. Something off that training program you've started." He gestures to the laptop again, and I can tell from his expression he wants to be helpful. "Lauren's at a friend's and your mom's busy with her campaign. The timing just seemed right."

I have to smile at my father because he's being so sweet. So I get up, put on my shoes, and head out with him for a walk, even though most of my brain would really rather go back to chat and wait for Paul, and talk to him forever.

Dad and I take a long walk, though, a lot longer than usual.

"Sharp shoes," I tell Dad as we circle the block for the third time. His breath comes in frosty puffs as the streetlights flicker to life. "They new?"

Dad grins at me, making his red freckled cheeks plump way out. "Had to do something to keep up with you." He's out of breath, and he's limping a little because one of his knees hurts him sometimes. "You're running me into the dirt. What's got you so motivated to exercise right now? Some new boy I should know about?"

I feel myself blushing.

Boy. Sort of. Man, more like it. But to Dad, Paul would still be a "boy," right?

I jog ahead of Dad to the end of the road, then circle back and jog around him. He grunts at me when I tag his shoulder.

"Maybe—about the boy." I tag him again and then take off.

"You know I'll want to know everything if it gets serious." He pumps his arms, trying to catch up to me. "If Mystery Boy hurts you like that Adam Pierpont kid did, I'll whip his ass. Just so you know."

"No mentioning the A-word." I wave my hands as I

slow to a walk beside him. "Bad mojo. No A-words allowed."

Dad presses his lips together and nods, then goes back to huffing and puffing.

When I told my parents about having herpes, I figured they would flip out, but they just . . . took care of things. Grim. No smiles. A lot of serious conversations about actions, consequences, condoms, and the pill that I had first gotten through Planned Parenthood, but I didn't get grounded or hollered at or anything.

The night I told them, I did hear Dad say to Mom, "Won't do any good to slam the barn door if the horses are already gone."

Weird. But . . . true, I guess. I didn't like how disappointed and sad he sounded, though.

I don't plan to tell him about Paul unless Paul and I are still together when I get out of college. I don't ever want to hear Dad sound that sad or disappointed again.

Dad reaches behind himself and massages his lower back. "Does your twirling coach focus on weight much?"

His question catches me off guard, and I almost spill the truth. As it is, I start to sweat big-time. The way Dad's looking at me with his green eyes all wide and steady as he puffs away, pumping those arms, I think he already knows the answer.

"Sort of," I say, as honest as I think I can be. "She wants us to stay healthy so we can be graceful and coordinated and have a shot at college twirling." I move my arms up and down, out and back in, like I would if I was marching in front of the band at halftime. "Most colleges have pretty strict height-weight requirements for twirlers, and you know Devin and I want to make the squad wherever we decide to go."

"That's college, though." Dad keeps trying to walk faster, but he's going slower and slower. "This is high school. I want you to enjoy yourself. Too much pressure—well, it's not good at your age. You'd tell me if you were under too much pressure, right?"

Dad stops walking and leans over, putting his hands on his thighs, but he keeps his head up, looking at me. So worried. I hate it when he worries.

"I'd tell you," I say, careful not to promise. "I know you'd help me."

Dad nods. "That's the most important thing," he says around gulps of air. "I'm here for you. Don't ever forget that, okay?"

I'm here for you.

His words bounce inside my head, bumping against the memories of him lying in that hospital bed, tubes running everywhere, and the doctor telling us things like *cardiac arrest* and *morbidly obese* and *shortened life span* and *critical to make changes in diet and lifestyle.*

"I won't forget." I make myself smile, even though I don't know how many changes he's really made. Well, the whole family. We'd all have to do stuff differently, right?

I never feel like Mom and Lauren and I are doing enough to help Dad.

Is our diet, our lifestyle, good enough now?

Are we helping Dad stick around—or still hurting him, or letting him hurt himself?

He smiles up at me, his face so red it looks like his freckles might catch on fire. "Ready to go back to the house?"

I nod, even though I have another lap to do.

I can always do it later.

MONDAY, OCTOBER 20

In American lit on Monday morning, after everyone else
has left the class, Devin waits to kill me.

Jets of fire blast out of her eyes.

Haggerty stands beside my desk, shaking her head
and telling me how disappointed she is that I didn't turn
in the outline for our Emily paper.

"It's not like you to be irresponsible, Chan." Haggerty's white eyebrows join over her nose, and her frown
reaches all the way to her neck.

"I just forgot," I say again, letting her—and Devin—
think I forgot to bring it, not that I totally forgot to do
the stupid thing, that it didn't even cross my mind even
after all her reminders. "The cards, the outline, I'll bring
it all tomorrow, I promise."

"You'll lose a letter grade." Haggerty shakes her head
again and sighs.

"I'll deliver," I say at the same time Devin says, "Our

cards are good. Just wait until you see what we've found out about Emily's private life."

Haggerty glances from Devin to me, and her eyebrows finally come apart. She looks interested. "I hope that's true."

Devin folds her hands like she's praying. "It's so totally true. Trust me. Right, Chan?"

That last part, Devin says through her teeth.

So much for protecting Emily's secret things. "The Wild Dyke of Amherst" it is.

"Right," I say, surprised I can talk with all the air squeezed out of my lungs.

By the time Haggerty lets us go and we get to the hallway, Devin's glare could wilt Mom's flowers in their pots.

She keeps it up, too, all the way to our lockers.

I know better than to open my mouth.

I can't believe I screwed up this badly. I've never, repeat never ever *ever*, forgotten a school assignment before. And English?

Emily, for God's sake?

Devin works her combination, then slams open her locker and throws her books inside. "I count on you for my A's in English, Chan," she says more to the locker than to me. "I'm sunk without you. You know that."

"I'm really, really, really sorry." I can't look at her, so I stare at the blue cinder block walls or the uglier blue hallway tile instead. I don't need anything out of my locker. "I'll make up for it on the final draft."

"You letters. Me numbers." Devin thumps her chest with her free hand. "*Comprende?*"

"*Comprende.* I'm so sorry."

She flashes me another look. Flowers wouldn't die from this one, but I'm not sure they'd bloom, either. "Well, I guess I forgive you, but only if you spill."

My heart skips and I almost step on a freshman who bumped into me. "About what?"

Devin rolls her eyes. "About the guy. Merwood Spitball. You're still hooked up with him, aren't you? You've been chatting nonstop, and that's why you didn't do the outline?"

"I—uh . . ." I fiddle with my lock even though I don't want to open it.

People elbow and bang around us. The noise in the hall seems like thunder and waterfalls made out of voices, and all of a sudden, the whole place smells like Pine-Sol and strawberry and bubble gum. I want to gag.

"Your salvation depends on your answer right here." Devin leans toward me, her face a few inches from mine, so close I can see each hair in her eyebrows. The flower-withering glare comes back. "Heave it up, honey, or stay in purgatory forever."

"I'm still hooked up with him," I admit, and hope Devin doesn't find a way to wilt me in my pot. "We've been chatting nonstop, and that's why I completely spaced on the outline."

Devin looks shocked for a few seconds, then worried, then a sly smile spreads across her face. "Honey, you are so gonna get busted and put in Mommy-prison forever."

"God, I know." I laugh, more from nerves and relief than anything else.

Devin laughs, too.

Oh, no. It can't be this easy. Why haven't I been telling her everything? I can't remember all of a sudden, because she's Devin, and she's my best friend.

I can be so stupid.

We close our lockers and start toward our next class. "He's so cute and sweet," I say, "And he's helping me and everything."

All the rest of the way down the hall, I tell her everything about Paul I can think of except for his age, and answer every question she fires at me. I kind of leave out the big stuff, though, like my confession to Paul about herpes. . . .

Paul and I will have to come up with something, to put Devin off the scent a little. He has to understand about best friends, even if he's twenty-three. It wasn't that long ago that he had best friends, right?

Does Paul have best friends? He said he got in trouble at my age. I wonder if he has best friends now, or if he lost most of them like I did last year. Guess there's more stuff to ask after all. . . .

By the time we get Devin to her next class, she seems satisfied—but she still says, "You need to be careful, Chan. Promise me you'll be careful and you *won't* go to meet him in person unless you take me."

"Yes, Mother."

"And you'll get the outline for the Emily paper done by tomorrow, too," Devin continues. "In straight-A style, right?"

Guilt jabs at me. Devin has dragged me through every math class we've ever had, and I *know* I owe her. "Absolutely. I promise."

She elbows me as she walks through the door to her class. "And we're definitely calling the paper 'The Wild Dyke of Amherst.' Total A. All the way."

Sorry, Emily.

"Done."

. . .

Monday afternoon, my weights come, but I refuse to "pay" Paul until I learn how to use them properly. Then I end up staying in my closet for two hours after I talk to him, working on that stupid Emily outline.

I've just given up for the night and gotten out of the closet when Lauren comes into my room again.

Only, it's a little different this time. She's not all wild-eyed and fully into panic-drama. In fact, she's only half-awake, scratching under both armpits like she's got a bunch of crawly, biting bugs.

"Bad dream," she mutters.

Then she just stands there and doesn't do anything pushy or angsty or demanding at all. She doesn't do a thing but dig at herself like a monkey.

After a second or two, I turn back the covers and pat the bed.

Lauren wanders forward.

I help her get in, then climb in beside her and shake her shoulder just enough to get her to quit scratching and look at me.

"What did you dream about?"

I can't be sure in the low moonlight slipping in over my shutters, but I think her face might be turning red. I definitely see tears pool in her big round eyes. Not the fake-freak-out kind, but real ones.

"People . . . people looking at me," she whispers. Her fists tighten, and she presses one against her cheek. She used to do that when she was really little, when she still sucked her thumb. "I was Brigitta and I started to sing 'Edelweiss' with my family at the big competition, only I didn't have any clothes on." She presses her other fist into her cheeks and starts to cry. "I was naked and everybody laughed at me."

"It's probably the stress from all your rehearsals." I wrap my arms around her. "Are you sure being in *Sound of Music* is worth all these bad dreams?"

"Yes," she mumbles into my shoulder.

What can I say?

Look at what I go through to beat myself half to death with a couple of spinning silver sticks.

"Okay. Well. If this kind of bad dream keeps happening, we're going to have to talk to Mom."

But Lauren's getting quiet already, waiting for me to start the princess story. So I tell it again until I hear her snoring. Then I roll over and do my best to doze off, too, in between Lauren's scratching and kicking. She gets my calf once, though, really frogs it, which keeps me up awhile. In the end, I get exactly two hours of sleep, but at least I get the Emily outline done during all that awake time.

. . .

On Tuesday, I turn the outline in before class and we get a major thumbs-up on our "Wild Dyke of Amherst" theme. Then I get sent to the principal's office for sleeping through physics.

Lectures I hate, yeah, but I can take them okay from school people, especially since nobody calls Mom. And Tuesday night, Paul and I agree to make 1:00 a.m. our limit, so I won't totally blow school.

Then I spend the rest of my week and the next week, too, eating and exercising according to the plan.

Well, the plans.

Nutrition, exercise, including Dad in the exercise

whenever he'll do it, keeping Mom off my back about
the computer, working through my competition routine
two thousand times, talking to Devin whenever she calls
so she won't get too uptight about Paul, talking to
Paul—

There *are* a lot of plans to keep up with.

THURSDAY, OCTOBER 30

Two weeks—and the Bear's grace period on my weighing in—really did just fly by, even though I haven't been having total fun.

The Thursday I have to step on the scales comes way too fast.

All my chances are up now. It's either make weight, or I'm out.

Devin and I both get to the gym early, but we get in line last. She holds my hand. I don't think I can breathe much longer. The gym-sock-cleanser smell hangs so strong in the locker room that it makes my eyes water, and Devin keeps sniffing. Can't tell much by that, though, because Devin sniffs whenever she gets nervous.

Over our heads, the ceiling lights flicker because the janitor keeps running his buffer across the gym floor. The loud hum of the machine blocks the whispers of the witch-monster and all the other girls, but I feel pretty sure they're talking about me and whether or not I'll make weight.

The Bear, dressed all in green today, has her clipboard out, along with her big red pen. Following Paul's instructions and the Bear's demands for *moderation*, I haven't weighed in all week, so I have no idea what that pen might write about me when I step on the scale.

I've eaten the calorie total I was supposed to eat, plus or minus no more than fifty. I did the strength training and exercises Paul recommended—and Dad did some of them with me. Of course, when we went walking, I had to go up and back, up and back every time since he couldn't keep up, but he did walk with me. Lauren went with us once, too, but she got irritated with Dad and called him slowpoke, so I didn't let her go the next time.

Have I been hungry enough?

I shift from one foot to the other.

Have I been tired enough when I exercised?

Girl after girl gets on the scale, and I hear the Bear saying, "Good. Yes. Good."

Ellis flounces by me after her turn, looking superior.

Wonder if she's got herpes yet. Please, universe? Can there be a little justice?

As each girl finishes, they leave the locker room and head out to warm up for practice. No doubt they would have hung around to stare at me if the Bear allowed that. She hardly ever does, though.

"Good. Excellent." The Bear smiles at Carny, who gives me a thumbs-up and a hopeful smile as she leaves.

Will I be good, too? Excellent's too much to hope for. Good would be fine.

Please, God, let Paul's plan work. Let me make weight.

Maybe I'll die of freaking out before my turn on the scale and it won't matter. If I don't die, Devin will. She grips my hand tighter, and I decide I'll lose all the weight I need to lose when my fingers fall off from lack of blood flow.

"You look like you're smaller," she whispers as she scrubs her free hand against her black practice leotard. "Your clothes fit looser, I think. They fit great before. It's hard to say. This is excruciating."

Because I can't focus at all, I have to dig through my brain to remember the definition of excruciating, but I finally get there. "Yeah. Excruciating."

Devin doesn't ease up any until we get to the scale— when she shoves me forward and almost makes me trip over the platform.

I steady myself, whirl back toward Devin, and start to get behind her, but she shakes her head.

"You go, Chan." She bites at one of her fingers. "I can't stand the suspense."

If the Bear weren't standing right behind me, I'd say a few things. The Bear doesn't tolerate swearing, though. *Svearing isn't ladylike.*

When I turn to the scale, the Bear's smiling at me.

My eyebrows shoot up. I've never seen her smile when I headed to the scale before. She usually looks angry or a little nervous, because I'm always *right* on the line. Today she looks positively cheerful.

I go from scared to terrified as she studies me with her magnified eyes, but I make myself step onto the metal platform.

My heart squeezes, then stops, squeezes, then stops as I swallow and try to move the weights with my shaking hands.

The balance line bounces between its metal stops, and finally quits moving.

At first, I can't believe what I'm seeing. My eyes must be lying. Maybe I screwed something up, because that can't be true.

No way.

Really fast, I get off the scale, get back on, and move the weights again.

Three pounds under.

I start to smile.

The Bear laughs out loud. Her pen squeaks against her clipboard as she says, "Excellent, Chan. I knew my faith vas not misplaced."

Devin lurches forward, stares at the scale, then claps and squeals. "Three pounds *down*. Stuuuu-pendous!"

I jump off the scale, think about turning a cartwheel, imagine breaking both my arms, and don't. Devin turns one for me. Then she almost runs out of the locker room without doing her own weight check.

As usual, she has no trouble coming in under the bar for her height, but for once, I don't feel jealous. I bounce out of weigh-in with her, singing and wanting to make faces at the witch-monster, who is so totally shocked by my happy mood.

Herpes soon. Justice will prevail.

After that, practice flows. I mean, it *really* flows. The Bear makes us integrate new steps into our routine to get ready for competition. I keep my rhythm and don't miss a single toss. My muscles don't hurt as much as usual, either, thanks to some strengthening exercises Paul added when I explained about how tired dance practice usually makes me. My head feels light, and I can't do enough, can't get enough. Like flying fast and doing dives and rolls. Total zone. Total perfection.

I don't even get flippy when Mom pops into the gym wearing a bright blue long-sleeve T-shirt that screams *Better DEAD than voting RED*, or when Lauren eats really ooey-gooey-wonderful-smelling chocolate chip cookies all the way home.

The minute we walk in the door, Mom gets absorbed with local campaign stuff, since the election's less than a week away. Lauren heads off to a friend's house, so I get to be alone awhile, and tell Paul the good news.

Perfect, and more perfect.

Dad comes home later, and he and I walk after dinner,

and he gets a kick out of me being goofy—and he doesn't ask me any hard questions.

No hard questions is definitely a plus.

I think he's walking a little faster, and he doesn't seem to be breathing as hard. After we get home, he gives me a kiss before I go up to my room, and he says, "Tonight was fun, doodlebug. I like it when you're happy."

"Me, too." I give him an extra kiss, because it's true, and because I like being happy a lot.

I can't wait to get to chat to tell Paul he's a genius, and I made it.

I owe him big-time.

Wild nights! Wild nights!
Were I with thee,
Wild nights should be
Our luxury!

Futile the winds
To a heart in port,—
Done with the compass,
Done with the chart.

Rowing in Eden!
Ah! the sea!
Might I but moor
To-night in thee!

Emily Dickinson

CONNECTION

Storms wake us in a moonless night.
We lie in silence,
Drowned by noise,
Lost in the screams of the wind.

Rain beats the windows
And we slide closer,
Staring at each other,
Breathing electric air.

I reach for you in the lightning,
You join me in the thunder,
And we rain and howl and crash,
We rumble and roll and roar.

Finally we cling to each other
And sleep in the dwindling mist,
    No longer awake.
        No longer threatened.
        Released.

Chan Shealy

SUNDAY, NOVEMBER 2

I think I'm ready.

I really do.

Everybody tells me good night and heads for bed. I linger downstairs, and I'm the last one to my room—and I pretty much run to my computer as soon as I'm sure Mom and Dad are settled.

I open the laptop right on my desk, after double-checking the door three times.

Five minutes late, but Paul's in chat, waiting for me.

"Evening," he says.

"You're still a genius," I write back, studying his shadowy outline. "I'm still so happy over weigh-in."

My heart thumps and bumps and rocks. I keep standing beside my desk even though I'm typing. Too nervous to sit down.

"No big deal." Paul's letters flash at me, bright purple, double normal size, followed by five rolling smileys. "I knew you could do it."

My fingers flex, but I can't think of anything to type back. When I try to swallow, my throat feels too tight.

"I really like your outfit," Paul says next.

Heat flows across my cheeks and moves down to my neck, sliding under the tight black tank top I've chosen for my little show tonight. I probably look like I've got third-degree burns. My black jeans feel too tight, but they hug in all the right places.

"You ready to pay up?" Paul types. This time he punctuates with a winking smiley and the one with its eyes bulging out.

No way I can answer him.

I just adjust the camera angle and walk to my weight bench, which I keep a little over an arm's length away from my bed.

The house seems way too silent as I sit down next to the lamp I placed on the floor when I first came into the room. Blood thunders in my ears. If Mom walks by outside, she'll be able to see the light under my door.

She'll probably come in.

I can always say I'm trying to get in an extra workout. She might believe that.

My head swims. Chills rush up and down my arms.

If I squint, I can make out Paul's outline in the little streaming window on the laptop on my desk. I can't see his handsome face clearly, but I know he's looking at me. I can feel his eyes burning across my face, my neck, the muscles in my arm as I pick up a small weight.

Just do a workout, he told me last night. *Go through the paces like I'm not even there.*

Right. Sure.

I feel like he's standing right behind me, ready to put his hands on my shoulders. My belly keeps turning flips, and I can't breathe right as I position myself to handle the weight.

Don't be stupid. You're not a virgin, for God's sake.

But somehow this is scarier.

Strange and exciting, and it feels way dangerous, even though I have my clothes on.

Paul's watching.

He's an older guy—and he thinks I'm sexy.

He thinks me lifting this weight is sexy.

I grin.

Oh, wait.

Is grinning sexy?

I erase the grin, try to think about the ways hot women look at men in movies, and pull my face into some kind of serious hot-movie-woman expression. I hope.

Then I put my free hand on my knee, lean forward, and curl the five-pound orange weight up toward my chin.

One, two, three, four . . . I curl hard and fast, like I'd do in a real workout, only if I were really working out, I'd let myself breathe better—and I'd definitely lose the tight pants.

But for now, I curl, and try not to gasp and sweat.

All the way to thirty. Other hand. *One, two, three, four . . .*

No noises in the hall.

I wonder if my heart can explode from just lifting weights.

The house is sooo quiet. The air seems still, a little cool, almost cold. I get more chills.

If Mom bursts in on me, she probably won't buy the workout thing, but she might not notice the computer being in chat. And even if she notices that, she might not notice the camera set to stream. Mom doesn't understand about how cameras work with the Internet, or she never would have let me get a laptop with a camera already in it.

I finish with the first set of lifts, pick up a second weight, lie back on the bench without looking at Paul, and push the weights up, up, up, like I'm pressing some serious iron.

What's he seeing?

Me, on my back, lifting orange dumbbells.

Maybe I look like a dumbbell.

My breasts look like some of Dad's pancakes inside the tank, but nothing's showing on the sides at least. I bring the weights down too fast and almost smack myself in the head.

If Paul could transport into my room, he might touch me somehow. Rest his hand on my leg, or massage my bicep as I jab my arms upward.

I'd probably like it, him touching me.

Doing my best not to giggle or turn any redder, I sit up and go to the next set of reps, making sure to face Paul and the camera as I lower the weights behind my head.

Now my boobs look better. Way better. Almost like they belong on my chest.

Not a total dumbbell.

Maybe he knows he didn't make a mistake, choosing me for his Red. I do have curves.

A few minutes later, I finish my show-workout, put down the weights, and have to grab a corner of my sheets to wipe the sweat off my forehead. Sweat isn't sexy, in my opinion, at least not on a girl.

My heart's still beating funny when I get back to Paul. He's typed stuff while I was working with the weights. Mostly "Oh, my God," in different sizes and colors, with lots of freaky multicolored smileys.

I laugh and pick up the computer. On the way to my closet, I shut off the lamp on the floor and put it back on my bedside table.

Did I look hot? I hope I looked hot.

Jeez, I need to breathe and settle down.

By the time I get comfortable in the closet and pull the door almost shut, Paul has typed, "You could make money doing that, Red. Amazing."

Air snorts out my nose as I gulp down a loud laugh. "You're nuts. You know that, right?"

"I'm totally not nuts!" Bright pink bouncing smiley. "Money. Lots of it. I swear."

I roll my eyes and lean back against the closet wall. When I take a breath, the air smells like cedar and detergent, kind of soft and comforting, but I still feel charged up. "Who would pay money to see me lift orange dumbbells?"

"ME!" Paul types back right away, with no smileys at all.

"Ha, ha," I write. The jumpy, electric zings in my stomach get worse, then change to something like a low, hot buzz. "You're supposed to like looking at me. You're my boyfriend."

Paul's shadowy outline leans back, then forward again as he types. "By this time tomorrow night, I bet I could have $300 in that Portal account, all from guys who paid to see that stream."

"What—you're talking about pervs?" The buzz in my stomach spreads out to my arms and legs, then turns cold.

Paul hesitates before he types. He turns his head to the side, like he's staring at his bedroom door.

Not now. Christ!

We're both old enough to know what we're doing. His dad needs to bug off and quit giving Paul crap. Paul's grown, for God's sake.

My eyes jerk toward the closet door, then toward the bedroom door I can see through the opening, as if the whole world just heard what Paul wrote about selling the video. As if my parents might explode into my space, grab my computer, and shatter the whole thing into hundreds of pieces. Chills—the bad kind—crawl all over my body. I don't know if I believe in premonitions, but if premonitions happen, I wonder if I'm having one.

Of Mom, standing in my door with a horrified look on her face. . . .

The blinking icon on my computer grabs my attention.

Paul is typing.

"Well, yeah. Some of them might be pervs, but perv-bucks spend just like everyone else's money, you know?"

Paul's shaded outline looks . . . tense.

Oh, God. Is he serious? "Don't show my video to pervs! No way!"

"You're dressed, Red." His shoulders lift and fall, like he's shrugging. "It's not like you did anything illegal."

I can't quit looking from the computer to the closet door to my bedroom door. "Hey, I did that show for *you*."

Weirdness drifts all around my brain like lightning, looking for a place to strike. If I half close my eyes, I bet I can see it. Something strange. Something I can't touch. Something I probably shouldn't let get anywhere near close enough to touch me.

Paul types, "I know you did that for me. I loved it, big-time. And if I loved it so much, I know other guys would cough up for it, too. Sorry. My dad's big into business. Can't help thinking that way. Who knows? Maybe someday I'll make a bunch of money and really make him proud."

The weird sensation in my head burns away as I think about how much pressure it would be to have a power-crazy dad who controls everything and treats you like a baby, even though you're an adult. Paul has it harder than me, for sure.

Besides . . .

A smile tugs at my lips.

It's sweet that he thinks other guys would find me sexy enough to pay money to see me. And a little exciting, to think about dozens of guys who look like Paul, all paying big bucks to drool over me. Another electric charge travels up and down my body, like when I was handling the weights. Like working out for Paul and knowing he's watching.

I've never felt so far away from the world, so totally in my own space. My closet seems like a magical place, where I can live the way I want to and not worry about anything. And where I have Paul, and he has me, and we have our secrets—safe together, completely.

God, I'm probably maroon, I'm blushing so hot and hard. Good thing Paul can't see much with just the light from my laptop.

Still . . .

"Don't you dare show that video to anybody."

His shoulders move again. Another shrug. "You're missing out on some major cash, Red. You have no idea how hot you really are."

"Come on. Do you really think you could make that much money off ten minutes of me lifting weights?

Paul's hands fly up, like, *Oh my God*. Then back to the keyboard. "I'm sure of it. I've got a friend who knows how to do that kind of stuff."

My eyes narrow as I stare at his profile in the streaming box. My next question pops out of my fingertips, and I press SEND in a hurry.

"Have you ever made money that way, Paul?"

He sits back. Looks at the door again. Seems to get more tense. Then his head droops a little, and I want to climb through the screen and give him a hug.

"Tell me," I type. "Like I promised before, I won't judge you if you just *tell* me stuff when I ask, I promise." I cue up a serious, businesslike smiley with little bifocal glasses. "This chat is a no-judgment zone."

Paul leans toward his keyboard again and writes, "Yeah, I've made a few bucks selling some pictures of myself with no shirt—you know, muscle shots—just to see if I could."

I gaze at Paul's words and his image for a while, then send: "You're a man of many secrets."

"I do have lots of secrets, Red. I warned you. Are we still okay?"

I touch his image in the streaming box, outlining him with my fingertip. So much about him I don't know . . . but I want to know.

Can I live with what I find out?

I think I can.

And I don't want Paul to feel bad. I so know what it's like to be the biggest freak on the block, thanks to Adam-P.

"Just because I don't want you to sell my video to pervs on the Net doesn't mean we're not okay. Of course we're okay." I hit a smiley, one that bounces and rolls.

He perks up a little. "Good." Then, after one of those heart-squeezing looks with his perfect mouth in a perfect smile: "I really can trust you, can't I?"

We spend the rest of the chat talking about Lauren and her nightmares, because I'm getting a little worried about her. Paul says he doesn't think I should tell Mom yet. Sibling-secret-loyalty and all that, and Lauren would be totally furious if Mom made her drop out of *Sound of Music*.

"This play stuff sounds as important to her as twirling is to you," he types. "You don't want to risk that."

"Yeah, but if she doesn't start sleeping soon, I've got to do something."

"Give it a little time. Sometimes things work themselves out." He sends me a winking smiley, and I kiss my fingers and press them against his image on the screen.

He makes me feel hot, even if I'm not. He makes me feel good, and better, and that's what matters.

As for the selling streaming video part—no, no, not happening, no way.

MONDAY, NOVEMBER 3

Monday morning, when I come downstairs for school, Mom's eyebrows lift the minute I walk into the kitchen. "Are you sure you want to wear that shirt? It's a little tight."

Drops of rain stream down the bay window of the breakfast nook. I focus on them to keep from rolling my eyes, work very hard not to shrug, and manage, "I like the way it fits," in a voice that I hope doesn't sound *argumentative* or *disrespectful*. Mom hates *argumentative* and *disrespectful*.

Her sweatshirt has a picture of the United States divided into red states and blue states. The blue states are labeled *United States of America*, while the red states are labeled *Dumbfoolistan*.

That one takes me a second.

Definitely wouldn't pass dress code at school, unlike *my* shirt. Mine's a long-sleeved black T-shirt that's a year old, and I haven't been able to wear it. Now I can because of starting to tone up with Paul's training program. The shirt has a high neck and no print or pictures at all, so it won't piss anyone off. Yeah, it hugs my curves a little, but I *have* curves. Isn't it okay to show them off? I'm not eight or anything, like Lauren, who's jabbing at her eggs with a fork.

Dad's chowing on an omelet, some bacon, and some toast. At my place is a single serving of eggs, one strip of bacon, and a grapefruit half. Just what I ordered. Dad's the best.

When Mom sits down with her omelet and bacon and toast and a bran muffin, she says, "That doesn't look like enough food for a growing girl, Chan—especially one as athletic as you are."

Don't be disrespectful. Don't be argumentative. Be responsible.

What would Paul say?

Paul talks like he has a knack for parent appeasement, maybe because he's older. Or smarter. Or something. I imagine him leaning back in his chair, imitate that laid-back adorable grin as best I can, and say, "Thanks for worrying so much about me, but I've been reading a lot about nutrition like you suggested, and I'm trying to eat five smaller meals a day instead of three large ones."

Mom blinks at me, opens her mouth, closes it, opens it again, and says, "Okay. What good does that do?"

I swallow a bite of grapefruit and give her another polite smile, or at least I hope that's how it looks. "It keeps my portion sizes more normal and reasonable so I don't get all stretched out and stay hungry, and it's better for active people like me. It's supposed to keep my blood sugar stable as I practice and work out. That kind of thing."

Thank you, Paul.

Thank you, Bear.

Thank you, Web sites.

"Well, okay." Mom wipes out her muffin, then fixes her gaze firmly on my face. "I just don't want you too obsessed with weight and body size and all of that. If twirling's going to cause that, then—"

"Please don't say you'll make me stop twirling." My voice is too quiet, and the words come out too fast. My back goes stiff, so do my arms and hands and face. My entire body. "Twirling's my life right now. Twirling's everything."

Lauren looks up from her scooted-around eggs, and I notice the dark circles under her eyes. "That's mean, Mom, threatening somebody with their worst fear to get your way. Isn't that unethical? Like what the Nazis did to Captain von Trapp, threatening his family and his home to force him into military service?" She lets out a breath and answers her own question. "Definitely unethical."

I don't know who starts gaping at Lauren first or biggest, me or Mom or Dad.

She shrugs. "I read Web sites, too. I knew I had a better chance of landing a role in the play if I really understood what it's about, understand the director's *vision*. I might need voice lessons, a voice coach, too, to work on my projection and carriage." Then she looks down at her plate, goes back to playing in her eggs, and just like that, we don't exist to her again.

We all take a bite of food, staring at the strange little eight-year-old, who, for whatever reason, just defended me better than I could defend myself. Better than most of Mom's politicians could have defended me. With a vocabulary better than Devin's.

Projection and carriage? Jeez. That had to come from her director.

Mom's not saying a word, but she's probably calculating ways to adjust Lauren's Internet filters to eliminate Web sites with the words *Nazi* and *ethics* and probably *voice coach*, too. Mom's opinion of voice coaching ranks just above—or maybe even below—her opinion on dieting and consulting nutritionists.

Extracurricular activities are fine, she tells us all the time. *I just don't want you girls to be so overinvested and anxious. We aren't raising you to be obsessive.*

"Are you sure that director's not putting ideas in your head?" Mom asks Lauren.

I glance at the United States of Dumbfoolistan once more, then close my eyes.

When I open them, I watch Dad finish his giant omelet. He eats a bite of Lauren's toast, tries my grapefruit, then starts cleaning off the table whistling tunes from *Sound of Music.*

The whole scene's just too weird for me. I actually can't wait to get to school.

Which happens soon enough. School, and class, and finally, practice.

Except, as I head into the gym, I see Adam-P in his football pads, lip-locked with Ellis.

I stop so fast that Alice, one of the freshmen, bumps into me from behind.

When she sees what slowed me up, she grabs my hand and gives me a tug.

"Gonorrhea, anyone?" she says loud enough to be heard two buildings away.

Why can't I ever think of good things like that to say—when they're right in front of me?

Ellis breaks off their kiss and smiles at me like a rich benefactor giving pity to a starving orphan. Then she tries to kiss Adam again, but he takes off down the hall toward the practice field. Ellis jogs after him, saying something about a time to get together later that night, but Alice and I don't stick around.

Later that day, I don't really want to leave practice and go home, but Devin comes with me, and we work on our competition routines in the garage. I go through mine too many times to count, but Devin keeps stopping me in the middle. "You've got to get that toss-illusion better, Chan. The whole performance hinges right there. It's pivotal. Nail that, and nail first place. Again."

She starts the music over.

"Again."

"Again."

"Again. . . ."

And so it goes.

I'm not any easier on her. Devin competes in the dance sections, and I stop and start her music twenty times. By the time we finish, both of us are sweating.

Yes, Devin's sweating.

When we get back inside the house, Lauren's playing on the computer, some computer game with a lot of bouncing puppies on a bright pink background. Mom's hovering close by, glancing over now and then.

After cooling off and sucking down a liter or two of water, Devin asks Mom for a ride home. When Devin hugs me good-bye, she reminds me that our first Emily rough draft is due next Monday. She doesn't get me in trouble with Mom by mentioning the outline I screwed up, but Devin's don't-you-do-it-again look is enough to keep me in line.

"I've already got a few paragraphs," I assure her. "I'll tell you as soon as I'm done."

After Mom leaves, I take a short walk with Dad.

When I come back in, Lauren's still on the computer. She jumps when she sees me, but when I glance at the screen, it's just the pink puppy game.

"Don't you have homework?" I ask.

Ohmygod. Did I just sound like Mom?

"I did it at school," she says without looking at me. "Are you finished with the garage?"

"Yeah, for the night."

Lauren shuts down the computer. She grabs her duffel, double-checks something inside it, and beats it out
the door to rehearse for her play.

Mom's voice rings in my mind.

We aren't raising you to be obsessive. . . .

Yeah, well, somebody should explain that to Lauren
a little better.

She starts warbling "The hiiii-iiiillls are aaaalliiiiiiive . . ."
before I even make it up the steps.

Fifteen minutes later, I'm sprawled on my bed, doing
stretches and chatting with Paul. This whole before-the-
middle-of-the-night-talking thing is too cool.

"I swear, that kid's really freaking herself out about
this play," I tell him, adding a cross-eyed smiley for effect,
even though he could see bits and pieces of me through
the webcam as I stretch.

"Don't you freak yourself out about games and competitions?" he types back. "I always did. She's just getting an early start."

Before I can say anything else, he adds, "That stretch
was a nice one," with a smiley that has big, bulging eyes.
"Put the computer on a pillow and do it again. Let me
see the whole thing."

I get that tingly feeling all over, and I can't help grinning. He makes me feel so . . . *all that.* I slide the laptop
up to my pillow, stretch on my side with my back to the
door, extend as tight as I can, and lift my left arm and leg
at the same time, until my fingers and toes touch.

Paul gives me a thumbs-up in the camera window, and we both laugh.

Another few smileys with giant eyes come through.

"Do it again," he writes. "In your underwear."

I roll my eyes.

Guys.

They really are *all* about one thing, most of the time.

Except I happen to like this guy, so I compromise. Since I have on a sports bra, I take off my shirt and toss it on the floor, but leave my sweats in place. Then I do the stretch for him again, really, really slowly.

It's so delicious, making him happy like that, with just my body. I don't feel as self-conscious now that I'm a little smaller—and with my sweatpants still on. I'm not too proud of my legs, but my upper body, it's not so bad.

Definitely not so bad, judging by Paul's reaction and the lines of smileys he fires through the chat.

Soon he might want to see more.

That thought gives me shivers, because soon I might want to show him more.

It doesn't feel like such a problem or a risk, showing off for him through a webcam. Like there's a barrier between us, a small one, but enough for me to feel safe and not so guilty. I mean, how much safer can sex get, just showing with no touching at all? I don't have to worry about anything like outbreaks or protection or pregnancy. It's just . . . fun.

I wonder what he looks like under his clothes.

With a grin, I lean forward and type, "Why don't you take off *your* shirt?"

Paul sits up straight, then smiles and shakes his head. In one fluid motion, he pulls off his black hoodie.

And oh, my God, the muscles.

He really is cut, just like a gym model. Tats crisscross his arms and pecs, some I've seen before in his pictures and some I haven't. I squint at the designs, trying to make them all out. If he could materialize in my bedroom, I'd trace them all, from his wrists down to his belly button. I like tattoos, especially artful, sexy ones like his.

Paul stands up and pulls off his jeans to show me thick, muscled legs sticking out of bright blue Scooby-Doo boxers.

I crack up.

He poses for the camera, curling his biceps like a bodybuilder at a photo shoot.

And I can't help noticing he's . . . a little excited.

Except, he doesn't look little at all.

Adam-P was, uh, interesting in that department, but now I realize he really is just a boy. Paul's definitely a grown man. Lots more interesting.

He sits back down and seems to realize what I'm staring at. I get another smile, along with a line of bulgy-eyed smileys.

"Did you like what you saw, Red?"

My face flushes, and my stomach jumps.

"Yeah," I type back. "You've got a lot of . . . muscle."

His eyes go wide and he laughs as he types, "You are so bad. You know that? But I like it. Don't stop."

"For tonight, we're stopping." I shake my finger at him on the webcam. "I'm worn out, and my mom will be home like, any second. Plus, Lauren will probably be up to get some leotards soon."

Though come to think of it, she hasn't been doing that as much lately. When she isn't on the computer, she's out in the garage, singing—or in my bed after a nightmare, kicking me stupid.

Paul is typing.

"We'll do more soon, right?" he writes. "I mean, it's safe and everything."

"Safe in one way," I answer. "Sure. But I don't want to go too fast."

On the camera, Paul shrugs and nods. "You're the boss," he types. "And you're sexy as hell in that sports bra. I'd settle for that and some tight shorts. . . ."

"You don't give up, do you?"

"Never."

I give him another long, slow stretch, letting my sports bra ride up just a little on one side, to tease him. I even cup my breasts, to show him the real shape.

"You're beautiful," he types in giant letters. "I want to see more. Now. You're teasing me to death."

I keep up my show and let him see a little more of my breast. "Don't you wish I'd show you what's underneath

194

this cloth?" I ask out loud, knowing he'll figure out what I mean. "But you've got to earn that."

Paul virtually jumps backward, and his camera window winks out. A message flashes, telling me he's left chat just about the time I hear my bedroom door bounce against the door jamb.

I forgot to turn the lock!

Paul must have seen the door opening through the webcam.

There's no time to flip up the screen concealer, and no way of hiding that I've been in chat. Worse yet, the streaming image of me is still active, even if Paul's gone. There I float in space on my computer, holding my breasts through the sports bra, looking like everybody's favorite hooker.

Let it be Lauren at the door.

The silence behind me feels like knives in my back.

Let it be Dad.

I slowly lower my hands to my sides and get ready to turn around.

When I do, I find Mom standing ice-statue still, arms folded, eyes wide, face completely pale. "Might I ask what *the hell* you were doing?" she says in a deadly quiet voice.

Sweat pops out on my face and neck and chest, where I feel the heat of Mom's gaze.

"I expect an answer, Chandra. Now."

My eyes close all on their own. "I was stretching," I say, hoping she still doesn't understand the streaming video. "Exercising. With support. You know, like at Weight Watchers or something, only this is online."

"With whom were you . . . *stretching?*"

Mom walks farther into my room, closer to the bed, closer to seeing what I don't want her to see. And if she sees the chat room name, she'll track it, and find Paul, and his age, and everything. He'll be dead. I'll be dead.

"A friend." Lame.

"One I've researched and approved?"

"No." I sigh. "This is a new friend."

"*Devin* is a friend, Chandra. A real, live person that you know, in real places and real times. People online aren't friends. They're gambles at best—risks. Dangers."

Fire catches in my chest. "I'm not that stupid, you know. I'm capable of talking to people and judging them for myself."

"You're sixteen years old," Mom says in that I-know-all-and-you-know-nothing tone I really hate. She moves closer behind me, and I know she's trying to see what's on the laptop. With each passing second, I'm getting madder. More mad than scared, even.

"What were you doing with that boy I saw on your screen? Tell me the truth, Chandra. He could *see* you—you could see him!" She starts toward the laptop. "There's some kind of video camera built into that machine."

I whirl toward the bed, grab my computer, and slam the top shut.

"Chan!" Mom reaches past me, snatches the laptop off the bed, and yanks the top back open. "I do not believe you just did that."

Relief washes through me when I see the black screen with the *Hibernating* logo. The programs I've downloaded to erase my Internet "tracks" are already at work, scrubbing away my history. Erasing Mom's access to Paul.

Tears push into my eyes. Almost out. Almost real teardrops.

Paul's safe. He's still mine and nobody else's, and Mom can't touch him. She drops the computer back on the bed and glares at me with an expression I've never seen before. Something like rage, but also disgust. And a little bit something else.

Fear, maybe?

Her eyes sweep over me, top to bottom, and disgust wins. Her upper lip curls, and all of a sudden, she looks like Ellis and the senior majorettes and every kid in school who calls me *skank* every time I turn a corner.

My eyes dry up before any tears fall, and so does my throat. My fists clench. I want to hit her. I actually want to hit my own mother.

It doesn't even freak me out.

"Put on your shirt," she says, ice-cold and whispery.

I can't move, because if I move, I'll hit her, so I don't twitch, not even a little twitch, or I'll do it, I swear.

Mom glances around, finds my shirt, snatches it off the floor, and throws it at me. It hits me across the chest and rests on my shoulder.

"Put it on!" Mom yells. Her fists clench just like mine. I grab the shirt off my shoulder, jam my hands into

197

the sleeves, and jerk it down to cover my bra and belly. "There. Happy?"

"Who was he?" Mom points to the computer. "That boy. I want his name."

"Merwood Spitball." I'm yelling loud enough for the neighbors to hear. "We don't use real names on the Net, remember?" I want her out of my room. I still want to hit her. And go take a shower, because of how she's looking at me.

"Damn it, Chan—who?" The questions land like punches. "How old? How long?"

This time, I don't say anything. I fold my arms and hug myself as tightly as I can. No hitting. If I stand like this, I can't move my hands.

She points at me. "How did you meet him? And that camera—why would you do something so stupid?"

"I'm sixteen! Don't I have a right to *some* life of my own? A little privacy? A teeny bit of respect for my intelligence?"

Mom's sarcastic laugh slices right through me. "Intelligence. I guess showing your boobs to some boy on the Internet constitutes smart behavior now?"

"That's my business, not yours!" I hug myself tighter, and feel myself flushing red all over. My face burns. Even my eyes burn. She's still giving me that you're-so-filthy stare, and I hate her for it. "That *boy* makes me happy. That *boy* doesn't look at me like you're looking at me. I'm not ratting him out to anybody—especially you!"

Mom draws her hand back like she's going to slap me.

My head snaps away and I cover my face and shout, even though she didn't do it. More heat pours through me, and my brain starts to burn.

"Get out of my room!" I yell as loud as I can. "I hate you! Get out, get out!"

Mom lowers her hand.

Her expression finally changes. She doesn't look disgusted anymore. Just blank, then almost surprised. She picks up the laptop and walks toward my door.

I gasp for air and keep yelling. "Get out! Stay out!"

She has my computer. She's taking it. Taking Paul away.

"You're grounded," Mom says with her back to me. "Indefinitely. School and practice only. No unsupervised computer time, no phone calls, no visits from Devin, except to finish the paper. This computer, I'm taking it to my tech friends at work. They'll track this boy and find him, and then we'll talk."

She says other stuff, too, but I barely hear it. I can't stop staring at the laptop and hating her long enough to pay attention.

Disappointed beyond belief . . .

Ashamed . . .

Scared for you . . .

I thought you were so much more mature than this, Chandra. I thought . . .

When your father hears about this . . .

Her voice melts into a total drone, and then she's gone. Just gone. With my computer. I stand there shaking, and staring out my open bedroom door, and hating Mom worse than I've ever hated anything.

Lauren drifts into view, standing just outside. She's wearing a baggy shirt and a dirty pair of warm-up pants, and her hair's ratty like she hasn't combed it all day.

I glare at her, waiting for her to laugh at me or tease me or freak out and start crying so I have to stop feeling anything and just go take care of her, but she just looks all messed up and tired and sad. After a minute, she slips into my room, puts her arms around me, and presses her face into my belly.

Surprised, I put my hands on her shoulders and hug her back.

"It'll be okay," she whispers. "It has to be okay, right?"

When she pulls back and looks at me, I wonder if she's been crying. Probably upset from all the yelling.

"It'll be okay," I mutter, because I don't know what else to say.

Lauren nods. She lets me go and leaves my room, closing the door softly behind her.

WEDNESDAY, NOVEMBER 5

"I so do not believe I'm helping you do this." Devin's got her back to me. Her arms are folded so tight over her black sweater that I can see her fingers digging into the cloth under her arms. Even without seeing her face, I know she's frowning. Her black skirt sways as her foot taps against the tiled lab floor.

"Hey, who took care of delivering the break-up note to Tevo?" I bend over the technology lab keyboard and type as fast as I can. "He *cried*, Devin."

She does that air-hissing-through-the-teeth thing. "Fine. Okay. We're gonna be late for marching."

"Just another minute."

"Doofus will catch us any second, Chan."

Dr. Dorfas leaves early on Wednesday. It's just his lab assistant, and she takes three smoke breaks before she comes back to tutor and close down.

We know about Doofus and the lab assistant because last year, we did some serious recon and pulled about fifteen computer raids for Devin, so she could e-mail her boyfriend while she was grounded over staying out past curfew. Only, her boyfriend lived a few blocks from my house, not in some other state. And he was only seventeen years old.

She made him cry, too. Poor guy.

Devin can be . . . a little mean to guys sometimes.

The air in the technology lab doesn't stir at all despite the hum of computer fans, and the big concrete space is dark except for the glow of fifteen monitors—one of which I'm staring at as I hack around the school safety filters to send Paul an e-mail.

God, I hate telling him about things like getting grounded and Mom confiscating the laptop. I sound like such a baby, and he's a grown man. Once I get through the filters and make it to my e-mail account, I can't even figure out what to say at all.

Hey.

Mom busted me and took the computer. I'm grounded, so I can't talk.

And what else am I supposed to say?

Sorry, but I probably can't talk ever again. Sorry, but I'm still an infant and my parents completely control every aspect of my existence.

I erase the first start and frown at the blank e-mail.

Hey.

Parental interference. Lost the computer. It may be a while before I can chat. Don't give up on me.

No. Stop. Erase. That sucks, too.

My stomach starts to hurt.

I can't believe I'll be going home tonight and I won't be able to talk to Paul. The frosty glares all morning from Mom and the I'm-disappointed-and-worried speech from Dad was bad enough, but tonight it'll be so, so bad. Sad and boring. So totally nothing, like my life after Adam-P and before Paul.

I'll do homework. I'll watch Lauren try on leotards. I'll probably work on my competition routine until I fall over—and then I'll just be there, in Mommy-prison.

How am I supposed to go from having everything to just . . . *nothing* again?

Sick feelings scrape my insides until I feel hollow, and I want to put my face on the keyboard and just stay there until somebody throws me out.

"Chan, for God's sake, get it done." Devin's foot-tapping gets a whole lot faster and a whole lot louder.

I chew on my lip.

Dear Paul,

Grounded. No computer.

An idea flickers in the back of my mind.

For a few seconds, I try to push it away.

I can't do what I'm thinking. No way. No how.

But if I do . . .

If I don't, I might not be able to talk to Paul for like, forever. I might lose him. I might never get to see Paul's dimple again, or his smile, or his muscles, or those stupid big-eyed smileys he sends whenever I show him something he likes.

My fingers hover over the keyboard as I try to decide if I really have the guts to tell him my idea.

"Today, Chan!" Devin's voice makes me jump half out of my skin.

"Okay!" I glance at the back of her head.

Eyes back to the computer.

Delete. Delete. Delete.

Paul,

Computer confiscated. No way to get out of the house to get anything else.

I stop again.

My fingers hover over the keyboard as I try to decide if I really have the guts to tell him my idea.

And even if I tell him, will he do it?

"Do you know the name of his school?" Devin's voice makes me jump half out of my skin.

"What?" I glance at the back of her head again.

"This boy. Paul. Do you know the name of his school, his town, his football team? Anything that we can check out and verify?"

Not now. *I can't have this conversation. No.*

I keep my eyes on the computer screen. "Yeah. Got it. I checked him out, top to bottom."

Delete. Delete. Delete.

Paul,

Computer confiscated. Remember the video of me and the weights?

I stop again.

Can I do this?

It isn't really that big a deal, is it? Paul's right. I've got clothes on in that video. And if it makes money, Mom can't keep me shut down. I can get stuff she doesn't even know about.

"You promise?" Devin startles me again.

"Promise *what?*"

She shakes her head and looks hurt. "That you checked out this guy. That he's safe."

"Yeah, I promise." My fingers curl against the keys. "Now give it a rest if you want us to get out of here. I can't think if you keep interrupting me."

Devin mumbles to herself, but goes back to watching the door.

My hands shake as I type, *Sell the video if you can. Put the money in my account and I'll get a Berry or a phone with video as soon as possible. And I'll need that I.D.*

After another few seconds of me breathing hard and Devin-the-guard staying stone silent except for accelerated foot-tapping, I type in my address, with: *I'll look for something from you starting Friday. If I don't see anything, I'll be back here next Tuesday, same time to e-mail you. I'll get on sooner if I can—might be able to check my box a few times, but I'll definitely have POS.*

Okay.

That's that.

I need to press SEND, but I feel so totally ridiculous.

Why would a twenty-three-year-old gorgeous guy keep fooling with me after I turn out to have such a pain in the ass life? I mean, he can have girls who don't have to fool with parents.

"Chan. Now." Devin's talking through her teeth.

That gets me moving enough to sign the post; *With love, Red*.

"Send the e-mail already!" Devin says, more urgent than ever, moving toward the door.

Terrified that Dr. Doofus didn't actually leave early, or that the lab assistant's on her way back into the main room early, I hit ENTER and the post disappears from my mailbox.

Another few seconds of erasing tracks and cookies, and I'm finished. I even manage to catch up with Devin before she closes the lab door.

We fly to the gym and dress in a hurry, but the band's already marching when we hit the field at a dead run.

The Bear glares in our general direction for a few seconds, but finally motions for us to take our places. We'll hear about it later, no doubt, but at least for the moment, she looks too relaxed to muster a first-class fit.

Thank God for whatever put her in a good mood.

Everything's okay.

Everything's good.

Until after dance practice, when the Bear calls me into her office. Without Devin.

As Devin leaves the gym with her father, she gives me a desperate wish-I-could-help look, but I just shrug and mouth, *Don't worry*.

Devin's return look says, *Yeah, right*, before the gym door closes.

Then I'm back in the little concrete office with the dusty trophies on the high shelves, and the Bear's behind her desk. She has on crimson warm-ups today, and her lipstick and nail polish match the color perfectly.

When I sit down in the chair on the other side of her desk, she looks at me steadily, and I wait for her to cut loose about Devin and me being late for marching practice. I'm not even that nervous about it. I've thought of about five good lies.

Unless somebody saw us in the tech lab.

God, what if they've put up security cameras? They could have them right in the computers. I wouldn't even know!

But unless the cameras were focused right on the screen, I could say I was checking the price on new batons, or getting some workout and diet info—anything my mom might object to. Anything that somebody might believe.

Lying's getting easier by the minute. Still, by the time the Bear looks ready to speak, my head feels close to exploding.

"Your father vill be a few minutes late picking you up," she says.

I gaze at her, surprised, especially when she doesn't say anything else right away.

Usually, if parents are late, we just wait for them outside in the gym parking lot. A little extra time to go through our routines—no biggie.

The Bear folds her hands in front of her and leans forward, studying me with more intensity. The lines on her face get so tight I wonder if her skin will crack. "Your mother, she is caught up in her campaign wrap-up. She called and asked me to keep an eye on you until he arrives."

Oh, great. My cheeks start burning. *I'm not five! God, sometimes, I really do hate my mother.*

I want to close my eyes, but the Bear has me in her sights. "You're in trouble. It's serious, yes?"

"Yes. I mean, no." I shrug. "It's nothing. Just grounded. You know, normal stuff."

"Ah. Good, good." The Bear sits back in her chair, and the tight lines on her face relax. "Your mother's voice—I vorried it might be real trouble. That you might not twirl at Regionals."

"What?" My eyes go wide. It's my turn to lean forward. "Oh, no way. I'll be there. That's like the most important thing in my life other than—well, never mind. It's the most important thing."

The Bear keeps her relaxed position, but her face tenses again. "This trouble, it's over a boy?"

That surprises me so much I just say, "Yes, ma'am."

Her eyes draw down to tiny slits. "Not that football blockhead. Tell me no, not *him*."

I look straight into the Bear's slitted eyes. "Trust me, I'm never going there again. Not for any reason."

The Bear's smile comes so fast I almost sit back in terror. But she nods and keeps smiling, then gestures at a spot on the wall over my left shoulder, in the general direction of the practice field. "You're looking so good, he gives you quite the eye earlier, Mr. Blockhead Football. I'm thinking he regrets himself."

I have no idea what to say to the idea of Adam-P noticing how I look or maybe regretting the choices he's made, or that piece of mangled grammar from the Bear, so I don't say anything at all.

She leans forward again and fixes me with another one of her intense stares. Suddenly, I can see her younger, still beautiful, at some smoky bar with a drink in her hand, telling her best friend all the problems in the world, and maybe even laughing over some of them. Even when I blink, that image won't go away.

"Vhat that boy did to you last year, that Adam, he should be shot." She shakes her head, purses her crimson-painted lips, then adds, "His terrible lies and the other children being so—" She waves one hand with a frown. "Anyvay, I admire how you handled yourself."

All I can do is sit quietly and stare at the Bear.

I've fallen into some alternate universe. Who is this woman, and what has she done with my real coach?

"You've come a long vay from all that. Another thing I admire. And vhen you take Regionals—and you vill—yet another proud time, for you and for me." She smiles some more. Her right hand twitches, like she wants to reach out and pat my head. "Redemption."

Instead of some Russian good-wishing, she says, "Vould you like to step through your competition routine until your father comes?"

I almost jump out of my chair. "Yes, please."

Anything but this—whatever this is.

Before the Bear can change her mind, I hurry out of her office, grab my bag, unzip it, and take out my batons. She walks slowly to her usual competition-training position and leans back against the first folded bleacher in the gym, right around where the judges' table would be.

I get into ready pose and start humming the music to myself, but before my first move, the Bear interrupts me with, "Once, I had a hard time, too, Chan Shealy. Around your age."

My arms lower slowly. I'm not sure if I'm supposed to answer, or what I should do next, but the Bear gestures for me to get my sticks up again.

I do.

She says, "Don't forget I know about hard times, yes?"

Yes. No.

"Um, okay." I hold both batons steady and give her what I hope is a smile instead of nervous, twitching lips.

Then she starts me fast, clapping and shouting, "One, two, three, four!"

. . .

A-gain! is still ringing in my ears as I drag my exhausted self down the hall toward the parking lot, where I hope Dad's waiting. My bag and batons must weigh three hundred pounds, and my feet don't want to work at all.

Which is why I don't launch the world's best karate kick when Adam-P steps out of the shadows and stops me near the door with a quiet, "Chan, wait. You got a second?"

I quit walking so fast I almost stumble.

Then I'm just standing there like a mute idiot, looking up into his handsome face.

That I hate.

I hate his face. And him. Yes, I do. I'm remembering that.

He's all dressed in his football gear, and smeared up with grass and dirt like he doesn't do any better in practice than he does during games. Automatically, I check all around me for Ellis, but there's no sign of the witch-monster.

Sarcasm, please don't desert me now. Let me sneer something masterful and cutting and brilliant like Carny. Even one of Devin's too-long words. Something?

"What do you want?" I manage to ask, but my voice comes out a mumble.

Adam-P studies his dirty cleats. "I—I've been wanting to say, well, thought I should say—"

He stops. Chews on his lip. Looks . . . like he did the whole time we were dating.

Which is adorable.

I hate him. I hate him.

He's so close to me I could reach out and put my hands on his green-and-brown-streaked jersey. I could touch him because he's real and not on a computer and right here. My stomach twists all up and cramps, but at the same time, it feels all fluttery.

Yeah, I could touch the jerk. I could punch him in the face.

Only, I'm not feeling that mad.

My legs seem a little stronger. A little less tired. Maybe I could pull off that karate kick after all?

But my heart's not in it.

Exactly where my heart is, I can't say right this second.

All I can do is keep looking at Adam-P, who says, "I'm, uh, sorry, Chan. For everything last year. When the rumors got out and everybody started asking me if I, you know, had *it* and stuff—I flipped out. I shouldn't have—well, like I said. Sorry. I was way wrong."

My muscles loosen like somebody sucked all the juice out of my cells.

When Adam raises his head, he meets my gaze, and he *does* look sorry.

And adorable again.

I hate him. I do. I really, really do.

I want to cry. Or maybe scream. "Okay," is all that comes out of my mouth. Kind of automatically.

Not *Screw you*, or *Drop dead*, or even *Fine, I accept, now blow off.* A tongueless second grader could have done better than *Okay*.

"I've got to meet Ellis," Adam-P says, and he walks off just in time for me to see Dad out in the parking lot, heading toward the door.

I'm looking at Dad, but I'm hearing Adam-P say he's meeting Ellis over and over, and imagine them tonguing like they always do in the hallway and I wish I could think of *something* to yell at Adam-P's retreating back.

But he said he was sorry. I didn't imagine that, did I?

Devin is so never going to believe that just happened.

I don't think Dad sees Adam-P hustling down the hall, which is good, because my father *can* lose his temper every now and then. Even though I want to bash Adam-P with something, I don't want Dad going to jail for punching him in the face.

So I suck it up and don't say anything, and I go meet Dad outside. He walks me to the SUV, and I climb into the passenger seat.

Dad gets in on his side, fights with the extender on his seat belt, and finally gets it fastened. When he looks over at me, he seems uncomfortable, probably still stressed from all the stuff last night and this morning, with Mom and me and the computer—which, thanks to Adam-P, I had actually managed to forget until this second.

Dad says, "Man, Coach Baratynsky really worked you hard this evening, didn't she?"

I nod and rub my aching hands. "Regionals are just a couple of weeks away."

Dad starts the SUV. "Want to go somewhere? You know, out for dinner?"

"No, thanks. I really need a shower. Besides, Mom would pop a spring. I'm grounded, remember?"

"Oh, yeah."

Dad goes right back to looking uncomfortable, so I close my eyes.

We drive without talking for about a minute before Dad asks, "This boy on the computer, is he important to you?"

I think for a few seconds, then figure it can't hurt to answer. "Yes. He's important. Not that it matters, since I'll probably never get to talk to him again."

After a second or two, I risk a glance at Dad. He's watching the road, but also looking a little sad. He clears his throat.

"Does he live around here?"

That makes me laugh. "Of course not. Nobody around here would have anything to do with dating me. You know that."

Dad's cheeks flush, just like mine always do when I'm mad or embarrassed. "Still? I mean, that's the whole Adam Pierpont problem—that's still such a big issue?"

"Not Adam-P. Herpes. Yes, everybody knowing I got herpes is still a major issue, at least as far as dates are concerned."

Every time I say the h-word, Dad actually winces. He clenches the steering wheel hard. "If I could pound that damned Adam Pierpont and get away with it, I swear, Chan, I would."

Usually, I love hearing that. Today, after that whole I'm-sorry scene, which is still swimming through my consciousness, it just makes me feel weird.

"The offensive line sucks so bad this year, some football team will do it for us." I glance from Dad to the road, hoping that ends the discussion.

"I like watching him get plastered," Dad admits. "Best part of the game. Your mother says I'm being vengeful and holding grudges."

"Yeah, well, me too." I laugh, but it feels phony. "When the Bear's not listening, I cheer for the other team."

Dad smiles. "What's his name, this new boy?"

An arctic wave crashes across my skin, and I clamp my mouth shut. When I glare at Dad, he raises one hand off the steering wheel. "I'm not conducting a background check, I swear. I just don't want to be left out of your life, Chan."

215

He looks sincere enough, but with parents, who can tell? No way am I sharing anything else about Paul. Too risky for him—and for me.

"Some things are just private, Dad." I look out my window to avoid the hurt expression on his face. "It's nothing against you. It's just that I'm older now. I don't want to share every little thing, especially after how Adam-P used me and lied about me last year."

This makes him drop the subject completely, of course. Talking about me having sexual experiences and getting an STD, then getting betrayed by a guy, that's almost as bad as talking about tampons, in my father's book. He tries, but I know he just can't take it.

We spend the rest of the drive home talking about the weather, my Emily paper, Regionals, and finally Lauren's nightmares.

"Her play stuff gets more intense next week," Dad says as we pull into the driveway. "Her dress rehearsals are the same day as your Regionals. Honestly, I don't know whether to hope she does well—or hope she drops out."

"Same here." I squint at the door as it opens. Brenda the babysitter pops out, waves at us, then takes off across the front yard with her backpack before we can even wave back.

From the strains of karaoke "Do-Re-Mi" blasting from the garage, I know exactly where Lauren is, and exactly what I hope about that play, and I sort of feel awful about it. We've dealt with Lauren and me having important stuff on the same day before, with Mom usually going with Lauren and Dad usually going with me—or sometimes both of them go with Lauren because she gets so stressed out. This time, though, I wish it could be about me, just me, for November 20.

It's mean, I guess, but I just want Lauren's whole play thing to be over.

As I follow Dad inside, I wonder if Lauren and my parents ever feel that way about my competitions, and how tense I get over every little thing related to twirling.

Which of course gets me thinking about Paul, and the fact that I won't be able to talk to him about any of it, because I have no computer.

All of a sudden, I just want to go to bed.

Except, with Dad here and Lauren in the garage, and Mom not home yet . . .

It only takes me a few minutes to make an excuse about working on the Emily paper, sit down at the computer downstairs, open two screens, pull up a search engine on Emily Dickinson on one screen, and open my in-box on the other—which I keep small and down in the right-hand corner.

My heart almost stops when I see there's a message waiting. In among the spam. Just one, but it's from KnightHawk859.

All it says is,

POS understood. Will do everything. Miss you. Love you.

Then: *At least 'tis mutual risk,* and a smiley.

At least 'tis mutual risk . . . I stare at that for a while before shutting down my e-mail and realizing I've got my hand on my chest, pressing against my heart.

Paul didn't blow me off.

He got my message.

Breathing slowly, staying alert for Dad, I make myself quit pushing on my chest, erase my tracks, leave the Emily search engine up, and go upstairs to check my compendium.

I can't find the poem. It's hard to concentrate, and I flip pages until I get irritated, then fetch the smaller collection of love poems out of my closet, the one Adam-P gave back to me.

Using the smaller book makes it easier, and in seconds, I've got it.

Emily's poems, of course, don't have titles, but most people refer to the first lines like titles.

The poem Paul quoted is "I Gave Myself to Him."

If I could, I'd give myself to Paul right this second, and I wouldn't be thinking about Adam-P or last year or his stupid apology at all.

Not at all.

THURSDAY, NOVEMBER 6

"Again!"

The Bear punches off my music and starts me at the beginning of my competition routine.

Maybe dancing—even the short parts of my competition routine—should be moved into the top three things I despise more than anything else in the universe, right next to Ellis and Adam-P.

Ellis is still in the gym, and the seniors, and Adam-P's here, too, over by the bleachers with all of them. I'm trying not to notice him as sweat gathers on my forehead. The salt stings my eyes, then slides down my dry skin.

Obviously, the jerk's apology didn't change anything, did it?

Big surprise.

I'm huffing like a track jock after a twenty-mile haul, and Adam-P's watching me as Ellis dangles off his neck—but I fold my batons back against my elbows, stand at the ready, and pick up the first beat as it fills the air.

Devin's gone home after having six small strokes when I told her about Adam-P's weird I'm-sorry speech yesterday. I asked to stay an extra hour for help with the competition routine, especially the illusions, where I need to bend fluidly and swap the batons between my legs. It gives the illusion that I'm walking straight through the twirling sticks.

"Lower!" the Bear calls as I move into the deep bow, leg extended, batons moving. The second baton bashes against my knee and goes flying. I crash down hard, curse a lot in my brain, then jump up and keep twirling.

Never stop.

No matter what, never stop.

So what if Adam-P's still staring and Ellis is hooting and laughing. So what if I'm hungry, I haven't been able to talk to Paul in days, and Lauren's barely letting me sleep at all. With every passing day, Regionals get closer, and I don't seem to be getting any better.

Ellis manages to position herself in front of Adam-P and flip me off with both hands. Then she turns away and I hear the words *fat* and *useless* really loud out of her next sentence.

God, I want to beat her at competition.

I drop my baton again.

The Bear pops her hand against the STOP button and hits RESET. "Where is your mind, Chan Shealy? On some boy? Some family problem? No matter. The judges von't care, no? Own this routine. Ownership, now!" She claps her hands sharply. "Again. Again!"

I fetch my dropped baton, race back to position, and force myself through the opening for at least the tenth time. This time, I make it through the illusion, then the toss illusion, and drop on a complicated throw.

Off goes the music. "Again."

Again.

Again.

Always again. It never stops. I never get it quite right, quite good enough—but I *have* to. I *do* own the routine. I *am* going to slaughter Ellis and everybody else in Advanced Trick. No way I'm settling for less.

By the time Dad shows up, I'm limping and dripping and wheezing, but at least I've made two run-throughs the Bear actually complimented. As she turns me over to Dad, she says, "Your girl, she vorks hard for this. She has heart. A vinner's heart." She thumps her chest with her fist.

"I know." Dad smiles at me in that way that says, *My daughter is perfect to me.*

I smile back at him and let him pick up my baton case and take my hand like he used to when I was still a little girl.

It's impossible not to love my father. Okay, so he can be a pain, and he doesn't take great care of himself. There's a lot wrong with Dad. But there's so much right about him, too. I hope I can be like that someday, where the so-much-right is bigger than the so-much-wrong.

Unlike Adam-P, who's pushing Ellis off him and keeping his eyes on me and frowning as Dad and I head out of the gym.

Dad's chatting about his day at work, but I'm hardly listening because I'm too busy wondering what's *with* Adam-P, anyway?

Is that jerk *trying* to trigger a witch-monster rampage?

I actually feel his gaze traveling along beside me until the door slams, cutting off his view. His attention gives me the creeps, along with a tumble of hot-cold sensations in my belly. I start thinking about the poetry book at home, the one now buried in my closet, and how I spent hours coming up with just the right thing to write to him before I wrapped it.

Was that before or after he started sleeping with the cheerleader who gave us both a disease?

And why doesn't Ellis ever pick on *that* twit?

My thigh itches, but I refuse to scratch it as I open the door to Dad's SUV.

The scent of pizza almost knocks me backward.

"Dad, no." I stand outside and hold my nose. "I can't get in there. I can't eat that! It's torture to even smell it."

His face falls, and I swear he looks like he might cry, which makes me feel like a total ass. "I got you a small spinach and garlic cheese. Thin crust." He fumbles in his pocket and pulls out a piece of paper. "Here's the nutritional information. I know you're keeping up with that."

I am a total ass.

I take the paper from him and get in the car.

"Sorry, Chan. I just wanted to get you girls a treat since your Mom is tied up again. They're really launching into next year's local races now, since it's only eleven months 'til that election."

"Yeah. No worries. I know the drill—and thanks for getting this stuff for me, Dad. It means a lot."

That makes him smile, and the knots in my chest untie a few loops.

As we drive, I read. Then I take a deep breath, and try again. "See, this is the problem with pizza." I glance at him. He looks attentive instead of crushed for the moment, so I go with it. "I've eaten other meals today, so even if I count all the exercise I did, an eighteen-hundred-calorie pizza will put me like, a thousand calories over for the day. That's a third of a pound."

Dad drives another few miles, then offers, "What if you eat half the pizza?"

This time, he looks so pleased with himself and hopeful, all I can do is shrug. "Yeah. I guess I can do that."

Never mind the fat, the saturated fat, the carbs . . .

And how will I ever stop with half a pizza? Or manage to eat nothing *else the rest of the night?*

"You've been sticking to this training regimen for a while now, pretty near perfect from what I can see. Doesn't that earn you a day off every now and then?"

Every muscle in my body tenses. Before I got cut off from Paul, we talked about that—and I've talked it out with Devin and the Bear, too. That's dangerous thinking. Kind of like an alcoholic saying, *Oh, one drink won't hurt.*

Too easy to keep going. Too easy to fall all the way back into the hole. But I can't say that. I've watched Dad do it too many times—and he'll hear it in my voice.

"Maybe after Regionals," I say. "I need to be in top form on November twentieth. You know that."

Dad gives me a quick look, and I see resignation. Maybe a little embarrassment or worry, but acceptance. "Okay, then. I won't buy pizza again until after Regionals. But if you win, maybe we can go get a great dinner at Zoby's to celebrate. If you win, you definitely deserve the Crave-Buster and a Bomb."

My head bounces off my car window, and I have to make myself not whack it again. Zoby's Crave-Buster is a twenty-ounce porterhouse steak, and the Bomb is short for *Chocolate Bomb.* A dessert with cake and syrup and cherries and nuts and ice cream, and a layer or two of caramel on top of that.

My stomach roars at the thought. Then it roars at the delicious, buttery, meaty smell of the pizzas in the backseat. If Dad doesn't get us home soon, I'll leap back there and chew through the boxes.

His clueless, pleased expression is driving me crazy.

Dad doesn't get it.

How will I ever help him get it?

And if he doesn't ever understand, how will I be able to keep all the progress I've made since I started on Paul's program?

By the time we get home, the knots in my chest have tied themselves in my belly, too, and I'm not even that hungry. I manage to cut my pizza in half, and when Dad walks Lauren's sitter to the door, I feed the other half to the garbage disposal. If I don't do that, I'll eat it later, or Dad will, and I don't want him to. Especially not after he comes back to the kitchen, picks up his large deluxe supreme, and lugs it off to his bedroom. That pizza's enough to feed four people. Seriously.

Lauren's pizza has to go into the oven for safekeeping because she's out in the garage again with her music blaring. I pass by the door on the way to the stairs, but I don't hear her singing at all. Just the music. No voice.

Weird.

I knock on the garage door to see if she's okay.

No answer. I try the handle, but the door's locked.

I snarf a bite of pizza, chew it, swallow, then set the rest on the coffee table. Back I go to the garage door, and this time I bang on it.

The music shuts off.

"Yes?" Lauren calls in a quivery-nervous voice.

"What are you doing in there?" I ask. "I didn't hear you singing. Are you okay?"

Silence.

Then, "Nothing. I'm fine."

This time the tone's calmer . . . but something feels off.

Confused and a little worried, I lean against the door. "Open the door. We brought home pizza."

Silence.

"Is Mom with you?" Lauren asks.

"No. Just me. Open the door."

"I'm busy."

Okay, now she's sounding way too nervous again, in a real way instead of a fake goth-princess way, and I really am starting to worry about her.

"Hey, look. That's my practice garage, and I said open the door. Now. Or you can't use it anymore."

"Mom said I could! Dad, too! No fair. You're not my boss, Chan."

Dad comes out of the kitchen. "Hey. I heard the yelling from my room. What's wrong?"

I jerk a thumb toward the locked garage door. "She's up to something, or something's wrong. And she won't open the door."

"Tattletale!" Lauren yells, punctuated by a lot of banging and thumping and shuffling.

Dad's eyebrows rise. He gives me an oh-great look, strides up to the door, and knocks more gently than I did. "Let us in, sweet pea. We just want to see your smiling face."

Silence.

More shuffling.

Some muttering.

Then the door opens.

And there stands Lauren, in my new purple leotard. This year's leotard!

Dad grabs my arm before I can grab her, but he can't stop me from saying, "Lauren, you have to take that off. Now!"

She bursts into tears, pushes past us, banging us both with her rock-heavy duffel, and hauls the bag up the stairs, sobbing.

The sobs are kind of quiet. Way too subdued for usual Lauren behavior.

Dad and I are both too shocked to move for a second.

Then Dad says, "Chan, is it too early for Lauren to be going through . . . you know, the change? To, um, womanhood?"

He lets go of my arm, and I pat him on the hand. "Yeah, a little. I think. It's probably the play pressure."

"Is it worth it, all this craziness?" Dad's expression looks earnest, and I can tell he really doesn't understand what it feels like to want to win, to want to get that prize, that part, or that trophy. To go for it and actually succeed. "Do you girls really feel like you have to do all this—the twirling, the musicals?"

"It's not a have to, really. It's . . . a want to." I rub my hands together as I dig through my brain for the right words. "A drive to, way down inside."

"But you know you're good enough, you're just perfect, even if you don't win a competition or get a part in a little play, right?"

"Sure," I say, then wonder if I'm lying.

We stand there another few seconds.

I keep listening for Lauren to start her give-me-attention hysterical crying, but there's only silence, and that bugs me way worse than her theatrics.

"Can you, uh—" Dad nods to the stairs. "I know you're mad at her over the leotard, but this might be out of my league."

"I'll handle it. And I won't kill her over the leotard, I swear. So long as you promise to send the Wrath of Mom upstairs later, after she gets home."

Dad wipes his forehead with his hand and looks relieved. "Deal. Done. And I still owe you."

He heads back for his room and his pizza, and I climb the stairs trying to figure out how to comfort Lauren and still find out what's wrong. When I get to my room, I find the purple marching leotard stretched neatly across my bed, and it doesn't look any worse for the wear.

Lauren surrendered it voluntarily? No fight? No

speech about entitlement and privilege how it's *just not fair* I get all the good leotards?

Have aliens kidnapped my little sister?

Muscles tensing, I turn toward her room, but the door's closed. I know without even trying the handle that Lauren has barricaded herself in her Cave of Doom.

But why?

I knock but I don't ask her to open the door.

When she doesn't answer, I sit down in the hall on the other side and ask, "You want to talk?"

"No." A slight sniff punctuates her answer. "I—I'm sorry about the leotard."

Okay, yeah, the aliens came and stole Lauren. I must have missed the flashing lights.

"Why did you take that leotard, Lauren?"

Like before, she doesn't answer. I didn't figure she would, but after a minute or so, she surprises me with: "I just wanted to feel pretty. Like you. Grown-up and pretty, and like I can win something, too."

I lean my head against her door. "You are pretty, silly, and you're plenty good at singing." I pause and listen for sniffling, but I don't hear any. "The growing up part, that comes later. You'll get older every year, right?"

Long silence. Then: "You're telling Mom about the leotard, aren't you?"

Ah. Leverage. Finally. "Not if you tell me what's really going on."

Another long silence, but this time, the clicking of

229

her door lock gets my attention. She pulls open the door to the Cave of Doom and sits down in front of me. Behind her, posters of cats and dogs and princesses in poofy costumes glow weird purple in her black lights.

My worry ratchets up another notch, because Lauren's a wreck. And not the whole goth-black-makeup-fake-blood-tattoo kind of wreck. I mean pale, massive circles under her eyes, and her brown hair sticking up in every direction. She must have swiped some of Mom's real makeup, because she's wearing (badly applied) base instead of white powdery stuff like usual, and both of her cheeks are streaked with mascara. Tears glisten in the corners of her eyes, and she's looking off to the side instead of at me.

"I know you think it's stupid," she says, a genuine shake in her voice as she looks at the floor, "but I really want to be a movie star. Maybe on Broadway, or a singing star. Something. Something—more."

"I don't think it's stupid." I strangle the urge to tease her even a little bit. For all the times Lauren's played drama queen or pretended to be totally fragile, this time, she really does seem breakable. "But what does that have to do with all this stressing out?"

She leans forward and speaks in a low whisper. "I heard some important people might come to the play, once we're really doing it. You know. Producers and talent scouts looking for kids to be in commercials, or maybe even have some movie tryouts."

"Who told you that?"

"My boyfriend."

"You have a boyfriend?" It comes out deadpan, which is good, but totally an accident, because I'm really, really shocked. It's all I can do to keep my face from twitching, not smile, not laugh, and not just let my jaw drop open like it wants to.

"His name's David." She looks up at me with tear-swollen eyes. "*Please* don't tell Mom. She wouldn't let me talk to him or see him or anything."

Instantly, I'm right there with her.

No, Mom would cut her off in a heartbeat, just like I'm cut off from Paul.

I think about my conversations with Paul about sibling loyalty, and I switch from Mom questions to Dad questions. "Does this boyfriend person make you happy?"

Lauren's tense face eases into a smile, and a blush colors her cheeks. "Yeah. He's ten. It's a little old, I know, but he's nice. He has a voice coach, too, and he might try to get me some free lessons when we see each other at the dress rehearsal."

"That's pretty cool." I reach out and ruffle her messy hair. "But you've gotta ease up. You're totally blowing your own mind."

"I need a voice coach for real," she says, getting serious again. "If I'm ever going to make it, I just have to get real lessons, but you know how Mom is. I'm trying to save my money, but it's so expensive."

My mind shifts to Paul and paying him back for the stuff he's sending. If I made a second streaming video, or maybe even more . . .

"Well, maybe I can help some with that, Lauren. We'll see, okay?"

Lauren relaxes a little more. "I really am sorry about the leotard. I won't wear it again."

I shrug one shoulder, then hear myself saying, "It's only a costume. If you need it, just be careful with it, or my ass will be grass with the Bear."

Lauren's lips tremble, then she smiles really big, and throws her scrawny arms around my neck.

"Sometimes I hate your guts," she says against my neck, "but sometimes you're the best big sister ever."

It takes me a few more minutes to get her settled down and eating her pizza in front of the latest Disney flick, and a few more minutes to cancel the Wrath of Mom agreement with Dad. After that, I steal a few unsupervised minutes on the downstairs computer and check my in-box—but it's empty.

I look around at Lauren, who seems more relaxed and happy now. And Dad, back in his room, stuffed from his humongous pizza, he's probably all relaxed and happy, too. Mom at work with her politically correct friends—no doubt she's having a blast.

As for me, I'm sore and tired and a little hungry, and hollowed out from missing Paul. I wish I could talk to Devin. I wish it so hard nobody even notices when I snitch the phone and take it upstairs, and sit talking to her for over half an hour, all the while keeping a lookout for Mom to come home.

She never does, and I go to bed and have a major nightmare about Lauren in my purple leotard, dancing for big-time movie producers while she cries about everyone staring at her. I'm still having that bad dream when she wakes me up crawling into bed with me. She doesn't even ask permission anymore, and I don't make her. I just get up and cover her after she gets settled, go to my desk to write a poem, and hope really hard that Lauren doesn't have the same nightmare she saved me from dreaming.

A wounded deer leaps highest,
I've heard the hunter tell;
'Tis but the ecstasy of death,
And then the brake is still.

The smitten rock that gushes,
The trampled steel that springs:
A cheek is always redder
Just where the hectic stings!

Mirth is the mail of anguish,
In which it caution arm,
Lest anybody spy the blood
And "You're hurt" exclaim!

Emily Dickinson

CYCLES

And then there was the time
Of growing,
Of getting to know
All the smiles and all the whispers.

And then there was the time
Of knowing.
The reaching and holding
All the sighs and all the winks.

And then there was the time
Of losing.
The searching and surviving
All the tears and all the sobbing.

And then there was the time
Of turning.
The pleading and shouting
All those words and all those lies
And all those echoes

   drifting

      slowly

         back.

Chan Shealy

FRIDAY, NOVEMBER 7

Friday, the football team has a bye, so we get a break from practice. That only happens twice all during the season, and I'm glad for the chance to let my twirling bruises heal for a day or two.

Last thing before we leave school, out in the main drive-around, Devin loads my backpack with two huge stacks of rubber-banded note cards, a pad of scribbled notes (with references, no less), and pictures of Emily Dickinson printed off Internet sites.

"I'm thinking write the paper normal, see, but also do a little newspaper-looking spread we could use for a cover—you know?" Devin shapes a square in the air with both hands, and her dark eyes flash with excitement. "You're so good with stuff like that. Make it look like some gossip rag? That'll totally get us some extra points, and make up for that abysmal outline."

"Sure." My breath makes a cloud in the cold air as I turn toward Mom's politically correct car, wishing that she'd stayed late at work again, like she had every day this week.

Abysmal.

Devin's big word echoes in my brain as I stand still beside her. The sun's so bright I have to squint against the glare off dozens of windshields. Of course, on the one day I need Mom not to be home, here she is. My heart's already beating so fast I can barely breathe.

Mom always takes me straight home, then watches what I do all the rest of the day. How can I get to the mailbox before her—or without her seeing?

Everything I'm waiting for should be here today, and I'll be free again, and talking to Paul—if I can get to the mailbox. And I've got to get to the mailbox. I can't take it anymore, missing him so much. Or feeling so trapped.

Abysmal.

I start toward the car.

Devin tugs on my arm hard enough to break my stride. I stop and turn back toward her. "Huh?"

"Did you hear anything I said?" She frowns as she lets go of my arm. "Sometimes, I swear you're on some other planet in your brain."

"I heard you," I insist, then try to remember exactly what she *did* say. If she wants me to repeat it, I'm toast.

Devin's eyes narrow. "Planet Paul, maybe?"

Tension grips my neck and back. "I'm not allowed to talk to him. You know I'm still grounded."

Total slit-eyes now, with pursed lips. Not good. "But you're thinking about him. Admit it. You're thinking about him all the time, even though you're not telling me. You don't tell me *anything* anymore."

"I do too!" I glare at her and open my mouth again, intending to lie about the whole Paul-obsessing thing, then change my mind. "I think about the fact he'll probably blow me off because of this. That he might just move on to somebody who can't get grounded. A girl who doesn't have to deal with parents."

Devin's eyes get a fraction wider. She lets out a breath, and her shoulders sag. "Would the world stop spinning if he does, Chan? I mean, I know you're having trouble around here because of—well, Adam-P and all that. But it's not like you'll ever really get to meet Paul. He lives hours from here. Plus, your parents—you know?"

I hold my breath to keep from yelling, which makes it hard to say, "I know."

"So, when I stopped you a second ago, *did* you hear anything I said?"

"Not all of it, probably."

Devin puts her icy fingers on my cheeks and makes me look at her as she repeats herself. "I want that headline," she adds as she lets me go. "'The Wild Dyke of Amherst.' You owe me that headline. Don't forget. And don't forget it's due Monday."

My stomach tenses along with the rest of my muscles, but I nod. "Done."

As I start for the car again, Devin says, "I'm calling to remind you every day this weekend, even if I can't talk to you!"

I wave at her over my head, like, *Yeah, okay, you do that*, and hear her laugh. The sound sort of fortifies me as I face the prospect of riding home with Mom. We haven't been talking much since the whole laptop-confiscating incident—need-to-use-words moments only, and even then, as few words as possible.

Oh, and that big threat about tracing Paul—she hasn't been able to do that, best I can tell.

Trying not to scowl, I get into the front seat.

Keeping her eyes straight ahead, Mom asks, "School okay?"

"Fine." I rub my hand across the beige upholstery on the door and watch Devin through my window as she runs toward her boyfriend. This week it's Mac "Mack-daddy" Brown, one of the football players. Total player in every sense of the word, but Devin knows that.

He's just arm candy, honey. I get to do arm candy every now and then, don't I?

One day, I'm going to tell her what I really think about how she treats guys. Maybe.

Mom eases us into the flow of traffic, and the air in the car seems to get a little colder despite the heat pouring out of the vents.

No secret. Mom doesn't want to be in the car with me any more than I want to be in the car with her. Only, she's the mom, so it doesn't seem right that she gets to act like this. I try not to look at her, but it's hard in such a little car, and because I'm working like mad to figure a way to get out of the house to get my mail, and get it back inside without her catching me. Like that'll ever happen.

Every minute or so, Mom lets out a big loud sigh, which makes me turn my head in her direction.

Finally, about three miles from the house, Mom says, "You can stop worrying. The tech guys at headquarters couldn't follow your tracks on the laptop. But then, you know that, because you downloaded hacker programs to make sure everything got erased *and* purged."

Okay, yeah.

I knew that.

But still, my heart jumps on top of its pound-pounding about getting to the mail.

"Who put that idea in your head, Chan? About the eraser programs?"

I'm so not having this conversation again. If Mom chooses to think I'm too intellectually impaired to come up with anything smart on my own, well, she can just be that way. I turn my head away from her and watch neighborhoods fly by as she accelerates—probably more than she should.

"Your computer had two worms and a Trojan on it, though, so you weren't *that* careful. It's a bad idea, disabling your virus program."

My attention stays on the outside world. Who cares

about worms and Trojans? Worms and Trojans only matter when a person has a computer. I don't have one. I'll probably never have one again, at least not one I get from Mom.

Another sigh floats through the car. "Do you think this silent routine will keep me from punishing you more?"

I think it doesn't matter one way or the other.

The inside of the car crushes in on me. I want to roll down the windows so I can breathe air Mom's not breathing. My chest actually hurts. We're about three minutes from home. From the driveway.

Mom says, "As soon as football season's over, you're grounded to your room, except for competition practice, assuming you make it through Regionals."

That brings my head around in a hurry. "Assuming? Gee, thanks for all your faith, Mom."

Her sweatshirt reads *Stop using Jesus as an excuse for being a narrow-minded bigot.* Her face reads *Finally I got Moody Brat to talk to me.*

I really want to tear off that stupid sweatshirt and cover her face with it, just so I don't have to see the look she's giving me.

"Sorry, Chan," she says with another huge sigh. "I didn't mean it like that. You're so oversensitive with me all the time. Why do you blame me for everything you're going through when *you're* the one who broke the rules?"

"I don't blame you for everything," I say before I can

shut myself up. "I blame you for the stuff *you* did. The stuff *you* said. The stuff *you* think."

Mom pulls to a halt at the mailbox at the edge of our driveway and glares at me. "Just exactly what is it that I think?"

"That I'm dirty because I had sex and got herpes." I force myself to look at her and not the mailbox as I fumble with my seat belt. "Go ahead. Say you don't think that."

But she doesn't have a chance, because my mouth slips a gear and just keeps going. "You look at me like I'm filthy because I still want a boyfriend even though I have a disease. You treated me like I was ridiculous and gross because I showed my boobs to somebody *I* chose, that *I* like and wanted to share part of myself with. It's my body, isn't it?"

Mom's eyes go wide. She blinks a few times. "Chan. At sixteen, you—"

"I what? I don't know who I like? I'm not allowed to be attracted to somebody?"

"No—I—I . . ." Mom's mouth keeps moving, but she's not making sounds. It's like she can't quite figure out what to say.

"You stick your nose in everything, and I hate it. I have *no* life, and that's what I blame you for!" With that, I jump out of the car, stalk over to the mailbox holding my breath, grab the mail out, and march inside. I slam the front door behind me and lock it, too, half to slow

Mom down, and half because I'm so mad. I storm all the way to the kitchen and throw the pile of stuff on the counter. It takes me a few seconds to paw through a bunch of junk mail, some newspaper flyers, a thin, square box for Lauren from her friend Michelle—complete with little heart and puppy stickers all over the brown paper—but there's only one thing for me. A bulky white envelope that has my whole name typed neatly on the front, and my school's return address in the upper left-hand corner.

Baratynsky is printed neatly under the address.

Totally not the Bear's wavy scrawl, though.

Okay, I'm confused. And so disappointed I can barely see straight.

What would the Bear send me?

Or . . . is this from Paul?

How did he know my school's address—wait, wait. I told him the name of my school and the name of my coach. He probably got the rest off the Internet and did this to make sure my parents wouldn't raid the package.

Genius. Total brilliance. I'm amazed.

I start for the stairs, but right about then, Mom slams through the front door, blasts down the hall, and storms into the kitchen.

It's all I can do not to stick the white envelope behind my back.

Why didn't I just take it and go upstairs? I'm such an idiot!

Mom's eyes blaze, and she looks ready to spit fire.

When she speaks, her voice shakes. "Just so you know, I don't think you're filthy because of what happened last year. You just made a mistake, that's all." She takes a breath, not so loud or dramatic. "I'd like to help you avoid a few more. That's why we have the rules we have."

Her eyes drift from my face to the envelope in my hands. "What is that?"

"It's from Coach Baratynsky." My voice comes out way too loud, and blood rushes hard against my eardrums. "Here." I thrust it toward her. "Would you like to open it and examine the contents to be sure they don't break any *rules?*"

Mom looks mad for a second, then like she just might start crying for real.

I hold my breath until I wonder if I might actually turn blue.

Mom glances at the envelope, long enough to see the return address and the way-too-neat *Baratynsky* written beneath it.

"No, Chan. I don't need to open it." She sounds like she's been a few rounds with a boxer and lost. Really bad. "Why don't you get yourself a snack and go upstairs. We both could use some cooling off time, I think. Besides, I have to go pick up Lauren from Michelle's house. I'll be back in under an hour."

A few smart remarks pop into my brain, but I stifle them all, grab an apple, and run for the upstairs. For the sanctuary of my room.

My heart's still pounding, and I'm sort of hot and mad and weird all over. Part of me feels like I was watching myself do everything, like I'm really some person on a balcony, way up high over my own head. I stare down at myself as I lock my bedroom door, listen for the sound of Mom's car pulling out of the driveway, then sprawl on my bed and pull open my envelope.

Out falls a small box and a photo I.D. of me, with my real name and everything, that looks just like something the DMV gives people for identification. All the information's correct, except my birthday, which has been adjusted two years, to make me eighteen.

I stare at the I.D. for a second, not quite believing it. Then I pick it up. It's all plastic and laminated like the real thing. Just holding it feels wrong and exciting all at the same time. It takes me at least a minute, maybe two, before I can make myself slide it into my pocket—and I can't even begin thinking about how I'll get out of the house to open a personal mailbox down at the mailbox place a mile or two away.

In the white box I find a new Berry3000, the B-3k, the very latest wireless handheld. I stare at the black-pearl-colored machine that fits neatly in my palm and still can't believe what I'm seeing. It has a full-color screen that covers my fingers, and on the bottom, a mini keyboard. Little icons let me know how many functions it has—the thing's like a complete laptop, except I can hold it in one hand. I can hide it in a jacket, or under my pillow.

God, how much did it cost?

And the plan—does it have a plan?

As fast as I can, I flip through the manual, then press the power button and wait as the screen brightens.

All the icons shuffle into place, the signal meter lights up strong, and the screen's already labeled.

Red's Talkbox.

My face flushes.

Paul obviously played with the machine a little before he sent it, got it all set up for me. How sweet!

I use the middle button to move a teeny cursor to the upper right-hand corner and click on *check plan*.

Minutes used: 1

Plan Type: Unlimited.

"Oh, no way!" What does that cost? Hundreds a month?

But I'm already flipping pages in the manual again and working my way toward logging on to my e-mail.

When I figure it out, I squint at the screen to see I have a post. From KnightHawk859.

The post has only one sentence:

I didn't buy it—you did.

No sig line.

He didn't buy it? What does he—oh.

Oh, no way.

As fast as I can with the tiny keys, I punch over to Portalpay and log into my account.

And drop the handheld on my bed.

This has to be some way freaked-out mistake. I can't have seen what I thought I saw. Absolutely not.

But when I pick up the B-3k and stare down at the tiny numbers from Portalpay, the balance in my account is over a thousand dollars.

Mouth dry, chest squeezing so tight I can barely move, I call up a transaction history.

Paul has been putting money in my account a little at a time since I e-mailed him Tuesday morning. All the transactions are marked *LovelyLifter*.

My weightlifting video.

He sold it. He actually did it—and just like he had promised, he made me some major money, probably from freaks and pervs and who knew what else, but oh, my God. I have a Berry3000. I have a way to talk to Paul, a way Mom doesn't even know about. And I have some major cash to pay for the plan, at least for a few months. I can almost buy a new laptop, and I would, if I thought for one second I could get it past Mom.

OhmyGodohmyGod . . .

The hour Mom's gone whirls by in a total blur as I read the manual and figure out how to move all over the Net, how to download the hacker programs to cover my tracks in case anyone ever does catch me with the B-3k, how to access my e-mail, the fastest ways to type—and even how to log into my B-3k account. It's in my name, and the password hint is *I'mnobody*. So, I type in *Whoareyou*, and check the cost of my plan, which is nearly two hundred dollars a month.

I can afford it for at least five months, if Paul doesn't put another dime in the account.

My brain pings and bounces and I can barely concentrate to make my fingers press the tiny buttons as I enter Paul's e-mail address on a post and write:

OMG.

Can't believe this. How did you do it all?

I'm here! I'm here! Are you there? Missed you so much.

Did I really make that much? All done? More to come?

Unreal.

I sign *Red*, with a P.S. of *admiring bog* from the poem, so he'll know for sure it's me.

About twenty seconds later, I get a post back with a time to be in chat later, after everyone else will be in bed. It's signed with a smiley.

Mom and Lauren clatter and bang as they come in downstairs. I hug the B-3k to my chest as my gaze moves to the locked bedroom door. If Mom tries to come in, I'll have plenty of time to react. I have to be sure it's always that way, from now on.

Paul's back in my life, and no matter what I have to do, Mom's not taking him away from me again.

TUESDAY, NOVEMBER 11

"A C, Chan?" Devin's tear ducts definitely aren't broken like mine. Water splashes from her cheeks to the fold-out bleachers. The gym seems eerie-quiet, since everyone else is out marching. The Bear noticed something was wrong the minute we showed up for practice, and gave Devin and me permission to be a little late to the field, so long as we *vorked things out.*

Are we vorking things out?

It doesn't feel like we're vorking things out.

This feels awful.

Devin sniffs, then explodes again. "We'll have to make, like a perfect score on the final draft to even pull a B on the project, and it's half our grade! With what I make on other stuff, I'll be lucky to pull a C overall. God!"

I hold the paper in my lap, the "Wild Dyke of Amherst," with its garish *Tattler* cover just like Devin ordered. Inside, on the first page, there's a note from Haggerty, written in sloping red letters.

Disappointing. Research is solid, but you didn't support your conclusions beyond assumption and innuendo. Chan, this paper doesn't have your usual flair. Do better on the final draft.

Below that's the grade.

A C.

Actually, it's a C–, but I don't want to make things worse by pointing that out.

Devin punches a finger at the paper. "This thing sounds so totally flat. Nothing connects. *I* could have written this. Maybe I should have!"

"I did my best," I mumble.

Total lie.

But Devin doesn't glare at me, so maybe she doesn't realize I'm not telling the truth. Not for sure, at least.

"I'm sorry," I say for like the twenty-fourth time.

Only Devin has no idea how sorry I really am. I already told her how Lauren's so into the Community Theater's *Sound of Music* that she's pounding my eardrums with constant rehearsals, not to mention the whole waking me up almost every night because of her bad dreams thing. I already told Devin about Mom's endless bitchery and how Mom won't let *anything* go, and even about Dad's pizza fetish driving me crazy, especially when I'm starving-hungry most of the time thanks to the training program.

But, of course, I didn't tell Devin about being back in touch with Paul or the B-3k.

Most of all, I didn't tell Devin how I kept putting off

the Emily rough draft and putting it off and putting it off until finally, sometime early Sunday morning, I paid one of those term paper sites twenty-five dollars a page for a rush job.

Since the paper has to be so long, with references and everything, paying for it really put a dent in my Portal-pay account. And, like the site promised, I got a sound paper from a native English speaker that followed all the rules and guidelines—but I could have done better.

I should have done better.

Assuming for one second I could have concentrated on it at all.

"Were my notes not good enough?" Devin's dark eyes are wide and teary as she looks up at me from the bleacher step below mine. "I thought I did my part, that I gave you enough."

Total ass. That should be my middle name instead of At-wood. Chan TotalAss Shealy. Just plain Ass would do for a nickname.

"You did great. It was me." I'm starting to feel sick inside. "I'm so sorry. I really, really am. I guess being grounded is melting my brain."

Devin studies me. "Are you sure there's nothing else? I feel like all of a sudden, I don't know what's happening with you."

"Not being able to talk outside of school completely sucks." Sicker, and sicker, and sicker. Part of me wants to spill everything, but the rest of me—well, the rest of me knows Devin, and knows better. "Mom has to give it up sooner or later."

"Maybe," Devin mutters. "But you knew you'd end up in Mommy-jail the minute you made that profile. Was Paul worth it? I mean, really?"

Oh, yeah, totally he's worth it, I want to say, but as I gaze at her sad, half-angry expression, I wonder for the first time ever if I could actually lose Devin as my best friend. The thought makes my sick insides knot and double-knot and triple-knot.

Will Devin dump me like Adam-P did?

"Um, not really, I guess," I say, wishing I could shrivel up and disappear. "It was pretty stupid."

God, if she does dump me, I'll deserve it.

But Devin wouldn't do that. Best friends don't dump each other, right? We have plans. We're going to college together, without my mom and her dad breathing down our necks every second of our lives.

I need to go home right after practice and work on another draft of the Emily paper. Maybe if I turn in something better, Haggerty might up our grade a tad, and give us a shot at a better final grade. I could give her some story about family problems.

It might work. It has to work.

"I'll do something, I swear," I say to Devin, who has started staring at the back of her hands instead of looking at me. "Somehow I'll fix this and I'll make the final draft rock."

She gives me a smile, even though it doesn't look like a normal glowing Devin-grin. "You make me believe you, you know that?"

"Because I mean it." I pick up my backpack and stuff the report down inside. "Wait and see."

Am I lying? I hope I'm not lying.

Devin stares down at her hands again, and seems to be making up her mind. When she looks up this time, all she says is, "Okay."

That's enough for the moment.

Devin doesn't have to say anything else. I know the rest is up to me. I just wish I could get off the ceiling and stop staring at myself. I just wish life would start feeling real again, and all mine, and like I'm in charge of it.

The rest is up to me.

It really is up to me.

.   .   .

"I don't know if I can take much more of Lauren's singing," I type to Paul that evening on the B-3k. I'm sitting at my desk with my notebooks open, my compendium open, and the Emily paper spread every which way.

Rising from the garage like some insanely annoying movie soundtrack, endless strains of "Edelweiss" have been assaulting me for over an hour. Sometimes Lauren sings with the karaoke music. Sometimes she doesn't. It's enough to make me want to jump out my window.

"Give the kid a break," Paul writes back. "She's just

being as dedicated as you are, right? Sounds like Lauren just wants to be a winner."

"Or the first member of our family to actually get committed to a mental institution," I send before he can start typing again.

"That's harsh, Red!" But he sends lots of smileys.

Talking to him is making me feel so much better. I tell him about screwing up with Devin, then fight guilt about telling Paul everything when I'm keeping so much from Devin.

"That's not good. You've got to work on that paper." No smileys now. Paul's being completely serious. "Want to set some limits on chat time, or maybe some rewards if you're a good girl?"

That makes me smile at him *that* way, like I know he's up to something. "What do you have in mind?"

He sends me a waggling-eyebrow smiley, and I swallow a laugh since I don't know where Mom is. My door's locked, but she could knock any second, especially if she hears me cracking up all alone in my room like some nutcase.

As if anyone can hear anything over yet another round of "Edelweiss." God.

"You have a one-track mind," I type as I seriously consider buying some earplugs, then send him a red-faced smiley. "Yeah, I do need to work on the paper. Tonight, in fact. I hate it, but I really, really need to."

"I understand—and I agree, Red. I don't want to be bad for you."

Those words make me stare a while.

"You're not bad for me," I tell him. "No way."

He types a quick good-bye, but I stop him by waving at the camera and tapping out, "Hold on a sec. I needed to ask—has my video made any more money?"

Paul sends me a sad-face. "No, sorry. It's about tapped. Why? I thought you had plenty in the account."

I confess about spending the bucks to get the Emily rough draft, which earns me a stern frown, followed by, "I'm tight this month, too. I can't pay your plan for you."

He pauses while I considered the horror of having my account shut off for nonpayment, then writes, "We could do another video. Something spicier, that'll make even more money—something like what I told you I did that time. You know, without my shirt and stuff."

I gape at him. "What, me sit around with no shirt on—*live*? I can't do that!"

Paul is typing.

Yeah, well, he better be typing something better than that *idea.*

"Sure you can. Just do it for me like you did Tuesday night."

I totally blush remembering our sweaty little Tuesday night closet session. If it's possible to make second base without ever actually touching, we definitely did that Tuesday night. What a way to break in my awesome

little handheld. Just the memory of it gives me good tinglies.

But Tuesday night had been for Paul, not for a bunch
of panting pervs watching a video.

I want to be mad at Paul for even suggesting that, but
since he's done it himself, I don't want to say anything to
embarrass him or make him feel bad about it.

Paul is typing.

"You could do it tonight, while you work on that paper. Kill two birds with one stone. Well, three birds, if
you count me, because I'll love it, too."

Feeling way unreal, I write, "Everyone's still up. My
mom could come to the door."

"It's locked, right? Look, Red, I thought you trusted
me."

"I do trust you, but this is freaked out."

"It's not. I promise. I can blur your face, and nobody'll
know it's you except me. So, really, it will be just for me,
since I'm the only one who actually sees you doing it,
with your real face, in real time."

He sends me a line of smileys before I can type anything back.

When I do, I find myself asking, "How much did you
make when you did the no-shirt thing?"

"Around 2k, but I'm not a girl. You'll make more.
And if you touch yourself, you know, cup your boobs
and stuff, you could probably make a small fortune."

"No way I'm doing that!" My body goes red-hot, and I know I have to be fluorescent red all over.

"No problem! If you just do the no-shirt thing, just sit and work on the paper, I bet I can get you enough to pay the B-3k account for most of the year—long as you don't go buying any more crappy English papers. Please, Red. I don't think I can face losing you again."

Paul gazes straight into the screen, straight into my eyes. My heart twists, and all the knot-tying starts in my chest and stomach as I write, "I don't want to lose you again, either."

"Then do this. Right now, tonight, while you work. And just let it be for me. I promise I can protect your identity, and you'll have the money you need—assuming you don't spend it on another term paper."

I give him an I'm-sorry smile and nod. Not paying the account and being cut off from Paul again—unthinkable. Not happening. Just the idea gives me an awful, tired, the-world-is-ending feeling. He's right, and I know it. This is the only way, for now. If I have to flash a little skin to keep Paul, then flashing's what I'll do. Besides, it was my dumb-ass idea to waste those bucks in my account on a paper I should have written.

Paul gives me a thumbs-up before I turn around to get my desk organized.

Then I take fifteen whole minutes getting ready, doing a zillion little things that don't matter. With each passing second, my throat gets drier and the knots inside my body get tighter.

I can't do this. I can do this. I have to do this.

"It's just for Paul," I mumble out loud to myself as I dig in my backpack and get out the report. Then I grab a pen off the desk. I put them both on my bed next to the B-3k and my last year's backpack, where I'll stuff the B-3k if Mom knocks.

When I pick up the machine, I see Paul, patiently waiting. He blows me a kiss and gives me another thumbs-up.

I put down the B-3k, take a breath, and pull my shirt over my head, leaving just a bra between me and the world who'll see the video.

Gooseflesh breaks across my bare shoulders. Instant cold. Instant shivering. I stretch the shirt out on the bed so I can get into it fast, in case of a Mom attack.

My fingers fumble with the satin straps on my bra, but my hands don't want to work. I grind my teeth.

Quit being a baby. Just take it off like you did Tuesday. Paul likes looking at you. You know that.

The next time I try, I manage to slide the straps off my arms, first one and then the other. Then I reach around and unfasten the two hooks in the back.

For a few more seconds, I stand there, just stand there, not wanting to let go because when I do, I'll be naked from the waist up. Just wearing my khakis and socks. And I'd be making a video of my boobs. For Paul to sell.

But he's going to blur my face.

And I have to have the money, or I'll lose the B-3k, and lose him.

From where I am, I can't see the screen anymore, but I imagine Paul leaning forward, his eyes trained right on the place my falling bra will leave bare.

Good tinglies.

A few, at least.

I do like him. I'm totally in love with him, actually. And he loves me, too.

So, he'll protect me, just like he says he will. He'll distort my face and nobody'll know it's me. And the real scene, this scene, with me letting go and letting the bra drop to the floor—it's all for Paul.

Cold air grips my chest, and I clamp my teeth together from the sharp sensation.

Then I look toward the handheld, cup my breasts, and make my best effort at a naughty smile.

For Paul.

He's the only one watching.

The more I think about that, the more I feel like I can do it. Keep my shirt off. And maybe be even sexier.

After a minute or so, I do more.

It's not so cold after all. Not after I get used to it. And it's not so hard, either, once I get started.

The knots inside me start untying as I imagine Paul enjoying my little show.

After a little for-Paul-through-the-camera dance, I sit down on the bed and check the B-3k.

Paul's eyes look glazed. He's grinning like crazy, and he's typed, "You are so gonna be rich."

"Better be," I write back.

Then I finally, finally make myself work on that Emily paper, and I do a way good job, too.

TUESDAY, NOVEMBER 18

A week later, my bank account's looking better. Like amazingly, shockingly better, and it doesn't seem hard *at all* to give Paul a few more late-night videos.

And my new customized mini-notebook computer and premium webcam are already on order, due in ten to fourteen business days.

After I save our Emily paper grade with that second rough draft—which got an A, of course, to average with that C and give us a chance at a much better total grade—I make Devin happy by producing a beautiful final draft a whole day early, for us to go over, edit, and make completely perfect.

Even better, Mom's relenting on the grounding enough to allow Devin to come over this afternoon to help put the final polish on the paper before we print it out, and to run through our competition routines again since Regionals are in two days. The Bear has excused us from organized practice and games until after Regionals, but she expects us to be working hard on our own.

Call me if you need individual attention, and I vill come right over. . . .

Now it is up to you, my girls. . . .

Own your routines. . . .

Own your victories!

Lauren bangs on the garage door and yells, "Is it my turn yet? I've just *got* to go over my pieces again!"

Devin's eyes shift toward the door and she drops a baton. It bounces toward me on the padded flooring. I dodge it and it bashes into Lauren's karaoke machine, almost knocking the machine off the old suitcase she uses for a stand.

I get my balance again, punch off my boom box, and re-cue Devin's competition music CD as we both yell, "Not yet!"

Lauren thumps the door once, but doesn't say anything else.

Devin gives me a miserable look. "Oh, honey, I don't think I can take another round of 'Do-Re-Mi.' Do we really have to let that monstrosity back in this room to start singing again?"

"Sorry." I let out a groan at the thought. "She really needs the time, though. This is all so important to her."

Devin groans to match mine, then glances at her

watch. "We've got like ten more minutes before we switch. And I still think your sister needs serious pharmacological intervention."

"She needs Mom and Dad to pull her out of this play." I frown. "But at the same time, that would just kill her, so I don't know."

Devin's eyebrows lift, but she doesn't argue with me.

"Ready?" I ask.

When she nods, I push PLAY and start her music, stifling an urge to scream *Again*, just to invoke the spirit of the Bear.

Watching the routine for like the billionth time, it's hard to keep my mind from wandering. I keep thinking about my new computer, and how when I get it, the B-3k currently tucked inside my last year's backpack in my closet, safe up in my room, will become a backup. If Mom nabs the new computer, I'll still have that, and I can order myself whatever I need. After seeing what came in from that video, there's no question I'll have plenty of money to buy whatever I need. More than plenty.

Devin moves through her illusions without a single mistake. I smile, total reflex because I'm not paying close attention, but I really do feel happy for her, and not so worried about how I'll do.

Of course, the new computer can't be with me all the time. I'll have to take the B-3k when I'm going out of town or something, like to Regionals. But the laptop will be so much easier to use and see, and I can do school assignments on it, too, and not have to fool with the downstairs computer as long as I don't let Mom catch me.

As I try to keep my eyes from glazing over, Devin zips through her dance moves, totally clean, and executes a spectacular toss. More smiles from me. I even clap.

The new laptop will be easy enough to hide from Mom. The biggest issue will be getting it from my private mailbox to my room. Paul and I have already talked about the next video I need to make, and spicing it up a little. That'll probably give us enough money for him to come visit me. I need that soon. I want it soon.

Devin's into her wind-down, smile plastered on her pretty face, but she's starting to breathe hard from doing the routine so many times.

"Well?" she asks when she finishes, holding her batons and staring at me with big, hopeful eyes.

"Perfect," I announce as I shut off the boom box, hoping I didn't miss anything.

"Now, see, you've got that I'm-on-another-planet look again." Devin lowers her batons and keeps staring at me. "Were you really watching that last part?"

Heat floods my face, but I swallow and hold up my head and manage to look her straight in the eyes. "I was watching!"

Sort of.

"You did great, as always, Devin. You have the heart of a vinner." I stand and move my baton case and the CD player away from Lauren's karaoke setup. "Stack your stuff over here out of Lauren's way, and let's work on the paper in the living room, okay?"

Without comment, Devin walks over and puts her sticks in her case.

Okay, she's annoyed.

I should kick myself for spacing out like that. So much on my mind. So many plans to keep up with. It's hard. But for today, I need to stay on the Emily paper and Regionals. The videos and Paul and my computer ideas, I need to save for tonight, in between dinner and Lauren invading my room to kick me all night long.

I so need to come clean with Devin about Paul.

The second I have that thought, part of me longs to tell her everything, or really, to tell somebody other than Paul everything. But then two seconds later, I never want to tell anyone ever. It goes like that. Up and down and around and around in my head.

As Lauren brushes past us hurrying toward her karaoke machine, I glance at Devin's tight jaw and her slightly hurt expression. She's believing me, accepting what I said, but if I don't tell her the truth about talking to him again and she finds out on her own, that'll be bad.

After I meet Paul, I'll tell her.

I want to see him in person, make sure I'm not crazy and all that. Then I'll spill some stuff to Devin. Maybe not everything, but enough.

Mom meets us as we come into the living room. She's carrying a small plate of fruit, cheese, and wheat crackers. Two bottles of water are sticking out of her cooking-smock pockets. We grab those instantly. By the time I kill mine, Devin's already scarfing down apples and cheddar and saying "Thanks" to Mom with her mouth full.

Mom sets the plate on the desk next to the computer and gives me a hopeful look. "Half the plate has about two hundred fifty calories. I measured and checked." She glances at Devin, who snags another handful of food. "A third of the plate has under two hundred," Mom amends quickly. "Good enough?"

"Yes, thank you." The smile I give her isn't forced or fake. I appreciate that she's trying. And it so helps that she's not really able to take things away from me anymore, even though she thinks she can.

Devin and I settle down to eat and stop sweating before doing the paper, and Mom sits with us. "I've talked to your father, Devin, about Regionals. He's driving up behind the bus, and he'll look after you and Chan until Chan's father can get there."

We nod.

The sharp cheddar cheese makes my mouth pucker, and I steal some of Devin's water.

Dad's out of town, but he's driving straight to the gymnasium where Regionals are scheduled for this year. The competition's about two hours from West Estoria, and about three hours from where Dad's working.

"Doe, a deer, a feee-male deer," Lauren sings from the

garage, really, really loud. Her voice sounds great, no kidding, but it's so *loud*.

Devin freezes mid-chew.

Mom's face pinches, then relaxes into a blank mask. Her hands twitch like she wants to cover her ears.

"Are you sure you're okay with me staying home for her?" Mom shouts over the music.

"I'm sure," I yell back after swallowing a slice of apple. "I know she needs somebody. She's worked so hard—you can't just break her heart."

Mom glances toward the garage and looks absolutely persecuted and miserable. "No, I can't, can I?"

All three of us laugh. Then glance toward the garage again like, *Maybe she'll get tired of this.*

Fat chance.

The kid's too good. Lauren will stick this out, and by the time it's over, I'll forever hate that play and the movie version of it, too, for the rest of my natural life. We'll all hate it. We'll all have nightmares about it.

Mom puts on her best supportive-mother face, gets up, and wanders off toward the kitchen. Devin and I finish eating, glorying in the few seconds when the music actually stops. Then we move to the computer. I sit down at the keyboard and pull up the Emily paper, and we start reading and talking and making sure each word is absolutely perfect. If we ace this draft, we'll get at least a B, and maybe a low A for the project, which will help Devin's grade a ton.

"This part about her lesbianism with her sister-in-law." Devin points to the screen as I use the zoom function to make it larger. "Should we mention that article I found about her 'Wild Nights' poem being a reference to doing the nasty with a woman?"

"I don't know." I scroll to the end of the sentence and think about adding the citation. "That article talks about the poem being about sex, but not about lesbian sex."

Devin gives me a look. "Hello? What do you think *rowing in Eden* means? Come on."

I crack up. "It's not that simple. We've got to—"

Mom walks back into the room with two more bottles of water.

Out of reflex, I hit CONTROL-ENTER twice to conceal our screen, even though I don't have to, then feel stupid.

Except . . . something pops up.

Lauren's pink puppy game.

What . . . ?

"Hey, I didn't partially lift your grounding so you girls could play computer games," Mom says as she puts the waters down. "Get back to work."

"Uh, okay," Devin mumbles, giving me the do-something elbow right in the ribs.

My brain's completely frozen. It looks like a game. There's a counter running and everything, and now and then the puppies shift position really fast and the score changes, as if I moved them with my fingers on the keyboard.

Finally, I manage to hit CONTROL-ENTER twice again, and the pink puppy screen vanishes.

Out in the garage, Lauren switches to "Lonely Goatherd," the song with all the yodeling, which sounds so much better when Julie Andrews does it. Each note stabs into my ice-cold head.

"Phew. The paper didn't get wasted." Devin sounds relieved as Mom "humphs" and heads back toward the kitchen.

"What was that thing?" Devin adds in a whisper. "A screen concealer? Did you put some on this machine?"

I nod, then get confused and shake my head for no. Aloud, I say, "Yeah, a concealer, only I didn't put it on here. Lauren's been using it. I thought it was a game."

Both of us turn toward the garage door and stare at it.

"Wonder what that kid has been up to," Devin says, like she doesn't really care and wants to get back to the paper.

But the question makes my cheddar and apples and wheat crackers charge up my throat. My stomach cramps. My body cramps all over. I jump out of my chair, fly off to the downstairs bathroom, slam the door, and drop to my knees, hugging the toilet.

I can't quit thinking.

I can't quit remembering the night I downloaded my screen concealer.

That night I passed right by the cartoons and pink

puppies and picked the kittens. Mine doesn't look like a game, but the cartoons and puppies were different. They looked like games.

I thought Lauren was playing a game.

My guts heave, but nothing comes out. My eyes tear, but the water still won't slide down my face. I'm all jammed up inside. Blocked.

Lauren could have found out about those screen concealers from anybody. Lots of people use them.

But the same site as I used?

Screen concealers are completely common. It's just a coincidence.

The . . . same . . . site. . . .

Same site. . . .

"Chan?" Devin knocks on the bathroom door, but I ignore her.

Why *does* Lauren have a screen concealer?

Who told her about it?

Am I being Mom, thinking Lauren's too stupid to figure something out on her own, just because she's eight?

Who told her about it?

God, I'm definitely being Mom. I might as well just march out to the garage and ask Lauren who put that idea in her head.

Devin knocks again. "Chan, are you okay?"

I mean, I heard of screen concealers before Paul, but never really looked into it until he sent me that link.

Same site.

Who told Lauren about those concealers?

The screen concealer's a coincidence.

But the big question isn't just how Lauren found out about the pink puppies. No. The big question's the one Devin asked.

What is Lauren up to?

What's Lauren using that screen concealer to hide?

I heave again.

"Chan, I'm so not above breaking down this door." Now Devin sounds annoyed. "One good kick, I swear."

I can't say anything. I can't talk at all. I feel raw and hollow and rolled up in a little ball.

Reason this out. Just calm down and think it through.

Lauren has a little boyfriend. David, that's his name, right? They probably e-mail. That's all. She's hiding e-mails to David. I'm just freaking out because—because—

Because of what I'm doing.

Because of Paul.

Heat boils through me, and this time when I heave, stuff finally comes up. My fingers dig against the toilet seat, and I feel like half my body's hurling into the bowl.

Maybe I'm not okay.

Outside, Mom and Devin talk. I don't catch much other than, "nervous," "Regionals," and "paper looks good enough."

I have to get a grip.

If I don't get my act together, Mom'll ask more

questions than I can answer. And if I freak out and start running my mouth all over the place, I'll lose everything— for me *and* Lauren.

The voices move away from the bathroom.

Mom's probably walking Devin out. Lauren's music is still blasting. Back to "Edelweiss," which totally makes me want to scream.

I could go to the garage and ask her about the screen concealer, but she might flip out, and then the whole Mom problem would blow up in both of our faces.

Screw it.

Maybe I should just go straight to Mom.

Yeah, so she and Dad can lock me in my closet (with no electronic devices) and feed me through a hole in the door until I get out of high school.

Not happening.

Bit by bit, I get my stomach under control.

When I think I can handle it, I flush, get up, wash my face, then rinse out my mouth. When I grab for the towel, I catch sight of my pale, freckled face in the mirror.

I imagine some perv staring at my face, at my bare chest. Some ugly, drooly old goat, getting off over a video of *me*.

Back to the toilet.

Not okay, not okay, not okay.

This time, I stay through four rounds of "Edelweiss" and two rounds of that weird little good-bye song.

When I finally get it together enough to come out, Mom's waiting in the living room. She gets up immediately when I come into the room, zips across the floor, and hugs me so tight she smashes my face against her crumb-covered cooking smock.

"You all right?" she asks when she finally lets me breathe.

"Yeah," I say, and I'm surprised at how hoarse my voice sounds. "I think I just need to—just, I—I need to—"

"Lie down. Right now." She rubs a hand over my hair. "Honestly, honey, you and Lauren are both so stressed out I think I'll make doctor's appointments for both of you. Maybe you need vitamins."

I don't argue.

Which obviously surprises Mom and worries her even more.

"You go on upstairs. I'll print that paper out for you and get it organized, and I'll bring you some crackers and soup and soda up later." She kisses me on the cheek. "Sugar-free soda."

"Thanks." I squeeze my eyes shut as the music in the garage changes again.

Mom lets me go and heaves a sigh that rivals any I've ever heard from Lauren. "And we're giving that a rest, too," she says through clenched teeth as she starts for the garage door.

I run upstairs before the fight breaks out.

I know I need to talk to Lauren—but I don't know just when I can do that without causing a major catastrophe. But first, there's someone else I need to talk to.

Only, a few hours later, locked in my room with Mom's soup and crackers, with Paul in chat on the B-3k, I just can't ask him.

He's being so sweet, so himself, so totally Paul as he talks to me, and I can just imagine those dark eyes and that handsome smile.

How can I ask him if he's been perving my little sister?

My *eight-year-old* sister?

No way. Paul's not like that. I do know him after so many hours of talking to him.

The screen-concealer thing, that has to be a fluke.

Besides, I can't do that to him, ask him that question. I can't do that to our relationship. But, for the first time since we started talking, I sort of blow him off, using the paper (finished, printed by Mom, waiting on my desk) and Regionals (too much to think about, too too much) as an excuse.

I go to bed early, but I leave on my desk lamp and I make sure to leave my door open. And I fall hard asleep, with no dreams at all.

Until Lauren nudges me and starts crawling into my bed.

When I open my eyes and squint at the clock, it's after 2 a.m. Either she stayed up late or slept longer than usual—but here she is, just like I knew she would be.

"Tell me my story," she says, all quiet and sleepy.

I let her get in, wait for her to settle down, then give her shoulder a little pinch and shake. "Hey. Wake up a sec. I need to ask you something."

"I'm not a hey," she mutters sleepily. "I'm a Lauren."

Hearing that chokes me up for a second. An old game Dad used to play with us, calling us animal names or kidding names or silly names, and waiting for us to answer like Lauren had answered.

My sister's *eight*. She still plays that game with Dad.

"Lauren, I'm serious." I give her another pinch and shake. "Open your eyes."

She does, but I can tell she's still not completely awake.

"What?" she mumbles as she rubs one eye with her knuckles and scratches her belly with her other hand.

"Downstairs on the computer, that puppy game—I mean, screen concealer. Who told you about that site where you downloaded it?"

Lauren stops scratching and rubbing her eye. I might be imagining it, but I think she just stiffened up a little. "Nobody. I found it on my own."

The tone of her voice, the look on her face—am I *that* obvious when I lie to Devin? Oh, God. I probably am, aren't I?

After taking a slow breath to make sure I sound calm,

I say, "Look, if it was your boyfriend, David, that's fine. I just need to know, okay?"

Lauren squints at me in the low glow of the night-light. "Nobody told me," she insists. A lie, again. "I just don't want Mom seeing everything I do."

Another centering, calming breath. I try again. "Lauren, is there anything I need to know about David? A secret or something? You can tell me anything. I won't rat you out to Mom, I swear."

Now she's totally awake, and even in the bad light, I can see she's starting to get angsty. "You're being weird," she says and pushes away from me. "I'm going back to my own bed."

"Wait." I try to catch her arm, but she pulls away from me and calls me weird again.

In a few seconds, she's out my door and walking down the hall, her little feet making squeegee-noises on the wood floor as she goes.

I lie there wide-awake for probably half an hour, maybe more, before I get up, make my way to the Cave of Doom, and sit down beside Lauren's bed.

A few minutes pass, then a few more, and a few more. Lauren's easy, regular breathing lets me know she's totally asleep again.

I rub my stomach like Lauren did and wonder if Mom ever feels this way when she's worrying about us so much. Is this awful, gut-digging sensation what makes Mom act so freaky and neurotic all the time?

Susan Vaught

If it is, I'll have to hate her a little less even when I'm furious with her. Maybe a lot less.

For the rest of the night, I just watch my little sister sleep, like my being beside her might keep anything bad from happening to her, or erase anything bad that might have already happened.

I can't think of anything else to do.

WEDNESDAY, NOVEMBER 19

Devin and I turn our American lit paper in to Haggerty Wednesday morning, and go first with our presentation. Devin doesn't stumble over the poem she recites, and I don't let myself hesitate in exposing our radical theories about Emily's hermetic life and shunning of marriage.

The whole time I'm talking, my stomach hurts, and I feel dizzy. Worse, I feel achy and fevery, and my legs keep tingling. Burning, actually, all along my thighs, and higher, in bad places. And I know exactly what that means.

Herpes outbreak.

God, not now.

But why?

Am I getting sick? A cold or the flu or something? I always have an outbreak when I get sick. But maybe it's too much stress. That will definitely do it, too. Staying up all night staring at Lauren probably didn't help anything. I need to remember to take a second pill when I get home tonight or I'll be too miserable to compete by tomorrow.

When we finish, Haggerty absolutely beams at us. "Looks good, girls," she says, though her sharp eyes linger on me.

After class, she stops us at the door and asks, "You feeling okay, Chan? Hope you didn't stay up to all hours working on this."

Devin gives me the talk-fast eyebrow, and I shake my head. "No, ma'am. We were actually done early this time."

Devin flashes a majorly nervous grin.

Haggerty glances back toward her desk, where the paper's sitting. "I've already looked at the first few pages. Definitely first-class work. Glad to see you back in top form, Chan."

She pats my shoulder and I want to jerk away from her touch and vomit. It's all of a sudden, and I don't have a clue why. It's just weird, getting compliments on my work or anything when down inside, right under my skin—and at home, in the dark Cave of Doom—everything seems to be messing up completely. Like, crashing straight to the ground. All my energy leaves me. All the good things inside me seem to drain out to the floor and just dry up to nothing at all.

All through world history and geometry, I keep thinking about Lauren, about what I saw and how she acted when I tried to talk to her.

What's the right thing to do? What's the *responsible* thing?

Should I say something to Mom?

Should I have risked asking Paul if he's somehow spoken to Lauren?

I definitely should have pushed my sister a little harder, made her tell me what she was hiding. But she seemed so little and tense and close to snapping in half.

Right, wrong, responsible—this is all screwed up.

Before physics, Devin stops me in the hall. "You better go to the nurse, honey. You look like you're about to fall out right here, right now."

"I can't get sick. Regionals are—"

"Exactly. We've gotta leave at the armpit of dawn, and you better go get some sleep and get copacetic before we get on that bus."

"Mom's at work and Dad's out of town. I don't have a ride home."

"Then lie down in the nurse's office and I'll tell the Bear. She'll drive you home in a heartbeat."

Oh, joy.

The urge to be sick starts all over again, but I go to the nurse's office and tell her I think I've got an outbreak starting, and that I feel like crap. She puts me on her couch and leaves a message with Mom, and about five minutes later, the Bear sweeps in to whisk me home in her big-ass dual-axle tank of a white pickup truck. All she needs is big tires and she could outdo any of the truck-freak boys at school.

The Bear's so vierd sometimes. Thankfully, she doesn't talk much, not until we get close to my house.

"You have vorked very hard for tomorrow, Chan." She turns onto our road and keeps her eyes straight ahead. Today, she has on lavender silk sweats, and her black hair's pulled back like usual, only loosely, fastened with a brown leather tie. "Vork is finished now. You should . . . enjoy. Stay focused, but enjoy. You are still just a girl."

"Regionals are important," I say. God, my throat feels sore. "I need to win. I want to win. It's like you said—redemption. Plus a lot of other stuff."

"Yes, but do not let your nerves make you ill." She pulls into our driveway, stops the truck, shuts off the engine, and turns to look at me. "Perhaps I say too much sometimes." She gestures with one hand. "Put on too much pressure. I am sorry."

I shake my head. "You're fine. I'm pressuring me, not you."

Well, sort of true.

Do I even know how to be completely truthful anymore?

I don't need to think about that or I might hurl before I even get out of the Bear's truck.

"Is there more?" the Bear asks, just like she's reading my mind. I *hate* it when she does that. I hate it worse when Mom does it, though.

It takes all the energy I don't have, but I manage to give her a questioning look and say, "More?"

"You know." She gestures again, and her expression pinches into tense worry. "Bigger problems. You can tell me."

I don't answer. I just can't. My hand inches toward the door handle.

"Vhen I vas a girl," the Bear says, "*Coach* meant everything. Mother. Sister. Friend. Leader. I have tried to be that, for you and my other girls. You know this, no?"

"No. I mean, yes." I hate it when she does that *no* thing, too. At the moment, my brain's actually starting to hurt along with the rest of my body.

The Bear gazes at me for a time without saying a word. Then she nods and says, "Go rest. I vill see you in the morning."

Grateful, I open the door, then try to muster the energy to get out and go inside. Before I can close the door to the big white pickup, the Bear says, "I mean vhat I say, Chan Shealy. If you need me, if you need your coach, I vill be here."

Her and Dad, always with the I'm-here-for-you's. What am I supposed to do with that?

Take a chance and talk to them? a chirpy part of my head suggests as I struggle into the house. If I could strangle that chirp without killing myself, I so would do it.

Instead, I guzzle some orange juice, take some serious Theraflu, and go ahead and call my doctor and up the dose on my antiviral. I check the messages, but there's nothing from Mom yet. She'll call soon, probably, to check on me, so I tuck the phone into my pocket as I go upstairs.

My first urge is to lie down and fall dead asleep, but once I get to my room, I feel drawn to the closet, to my last year's backpack and the B-3k. When I take out the little machine, though, I don't want to turn it on. What I want to do is turn back the date to a month ago or maybe longer. If I'd never said yes to doing any of the picture stuff, or maybe if I'd never answered Paul's first e-mail, a lot of things might be different.

Some things worse, maybe. But some things better, too. And maybe I wouldn't have to be so worried about Lauren.

Coincidence.

But I don't know that for sure, do I?

And I feel completely weird about all of that, and Paul, and the Internet in general.

What if he isn't who I think he is?

What if all he wants is my naked pictures and my videos?

That's stupid. But . . .

After a few seconds, I tuck the B-3k back into my pack and zip it up tight.

Then I do the most responsible thing I can think of. I head straight into the Cave of Doom.

An hour and one worried phone call from Mom later, I've taken the Cave of Doom apart and put it back together and found nothing at all. I feel double-miserable from doing all that, and from, I don't know, breaking all into my little sister's privacy.

But she's hiding something.

Maybe something really bad.

Shouldn't I try to find out what it is?

I'm her big sister. It's kind of my job or something. At least it feels like it is.

The next place I go is downstairs to the computer, where I hack all over the place, but can't find out where she's been going, or access any of her accounts.

Of course not. The screen concealer erases all the tracks. Duh.

I sit there, head in my hands, aching.

What am I missing?

What am I not thinking about?

If I were Lauren, where would I feel safe hiding something nobody should see?

I already went through every one of her old backpacks upstairs. All the neat hiding places in her room I would have used, and some I thought of when I saw them. Zero. Zilch. Nada.

My increasingly feeble brain rambles back over the last few weeks, to all of Lauren's patterns and habits—at least the ones I know about.

And my skin goes cold all over.

The aches in my body immediately triple, and I run to the kitchen and take more Theraflu with a bunch more juice. If I were the type to take anything stronger, I'd find something right this second.

Because I think I know.

I don't want to know, all of a sudden, but that doesn't

matter, because as I stand here with my hands braced against the kitchen counter, I *know* where Lauren's hiding place has to be.

Knots tie inside my cold, miserable skin. My sick, churning belly. My tight, getting tighter chest. I need to go look. But now that I'm so sure where the hiding place is, I don't want to find what I think I'll find.

My legs burn and I wish I could cry. I wish something inside me would break loose and finally, finally let me sob for hours. All of last year's tears and all of this year's tears. All the right-now tears—and those would be plenty enough.

"Enough," I say out loud, and I force myself to walk to the garage.

The first thing I do is flip on the lights, and the second thing I do is lock all the doors and switch off the door-opener that's still hooked up even though my parents don't park cars in here anymore. I haven't heard from Mom again, and I can't take the chance that she'll come home and bust me. Well, bust me busting Lauren.

If I don't find anything bad, I actually don't want to get Lauren in trouble. I definitely don't want to cost her this whole being-in-the-big-play dream. Big sisters just don't do awful things like that to little sisters. I don't want to be awful to Lauren.

I turn toward the karaoke machine, or more to the point, to the suitcase underneath it.

"Maybe it won't be bad," I tell nobody, but when I get

to the old beat-up suitcase—it had been one of Dad's, I'm pretty sure—I discover it has a combination lock.

So, it's probably going to be bad.

It takes a while to hunt up a hammer and screwdriver, but I manage that, move the karaoke machine, and beat the suitcase lock until it finally breaks and pops open.

I'm holding my breath and it hurts, and I realize I've closed my eyes.

Open. Look. Pay attention.

But I don't want to. God, I really, really, really don't want to.

It's not like I have a choice, right? I have to find out. I have to see what's been happening, and figure out what to do. So I lay the hammer and screwdriver on the padded floor next to my leg, and up goes the lid.

A sleek blue laptop sits in the suitcase, the very newest model with all the gadgets included—like built-in webcams and full sound capacity. Almost just like the one I picked out for myself, only a little better. It's something like I thought I'd find, but I still suck in air through my teeth. I still feel absolutely shocked, way down deep, to my feet, to my toes. Stuff tips and teeters inside me.

When it falls, I don't know if I'll be able to move. Not now, or ever again.

Lauren has herself a computer worth a ton of money. Money she can't possibly have, unless someone's giving it to her.

Or unless she's selling . . . something. Like I've been doing.

"No." My voice is loud. Hoarse. "No, no, no!"

But I open the laptop.

Lauren's a little kid, so she hasn't thought through what might happen if somebody finds the computer—not all the way, anyway. She's got the concealer, but her files aren't password-protected, and what she has put passwords on, she's told the computer to remember. So, the minute I type the correct first letter, the rest of the password comes up and the files open.

I poke around through everything—her word processing documents. Her e-mail. And then, her picture files.

Oh, God. OhGodnonono . . .

I'm saying it out loud.

Yelling it.

Things crash down in my mind and explode. Pulverize. Definitely not in my body anymore. Definitely way up on the ceiling somewhere, staring down at that awful stuff from someplace far, far away.

"David" doesn't talk in the e-mails like any little boy I know.

The way he does talk is so familiar I want to tear out all my insides and use them to drown the computer so Lauren can't ever, ever, ever use it again.

Lauren's made some pictures of herself.

A lot of pictures.

Still-shot after still-shot clog up her files, mailed to this "David" in exchange for his "coaching" on her singing for the play. "David" compliments her on how beautiful she is, how much he loves her. He confesses to being "a little older." He plays into her whole vampire-goth thing, signing himself *Prince of Darkness*.

Vomit. Vomit!

She's got her clothes on—but it's still all wrong.

And "David—"

No, don't think about it.

But I have to.

"David" talks about how hard his life is. How his dad picks on him. How he knows how she can make a lot of money and have anything she wants. How he'll show her, teach her, be beside her every step of the way.

Sounds a lot like Paul, doesn't it?

No!

Coincidence.

My vision blurs until I can't even read the words anymore.

But they're burned into my brain, my heart.

Lauren. . . .

I drop the computer back into the suitcase. Before I really think about it, I've picked up the hammer and screwdriver, and I'm one second from bashing that stupid machine to bits when a rational thought or two nudges through my brain.

Police.

Prosecution.

Catching this sick perv like they do on those television news shows.

If I break all the evidence, nobody can hunt down "David" and leave him to rot in prison for trying to mess with Lauren.

And the timing. Oh, God.

From what I can tell, Lauren got the laptop about ten days after I got my weights. The first e-mails on that machine hinted that she and "David" have been boyfriend-girlfriend (*ohGodgross*) since right after that.

Another coincidence? Three in a row?

The screen saver site, the way the e-mails sound—and now the timeline, too?

Paul. . . .

Or . . . "Paul"?

"No," I chant like I've been doing since I first opened the computer. "It's not the same person. These are definitely coincidences."

But I'm going numb inside. Numb and cold and I think I might faint.

Okay, no. Really no. I can't faint out here in the garage holding a computer full of sick perv letters to my little sister. I have to do something. Right now. Call Mom. Call the police. Anything.

And yet . . .

The play.

I know what'll happen to Lauren when I rat her out

like I promised I wouldn't. Her life will be totally screwed. Everybody'll find out, and she'll have to live like I've lived all this last year, with witch-monsters calling her skank and treating her like she's a freak.

How can I do that to her? To my little sister?

Even if everybody doesn't find out, Mom and Dad will know, and *they'll* treat her like a freak. She'll lose everything. No way they'll let her out the door for *Sound of Music*. She'll be trapped in worse than Mommy-jail forever, with nothing.

But if I wait until tomorrow night when I get home from Regionals, I'll be finished with this year's big competition, and Lauren will be finished with dress rehearsal and ready for opening night. And maybe that'll work like twirling. They'll restrict her from everything but school and play practice, and at least she'll have that.

We'd both win, Lauren and me.

God only knows all the times I've been grounded, if I hadn't had twirling, I would have had less than no life. The least I can do is give her that play. And the least I can do for myself is finish Regionals.

Tomorrow night, everything will be a lot simpler, won't it?

My head gradually stops spinning, and I close the laptop and take it out of its suitcase. Then I close the suitcase, push the lock back into place, and set the karaoke machine back into position. It only takes me a second or two after that to put away the hammer and screwdriver, and open the garage again.

The computer's so small I can put it under my shirt, just in case Mom shows up before I get it upstairs.

For now, I have a plan.

Take the computer, and for tonight, hide it in my room. That way, Lauren can't get hurt anymore. She'll probably be focused on the play, anyway. Obsessed with that all night. If she realizes the laptop is gone, she won't dare say a single word.

Then, tomorrow, after Regionals and her dress rehearsal, I'll go to Mom and Dad.

About Lauren.

Not about me.

Not about Paul.

At least . . . not until I can make myself talk to him. Not until I know whether or not "David" is really Paul.

Maybe he isn't.

Besides, I need to be sure before I screw up my whole life even worse, and his, too. At least I think I do.

That seems like the responsible thing.

Isn't it?

Success is counted sweetest
By those who ne'er succeed.
To comprehend a nectar
Requires sorest need.

Not one of all the purple host
Who took the flag to-day
Can tell the definition,
So clear, of victory,

As he, defeated, dying,
On whose forbidden ear
The distant strains of triumph
Break, agonized and clear.

Emily Dickinson

AT THE TOP—OR THE BOTTOM

The rain
It's coming again I can
Feel it
On my shoulders
At my back
Wind
Scraping my cheek
A cold paintbrush
Stiff
With unknown pictures.

Chan Shealy

THURSDAY, NOVEMBER 20

Devin's "armpit of dawn" comes even earlier than I thought it would.

By the time I get up, pass Mom's health-check by lying like a total dog, and load myself with antiviral meds, Theraflu, and orange juice, Mom has Lauren in the shower.

I fell asleep early last night, throbbing and half-insane from the outbreak trying to take over my entire body, and from everything rammed and jammed into my head.

Of course, I dreamed. Weird, off-color nightmares about Lauren, singing and sobbing and screaming, then about me being in jail over what was on her computer.

Did I do this to her, somehow?

Is what happened to her my fault?

My hands shake the whole time I'm getting dressed and packing up my leotard and tights and makeup and batons.

I can't do this. I'm too sick. I'm too upset.

But it's Regionals. Devin's counting on me. The

Bear's counting on me. I've been counting on me, too, to beat Ellis in a major way and finally shut her up. And Lauren's counting on her dress rehearsal. The play's a big deal. Mom's getting Lauren an out-of-school pass for it and everything, since it's a major community event.

Lauren. . . .

Tonight, I'll do what I have to do, and everything will change, probably for the worse, and probably for the both of us. For today, Lauren and I still have life as we know it, and big things to do—moments we've been working really hard to achieve.

That thought carries me through the rest of my packing, and lugging my bags downstairs, including last year's backpack with all the illegal electronics inside. No way am I leaving any of this stuff for somebody to find. Not that Lauren would dare look for it with Mom stuck right up her nose.

About the time I get my stuff to the front door, Lauren comes out of her bedroom in her robe with her hair wet and sticking to her pale face. The sight of her makes me stand still and stop breathing. I can't stop staring at her as she walks down the stairs, but once she makes it to the living room, I can't look at her at all. I just turn around and open the door and start searching for Devin and Mr. Macy.

I have zero idea what to say to Lauren, or how to say it. Just the thought of trying to talk to her, ask the questions I need to ask, say anything at all—chokes me up completely.

I'm Mom. I'm everybody who hasn't been able to talk straight to me since they found out about Adam-P and the herpes thing. I'm . . . awful.

Lauren tugs at my warm-up jacket.

Oh, God.

I turn around, expecting—anything. For her to freak out. Demand her computer. Start yelling or crying and blow it all up, right here, right now. My stomach drops hard, and orange juice burns up my throat.

She looks so *little*.

"Can I go in your room and get your extra mascara?" She pushes a strand of brown hair out of her face and gazes at me with clear, wide eyes, exactly the same color as her hair.

"What?" My own voice sounds so alien it makes me jump.

"Mom said I had to ask." Lauren's acting nervous. Her hand shakes as she points upstairs. "About the makeup. Can I use it, or not?"

I tighten my grip on the straps of the pack with her computer in it. "Oh. Yeah. Sure. Use whatever you want."

Off she goes, back up the stairs again.

Something about the way she sounded and looked makes me wonder if the real Lauren's somewhere up on the ceiling with the real me, watching everything going on below.

The blare of a horn jerks me back to reality for a few seconds at least.

Devin and Mr. Macy have arrived. They're in the big black sedan today, and they both have on sunglasses for the perfect too-cool-for-our ride look.

I drag my bags out the door and Devin meets me halfway across the yard.

"You look like excrement," she says with all her usual tact.

"Thanks." I squint into the sunlight as we put the bags into the sedan's trunk. Look like excrement, feel like a total vampire. It's gonna be a great day.

She slams the trunk, then opens the back door for me. As I slide onto the seat and grab for the belt, she asks, "Can you do this?"

"I can do this," I say. But I don't talk much more on the way to the bus.

We get to the school a little early, but the Bear and the rest of the majorettes show up pretty fast, including Ellis, who, thankfully, ignores me. The jazz band arrives, too. They have a competition at the same place, so we're all riding together. A bunch of parents, including Mr. Macy, are lining up cars to drive behind the bus as I settle into the very back bench, which has a bit of extra room so I can lie down if I need to. Devin flops on the other end of the seat, and the Bear takes the seat directly in front of her. The rest of the majorettes and the jazz band mix up and sit down, chattering and clanging instruments and jawing about how much ass they're going to kick.

All the noise makes me want to scream, but I don't have the energy to waste. I need to rest as much as possible if I want a prayer of making it through my routine.

Don't think like that. You'll make it through. You're going to beat Ellis.

I lean back and close my eyes.

I have to get through the day, do my best, then face tonight.

The bus pulls out, leading the line of parent-cars, and the lurch makes my stomach flip. I chew my bottom lip to hold it together.

"Quit thinking about bad things," Devin says under all the noise and clanging and trumpet blasts.

I turn my head in her direction. "I'm not."

"Don't prevaricate, honey." She shakes her finger at me. "I can see negativity all over your face."

Don't lie. I smile at her. *So easy to say. And don't think about Paul. Yeah, okay. Right. I can do that.*

My head rolls back to center and I close my eyes. My legs hurt. My private parts itch a little and burn. It's a tiny bit better than yesterday, but not much. Without the Theraflu, which I probably shouldn't be taking, I'd fall right on my face and just stay down for the count.

As it is, I'm awake, but I wish I weren't. The bus seems first too hot, and then too cold, and definitely too, too noisy. The chatter won't stop. And the chatter in my head won't shut up, either.

When I do start talking about all this stuff, what

exactly am I going to say—to Mom, Dad, Lauren, Devin, the cops—to everyone?

I've been talking to this guy and I made some videos for money on the Internet. . . .

My fingers trace across the rough fabric of the old backpack.

Hey, I just happened to find this computer after beating open an old suitcase under a karaoke machine—no special reason—and hacked into my sister's computer files, and . . .

Images of Lauren's e-mails flicker through my mind and I try to shut them out.

"Chan, you look like you're sucking on a sour, rotten pickle," Devin says. "Give it a rest."

This time, the Bear turns around in her seat and gives me an endless, hard stare. I can't tell if she's mad or worried. Probably mad. Maybe everybody should be mad at me.

I rub my palm across the old backpack.

So, Lauren downloaded a screen concealer from the site Paul directed me to. And her perv's e-mails sound way too much like Paul talking. And the timing matches.

What else?

What else is it that's banging around in my brain, trying to be remembered?

I do my best to keep the pickle look off my face as Devin gives me a speech about motivation and positive thinking, and the majorettes chatter, and the Bear hollers at a trumpet player for emptying his trumpet's spit-valves on a drummer's head.

It's all too normal. I don't want normal. I don't feel normal.

I feel like I should be remembering something.

The nightmares and the Cave of Doom, for one thing.

Hadn't Lauren's nightmares and her goth phase gotten worse around the same time I started talking to Paul?

I shut my eyes and play back everything Paul and I discussed those first few times we talked, even though it's been weeks.

We talked about ourselves. About school (him lying at first, of course). And our families.

Did I mention Lauren by name?

My eyes come open.

I did mention her name. And I gave Paul my name and the name of my school. How hard would it have been for him to look up Lauren's school? To find her profile or her e-mail address?

I've even given Paul Lauren's BlahFest profile name—lots of times.

He could have gotten her e-mail address from that, if she included it.

Of course she did.

Paul might have even hacked it right off my computer. Mom said my laptop had some worms and a

Trojan. One of those programs could have fed Paul my entire address book.

He might not be a perv.

I might be adding up a whole bunch of things that don't add up.

I've never done a search for Lauren's name on the Net, either. Maybe her profile and e-mail come up. I'll have to check that.

My fault. It's probably all my fault.

But I could be making a whole bunch of mess out of absolutely nothing.

Those e-mails on Lauren's laptop aren't *nothing.* They're—they're everything. Everything awful in the whole world.

Somebody's trying to take advantage of my little sister.

I think about the envelope she got the same day I got my B-3k from Paul. The one with her friend's name on it, and the little hearts and stuff.

If Paul faked out people by using my school's address, could he have faked us all out by using the name and address of one of Lauren's friends?

No.

Yes. . . .

She said she had a boyfriend. That poor kid. Wanting her voice lessons, and the boyfriend—

Like Paul with me, and the training program. The money. The escape from Mom's rules. The whole I'm-okay-with-your-herpes thing.

"I'm not eight," I mutter out loud, then catch my-self.

Devin gazes at me. "Are you getting delirious?"

"No." I glance at her handbag. "Can I borrow your cell a minute?"

She leans back on her seat and holds up one hand. "Not if your mom will kill me or have me arrested or anything."

"It's Mom I want to call," I say.

Devin gives me a you're-way-past-nuts look, but she also gives me the phone.

I try Mom's number, but get her voice mail immediately. The phone's off. They're probably already at the dress rehearsal. I leave a message, try Dad next, but can't get him, either. After trying them both one more time and leaving messages on both voice mails, I hand the phone back to Devin.

What time is that rehearsal?

Would Mom stay with Lauren the whole time?

And after it was over, since it would be after school hours, would Mom leave Lauren with the babysitter and go to work?

Just for good measure, I take back Devin's phone and leave a message for Mom on her voice mail at work, too.

Miles roll by. And minutes. Nearly an hour.

I try to get my mind off things. Talk to Devin about the competition. About Haggerty and the paper. About how we would win our categories. About anything at all.

But my thoughts keep coming straight back to Lauren.

Devin names her biggest competition in the dance section and says, "I think my high kick can take hers any day."

Please *don't tell Mom*, Lauren had said when she told me about David. *She wouldn't let me talk to him or see him or anything.*

Did she actually use the phrase *see him?*

I sit up straighter.

She did. I'm sure of it.

I look at Devin. "So not good."

"What?" Devin's eyebrows come together. "My kick is totally better and you know it!"

Wait until tonight, Chan. The thought pops into my head and almost sounds convincing. *Today is too important for Lauren. And way too important for you.*

My heart starts a fast, steady, *pound-pound-pound*, and my gaze moves to the back of Ellis's head. She's got her hair up today, looking perfect, completely calm and ready to compete. She's blabbering to her friends, stopping only to dig me with a witchy frown a few times.

I . . . don't care.

I really don't think I do.

All of a sudden, Ellis and *skank* and Adam-P and herpes and tons of other things just don't seem that important.

Am I *really* willing to take a risk like Lauren not

having a grown-up right beside her just because I might not be able to compete and beat the witch-monster and get what I want?

Or just because I might get in trouble, too?

Please *don't tell Mom. She wouldn't let me talk to him or see him* . . .

God, what kind of person am I?

"Chan, baby, you're startin' to scare me." Devin's voice drifts through the craziness on the bus and in my head.

"I'm scaring myself," I say out loud, to her and the craziness. "I hate myself. You should hate me, too."

Devin's way-high eyebrows say, *You're completely delirious and I'm about to call an ambulance.*

When I had talked to Lauren about her "boyfriend," I had asked if he made her happy, and she said something like, *He'll get me free lessons when we see each other at the dress rehearsal.*

In a big hurry, I grab Devin's phone off the seat beside her and dial.

Mom's voice mail picks straight up again.

I swear.

Dad still doesn't answer, either.

Should I call the police?

Or maybe the place where Lauren's having the dress rehearsal?

Where *is* the dress rehearsal? I don't know!

It's probably at the theater, but I don't know for sure. The theater's pretty small, and it's a college auditorium

307

during the day. The college might have classes there or something.

Lauren. . . .

What am I doing on this bus? Am I out of my mind?

What have I done?

When we see each other at the dress rehearsal. . . .

Responsibility makes sense in a way it's never made sense before. The pounding in my chest becomes absolute thunder. I start to shake all over and slam the phone shut.

Devin jumps and snatches it back from me. "Easy on the phoneware," she says. "What's wrong with you, Chan?"

I hit myself in the head, hard, twice, with both fists.

"Everything!" I yell.

Then I start to cry. Really cry.

Tears stream down my face.

Devin freezes in place and the bus goes funeral-quiet.

The Bear wheels in her seat, but I don't wait for her to speak. "I need to go home, Coach." I stand, step forward, and grab the sleeve of her black competition-day warm-up suit. "I've got to go home *right now*."

THURSDAY, NOVEMBER 20, LATER

In less than ten minutes, the Bear orders the bus off at an exit, talks a majorette's mom out of her car, puts that mom in charge of the bus and the competition, asks Mr. Macy to help that mom, and gets us back on the road toward home.

She doesn't ask me any questions or try to argue with me, or even ask me to stop crying. She just drives. Very fast.

I guess that's why I start talking, because she's not pushing me, and she's taking me so seriously, and keeping her promise to be there for me if I ever need her. All the way back to West Estoria, I talk and cry. I tell the Bear everything, and I mean everything, right down to how much I hate myself for all the choices I've made, all the way back to Adam-P.

The Bear never wavers in her driving, or gives me any freaky looks, or anything. She keeps driving, and after I finish, she stays quiet while I use her cell to leave Mom and Dad increasingly more desperate messages.

"Call the police," she says after I hang up from the last call. "No, vait. Let me."

She gets the number for the West Estoria PD, and in her heavy accent, getting heavier as she speaks, she lays everything out for them, only lots shorter than my version.

"Yes," she says, nodding. "Lauren Shealy. No. Ve don't know vhere the rehearsal is, but it is a community theater production. Please. Yes. Thank you. Hurry."

She closes the phone. "They are sending officers."

A flash of relief blazes through me, then I just start crying again.

After a while, the Bear offers me her sleeve to wipe my face. I use my sleeve instead. She turns off the interstate at our exit, points the car toward town, and says, "I'm betting on the theater, or that big church next door to it. Ve go there, yes?"

"Yes."

"And if this Paul or David shows his face, either the police get him, or ve get him." She lifts one hand off the wheel and makes a throat-cutting gesture.

"Yes."

"You know, vhere I am from, people are very poor. People vant out, they vant to come here to the U.S. more than anything." She pops her hand against the steering wheel. "For years, it has been this vay."

I've heard her say this before, so I nod.

"Now, vith Internet, this type of thing—and vorse—happens to girls, all the time. You can't imagine." She glances at me. "Or maybe, maybe you can. If people vant a thing to be true badly enough, it makes them open. Like a veakness. It makes them prey for bastards like this. Vherever there is prey, there are predators."

"Please don't say I'm just a victim, that it's not my fault."

"I vould never insult you like that. You are too old, too smart. You have some responsibility, and much vork to do—vith your family, vith yourself." Another glance, this one more gentle. "But Chan Shealy, this is not all your fault. There are things you couldn't have known."

I'm about to argue with her when she starts talking again. "Going over the mountaintop blaming yourself, it's not helpful, to you, to Lauren. It vill only make things more difficult. It vould be . . . selfish. You don't vant selfish now."

By the time we get to the church next door to the theater, my entire body's completely in a knot. I feel dizzy and sick and scared, and I can't stop shaking. There are cars everywhere, and two police cars with flashers going. Dad's SUV is parked sideways in the middle of the road, right in front of them.

My heart jumps at the sight. Then plummets. I'm so glad Dad's here, and so miserable, too. He must have gotten one of my messages and drove straight here, even faster than the Bear.

No less than one minute after we find a parking spot across the street and start to get out of the car, Mr. Macy and Devin screech to a stop behind Dad's SUV. She bails out of the passenger seat and runs straight toward me, tears flowing down her pretty, worried face.

I grip the old backpack and watch her come, not quite believing she's here.

Mr. Macy looks totally worried and stressed. He's come out of his tie, his suit jacket's off, and his sleeves are rolled up. He points to us, then at the Bear. "Put them in my car. Keep them there."

The Bear nods.

Mr. Macy turns and runs toward the church, toward the commotion that's all of a sudden spilling out the side door, only a few yards away from us.

Devin and I glance at each other once, break away from the Bear, and run after him.

The Bear shouts after us, and I know she's probably following. That's okay. That's fine. We're a lot faster than her, and I have to see Lauren and my parents. I have to see if Lauren's okay, if anyone's tried to bother her—and if so, if it's Paul.

We pump our arms hard.

Two policemen in uniforms come out of the church. They have a guy in handcuffs, and even without looking too close, I know it is Paul.

Paul.

My Paul.

My insides sort of crack and shift as I run, and I want to keep running and cry and scream and die all at the same time. My heart hurts, and my belly and my whole body.

It can't be him, but it is him, and he's here, being led away. He came here to meet Lauren. To meet my eight-year-old sister, for God's sake.

Paul.

Or whatever his name really is.

Paul with a majorly smashed nose and blood spilling all down his shirt.

Just then, he catches sight of me.

Our eyes meet.

And he smiles, just like he's smiled at me so many times, through the camera on my computer.

Only this time, instead of *I love you* or *You're so beautiful*, the smile says, *You won't tell on me. I know you. I know way too much about you.*

Circuits fry in my brain.

I go all hot-cold and stop running. Devin pulls up sharply beside me and seems to recognize Paul, too. She grabs me by the arm. "Oh, my God, Chan."

Paul's still smiling at me as the officers push him forward.

And I'm breaking. I'm broken. I don't care anymore about him or me or anything at all except my sister. As if Paul has any clue what's in it, I hold up the old pack and shake it back and forth.

Paul stares at the bag as he stumbles, propelled by the officers, and he seems to get it all of a sudden. What I might have in the bag. What I might be willing to expose in order to help my sister, even if it cooks me in the process.

The officers push Paul forward as Devin makes me lower the pack.

"What's in there?" she whispers, eyeing it like it might explode.

I answer her by starting to cry again and standing on my tiptoes to see where my family is.

Two more police officers come into view.

These two have hold of my dad, one on either side, obviously working to keep him away from Paul.

That's where Mr. Macy goes, straight to Dad, hollering about being Dad's attorney, and I see one of the police officers move aside to let Mr. Macy closer to Dad. Dad's face looks scary red and furious as he stares at Paul, and I can tell he's breathing hard.

Mr. Macy starts talking to Dad, and I wonder if he's telling Dad that killing Paul isn't worth the jail sentence.

From the look on Dad's face, somebody better be telling him that, for sure.

The Bear catches up with us and snatches hold of our shoulders before I can call out to Dad. "You don't need to be here. Come. Come back to the car."

"I want to see my dad," I say. "I want to see Lauren and my mom."

And when they walk Paul past me, I want to kick him right in the balls, just as hard as I can. And then I want to go home, get in my bed, cover up my head, and never, ever get out again.

"And you vill see your family. In a few minutes." The Bear's tone turns hard as rocks, and sharp, like when she's shouting at us in practice. "For now, the car. No arguing!"

Devin and I go back to Mr. Macy's sedan without arguing.

The Bear sits us down, dries my face with her sleeves, then pushes us into the car and slams the doors as media trucks and cameras start arriving. At her gestures, we duck down in the backseat, and she stands guard while I spill everything—and I mean everything—to Devin.

"This is so not real," Devin says in a quiet voice as she huddles against the driver's-side door. "Chan, I can't believe it's happening."

"I'm sorry." I lean against my door cradling my old backpack and close my eyes. "It's my fault. I'm the one who kept chatting with him. I'm the one who answered his e-mail messages."

"I told you to!"

"You did not. You told me not to talk to him, that his name was probably Merwood Spitball."

"I told you he was a dreamboat hunk—are we really about to fight over this?" She bangs her head against the door. "I'm sorry. All this time, you've been talking to him again and I didn't figure it out."

315

"Because I didn't tell you. Because I'm an ass."

"If you were really an ass, we'd both be twirling at Regionals right now."

I wish it could be that easy, but that redemption thing the Bear's been talking about, that's a long, long way off.

"Do you think he . . . you know, got Lauren?"

I squeeze the pack. "He got her, all right. I just don't know how bad yet. I don't think it's terrible—but it's awful enough, right?"

That makes me start crying again.

Devin doesn't say anything else. She just ooches across the car seat, wraps her arms around me, and lets me sob all over her warm-up suit.

A few minutes later, more police cars pull up and a group of officers come to the car and escort Devin, the Bear, and me inside the church. They put us in a room, and one officer, a blond-haired lady, tells me she has my mother's permission to talk to me as long as the Bear's in the room. The Bear declares she's not going *anywhere*.

Which makes me feel better in ways I can't even explain.

Then the officer talks to me about what's in the backpack.

I do my best to explain, half wishing I could die rather than admit it, but glad, too, I've got some kind of proof that might help my sister.

The officer makes a few notes on a pad, takes the

pack, and tells me they'll have to talk to me more later, when my parents can be with me.

"Am I going to jail now?" I blurt, still not entirely sure how all this works.

The officer looks surprised. "No. We don't want you in jail, honey. We're hoping you can help us put this man behind bars—not you. Can you do that, Chan?"

I glance at Devin and the Bear and take a deep breath. "Oh, yeah, I can do that. Now can you please tell me if my sister's okay? Did Paul—did that guy—did he—you know?"

"We don't think your sister has been harmed," she assures me. "Physically at least. Your dad got here a few minutes before we did, and he and your mother found Lauren in the bathroom. The suspect—er—the man was in there with her. He was trying to take Lauren out the window to his car."

Oh, God.

"Oh, God," Devin echoes.

The Bear says something in Russian.

"Can I see Lauren?" I wrap my arms around my stomach to hold on to myself, to keep my spinning brain more on Earth. "Please? I need to say—I need to tell her how sorry I am. I need to tell her, well, a lot of things."

"She's been taken to the hospital by ambulance," the officer tells me, giving my shoulder a squeeze. "Just to check her out, make sure she's fine, and get her some crisis counseling. Your dad's going with her—he needs a few stitches on those knuckles."

"Go, Mr. Shealy," Devin says.

Before I can ask my next question, the officer answers it. "As soon as your mother finishes her statement, she's coming here, and we're taking you guys"—her eyes sweep over the Bear and Devin, too—"all of you, in for the crisis intervention."

Somebody knocks on the door, and my stomach cramps so badly I clamp my teeth shut to keep from crying out.

The Bear goes to the door and opens it.

My mom runs into the room, glances at Devin, glances at the officer, then looks straight at me.

My stomach hurts worse. I hang my head and stare at the floor and wish I could just vanish. "I'm so sorry," I mumble, then keep saying it until Mom grabs me into a fierce, smothering hug.

She's crying and shaking, like me.

Confusion tangles my brain, but I hug her back.

She must not know what I've done, all that I've done. She must not have listened to her messages, what I said when I was freaking out.

I really don't even know what I told my parents in those messages, but I'm pretty sure it's everything. Anything to convince them to get to Lauren, to stay right with her.

When Mom does listen to those messages later,

when she finds out the truth . . . well, I'll deal with that later.

For now, I just hug her back and feel really glad Lauren's alive and safe, that Dad's okay, and that Mom's here in this room with me.

"Thank you," she whispers. "That was way past brave." Mom kisses the top of my head. "I'm so proud of you. Calling us, laying yourself bare like that for Lauren's sake. I've never been more proud of you in my entire life. You did the right thing."

I pull back and stare at her, absolutely not believing what she just said. "Mom. I did so many wrong things. I did this. I—"

Mom holds my face and presses her hands into my skin hard. Almost too hard. "Stop it. You made mistakes and we'll have to deal with that, but you didn't hurt Lauren. That sociopath did."

The Bear's earlier words come back to me, about not going "over the mountaintop" blaming myself and being selfish. I can see what she means, a little bit. If I keep freaking out, I'll suck up attention from my parents, and Lauren's the one who needs most of it right now.

That's the truth, the truth I need to hold on to for now.

So I shut up and keep hugging Mom, and a little bit later, we all go to the hospital just like the officer said we would.

THURSDAY, DECEMBER 18

TEEN HELPS BREAK CHILD PORN RING

LOCAL EIGHT-YEAR-OLD VICTIMIZED BY PEDOPHILE

PICTURES, VIDEOTAPES, AND CHAT LOGS, OH MY

The headlines never stop. Even when they die down, they come right back whenever there's another step in all the legal cases.

So I'm kind of shell-shocked.

Kind of blown up and bombed out and weird.

That's me. That's what my life is now.

And I'm in the kitchen on the phone with, of all people, Adam-P.

"I'm glad your mom lets you talk," he says. "On the phone. To me, I mean."

I don't tell him Mom's probably just glad he's under-age, or that she probably hasn't said one word to Dad about any of it. Instead, I say, "Yeah. Thanks for calling again," and draw pictures on the kitchen counter in some salt I spilled.

Adam-P broke up with Ellis the day she came home with all her trophies and ribbons from Regionals, but he's never told me why. I can't believe he's called once a day every day since everything happened. Maybe he feels bad. Maybe he thinks it's partly his fault. I don't know. And I'm not really sure why I'm talking to him, except he's being nice and he's not wanting anything from me.

Adam sounds sincere and concerned like he always used to. "When do you have to testify?"

I make a frowny face in the salt. "Sometime next year."

He grunts. "Sucks."

"Yeah." Did I ever really give Adam-P a book of love poems? Guys like Adam-P don't do love poems. I should have given him a football. Or maybe a new helmet and better pads, or whatever it is guys really like.

Still, brilliant and stimulating conversations aside, talking to him's okay. Sort of. For now, at least.

When Devin shows up, it's my excuse to say good-bye. She grabs my hand and drags me out of the kitchen.

So, four weeks, two major outbreaks, and a lot of crisis counseling sessions later, Devin and I sit in the living room at my house, staring at the blinking red, blue, green, and yellow lights on our Christmas tree. There are lots of presents underneath it.

But I bet all the money the police confiscated out of my Portal account that there aren't any computers in those boxes.

The computer that used to be in the living room, it's gone. There aren't any computers in our house anywhere. My parents even took out the landlines and went to cell phones only at home, and Lauren and I don't have one of those, either. That might have been a problem with our school assignments and extracurricular activities, except my parents pulled Lauren and me out of school and extracurricular activities, too, and Mom's home-schooling us for now. The only "extra" thing we get to do is private twirling lessons with the Bear, who comes over every Monday, Wednesday, and Friday afternoon.

Because of all our counseling, Mom's working on the concept of being "flexible." We all have concepts. Lauren's is "confident," Dad's is "consistent," and mine is "accountable."

Accountable isn't much fun.

I'm managing it, though, just like I'm managing the headlines and all the television coverage and the fact I still miss . . . well, not Paul.

Definitely not Paul.

"I guess I miss what I thought Paul was," I tell Devin when she asks. "That special romantic person in my life I can love and adore and totally trust, who loves and adores and totally trusts me."

"Well," she says, straight-faced, "I still don't want to put pearls on your titties or anything, but you can totally trust me."

I almost smile at that. "I know. I'm—"

"Don't say you're sorry again." She holds up her hand. "I'm saturated with I'm-sorry." Then she tells me that one day, when I'm ready, I'll find a good man to give me pearls and it sure as hell won't be Paul. "Or Adam-P, even if he's calling you all the time. The freak."

"He called twice yesterday," I mention before I forget and she finds out and I have to start over with saying I'm sorry.

"Oh. My. God." Devin gapes at me, holding her ankles with both hands. "What did he want?"

I shift my gaze back to the blinking lights and presents. "He just asked if I'm okay, if there's anything he can do."

After a few seconds, Devin says, "I heard he's still broken up with Ellis."

"I don't want Adam-P back, Devin."

"No way. I know you don't."

And I really don't think I do. The guy I want, maybe he'd be like Dad, a little bit. Kind and gentle and sweet, but with a mean nose-crushing punch when his babies get threatened. Or like Devin, loyal and brilliant and energetic, and always there, more than anyone else in my life has ever been there. Or maybe he'll even be a little like the Bear, tough and focused and talented—though I'd rather he do without the big white pickup truck.

"Have they grounded you yet?" Devin fiddles with the bow on the closest package, the one that just happens to have her name on it. "My dad grounded me for a week and keeps threatening to do it again even though I didn't *do* anything. Other than lose it on the bus and make him follow you and the Bear back to West Estoria."

"Your dad should see our counselor. She'll have him working on 'flexible,' too."

Devin snorts. "Yeah. I wish. Life without computers sucks, and I don't think he'll be getting over that one any time soon. But you—your parents *really* haven't grounded you?"

"Not yet. I kind of keep waiting, but it doesn't happen." I lean back against the couch, battling with that me-on-the-ceiling feeling. It's getting a little better, but it's still there. "Maybe all of that will come later, when they're finished being thrilled that Lauren and I are alive and here with them. I'm not sure I even care, really. I don't get to leave home much anyway."

"Honey, I wouldn't go looking gift equines in the mouth." Devin pushes her package around a little. "At least I get to come over, and we get to talk on the phone. I'm just glad Lauren's okay, and you're not insane anymore."

"I'm still insane." I glance upstairs, to where Lauren's sealed inside the Cave of Doom. She hasn't talked much since that day at the church, since everything blew up, and she's pretty furious with me, partly for leading "Paul"—his real name is actually Jim—to her, and partly for "telling on her."

Maybe it'll get better as time passes, as she gets treatment. Or maybe as she gets older. I wonder . . . but I also hope it can be that way.

As for the things Paul/Jim did to me, I still have trouble with my counseling for that. Trouble seeing myself as a victim. The counselor tells me that part of learning accountability is understanding what I am and am not responsible for, but that's way past hard.

"Are you sure you're not mad at me?" I ask Devin for like the millionth time.

She finally picks up the present with her name on it and shakes it. "I promise I'm not mad—if this is a good present."

"It's good." I hope she'll think so, even when she finds out it's two books of poetry. One's a brand-new Emily compendium she can take with her even if we don't get to go to the same college. The other book is my own poems, twenty of them I've handwritten over the last month, bound together with the best cover I could make, considering I have no computer.

She hugs her present close to her, eyes fixed on the tree's blinking lights. "I don't know how you've been standing it, with your private life all splashed like—like—"

"Like we splashed the 'Wild Dyke of Amherst' all over American lit?"

"Oh, now, don't start with that karma stuff again or I swear I'll take you straight to church."

I point toward the door. "Just go check our mailbox. We get plenty of offers to teach me religion every day, especially after those gossip shows started showing bits of the videos."

"Uh, yeah. I saw some of that." Devin shakes her present again. "When do you testify? I want to mark that on my schedule."

"Thanks, but I don't know. The trial's next year. When somebody tells me a date, I'll tell you."

"I think what you're doing is brave."

Brave.

I don't feel brave. I feel like a complete idiot and an even bigger ass.

I'm the girl who fed her little sister to an Internet predator.

Devin and I spend the rest of the afternoon talking, and that, at least, feels real and right and sort of normal. It does seem totally weird to have nothing else going on in my life, but also not so bad. Sometimes I get so bored I think my brain might melt, but other times, it's nice to just write poems or read them or sit in front of the Christmas tree and run my mouth.

After Devin goes home, I check in with Mom, who's working from home on her cell, a bunch of papers scattered in an arc around her on her bed. She waves at me. And she looks at me straight in the face, which still feels important.

Then I go to find Dad, who's in the basement playing

a video game where he has to out-dance the characters on the screen. Like, actually dance, crazy-fast, and keep up. I like that game, too, but he always does better than me, even if he still orders way too many pizzas. He gives me a hug and a kiss, then asks me in a quiet voice, "Will you check on Lauren?"

I frown and look at my feet, but agree to do it, which gets me another hug. Dad feels a little bit smaller when I have my arms around him. I wonder if he is, or if I just want him to be—but I hope he is.

The climb up the stairs to Lauren's cave feels long and hard, and with each step I move more slowly. This part's messed up, dealing with her, especially without my parents. I know I need to, that I owe her that.

So I knock on her door and wait for her to tell me to go away, like she usually does.

No answer.

I knock again. "It's just me. Let me see your face because I promised Dad I'd check on you, then I'll take a hike if you want."

I hear a rattle and the door opens a fraction. Lauren puts her face in the crack. She has smudges of green and purple on her cheeks and chin, and she looks at me just long enough to say "Take a hike."

Even though it hurts, I try to smile and I hold up both hands. "Okay, okay. Like I said, just checking. Let me know if you need anything."

Lauren closes the door.

If every single electronic anything hadn't been taken out of our house, and if my parents hadn't obsessively searched our rooms and monitored all incoming correspondences and packages—and if my dad hadn't bought this weird spy thing from WireShack that told him if any wireless device was broadcasting in our house—I might worry.

These days, Lauren's not doing anything on the Internet, or singing, or dancing. She's drawing. Charcoals and pastels, and sometimes now, a little bit of watercolor. I guess it's like poetry for me, something good for her, maybe a way she can talk when the words won't come any other way.

I head toward my room, but just then, her door opens again.

The sound makes me stop, but I don't know if I should turn around.

"Would you bring me a bottle of water?" Lauren asks. "I'm right in the middle of a lion's face, and I don't want to stop, but I'm thirsty."

"Okay." I opt not to turn around, but I go get her water and bring it back to her.

She opens the door when I knock and doesn't say anything nasty, and she takes the water when I offer it to her.

Then she thanks me.

And she doesn't say anything sharp or nasty before she closes her door again.

Not bad, I think as I look at the piece of wood separating me from my little sister. *That's actually progress, maybe?*

I decide to take it as progress.

Fetching water for Lauren lifts my spirits enough that I decide to go back to the basement and challenge Dad to a dance-game tournament. I know he'll probably whip my butt like he usually does, but I'm okay with that.

And I'm okay with hauling a *lot* of water up the stairs to my little sister, if that's what it takes.

Maybe I'll even try drawing, too, to go along with my poetry. Maybe one day, Lauren will let me teach her how to write a poem, and about Emily Dickinson, and about anything else I know that she might want to learn. If I'm really lucky, she'll ask me to tell her the princess story again.

Like with everything else Lauren-related, I wonder, but I also hope it can be that way.

Dad sees me coming and resets the game for two people.

I line up beside him and get into ready position, just like I do when the Bear drills me at twirling.

And . . . as of this week, the steps to win this video game. . . .

"You ready to lose again, Chan?" Dad's pink freckled cheeks stretch as he gives me a "gonna getcha" smile and rubs his hands together. "Because you know I'm the king of this game."

I smile at him, because it's impossible not to smile at my dad—even when I'm about to dance him into the carpet fibers. "Hit the button, Your Majesty. We'll just see who rules."

ACKNOWLEDGMENTS

I cannot write a book without thanking my intrepid critique partners. To Debbie Federici, for going over this a thousand times, I owe you, as usual. Thanks to Christine Taylor-Butler, Tara Donn, and Sheri Gilbert and anyone I may have forgotten who read this book and gave me feedback—I bow to you all.

To my agent, Erin Murphy, who kept encouraging me, I definitely needed it. To my spectacular editor, Victoria Wells Arms, thanks for your patience and belief. Special thanks to Brittany Jepson, PA, for her help with the medical details.

Finally, much appreciation to my family, who tolerated me during this writing process. I know that wasn't easy, guys. You rock.

Susan Vaught is the highly acclaimed author of *My Big Fat Manifesto*, *Trigger*, *Stormwitch*, the Oathbreaker saga, and a number of books for adults. She is a practicing neuropsychologist and lives with her family in Kentucky.

www.susanvaught.com

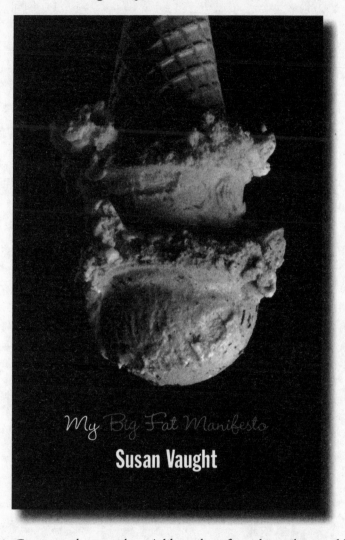

My Big Fat Manifesto

Susan Vaught

Jamie Carcaterra knows what it's like to be a fat girl in a thin world, and this year—her senior year—she's going to set the record straight.

"This zesty page-turner will hook readers with romance and energy."
—*Kirkus Reviews*

BACK TO SCHOOL SPECIAL EDITION
for publication Wednesday, August 8

Fat Girl Walking

JAMIE D. CARCATERRA

I am so sick of reading books and articles about fat girls written by skinny women. Or worse yet, skinny guys. Tell me, what in the name of all that's creamy and chocolate do skinny guys know about being a fat girl?

The fat girl never gets to be the main character. She never gets to talk, really talk, about her life and her feelings and her dreams. Nobody wants to publish books about fat girls, by fat girls, or for fat girls, except maybe diet books. No way.

We're not even supposed to mention the word *fat* in print, because we might get accused of supporting "overweightness" and contributing to the ongoing public health crisis in this country [insert hysterical gasp here], or because we might cause an eating disorder.

To heck with all of that.

I'm a fat girl!

And I'm not just any fat girl. I'm *the* Fat Girl, baby. I'm a senior, and I by God do own the world this year, so put that on ice and gulp it down. I'm *The Wire*'s new feature—the Fat Girl Manifesto. I'm large. I'm loud. Go big or go home!

Let me shoot down a few myths right now, before you even set up a stereotype:

Myth Number One. Speak gently to poor Fat Girl. She can't help her terrible disability. Okay, bullshit. I'm not chubby. I'm not chunky. I'm not hormonally challenged or endocrine-disordered. I do not prefer platitudes like "large" or "plus sized," or clinical words like *obese*.

I'm fat, fat, fat. If the word makes you uncomfortable, that's your problem. Go to www.naafa.org and get a *real* education. Yeah, that's right. The National Association to Advance Fat Acceptance. *F-A-T*. That's the word. Get used to it. Get over it. I have to. Every single day of my life.

Myth Number Two. Poor Fat Girl needs to be educated about her problem. Even more caca, this time on toast. I'm not clueless about nutrition and exercise or waiting for that wonderful aha moment to motivate me to "lose weight." I know how to eat. I know how to exercise.

Guess what? I'm still fat, and blond, with so-so skin and big feet, just like my mom, my dad, and most of my relatives. We're the Fat Family. Or the Blond Bombers. Maybe the Psoriasis Clan? Oh, wait. The Bigfeet. Actually, we're the Carcaterras, and we don't apologize for taking up two seats on airplanes. Well, my mom does, but she apologizes for everything, so don't take that too seriously.

Myth Number Three. Poor Fat Girl laughs to hide her tears. More and more poop just piling up in the corner. I'm not a jolly round person. I'm a peevish, sarcastic, smart, dramatic round person. I'm larger than life. I've had roles in Garwood's stage productions all four years of high school. I'm playing Evillene in *The Wiz* this year, and the role sooo suits me. I helped start our cable channel that my friend Frederica—Freddie—Acosta anchors now. I'm *The Wire*'s feature editor. When Fat Girl laughs, it's because something's funny. Usually something *I* said.

Myth Number Four. Poor lonely Fat Girl can't get a date. Big blare from the bullshit sensor. My boyfriend's name is Burke Westin, he's a starting tackle on our championship football team, and we clear the floor at every dance.

Being fat isn't always like those sappy

after-school specials and snot-rag sob books. Not every fat person is twisted up about how their outsides don't match their insides.

Myth Number Five. All poor Fat Girl wants to do is lose weight. So not true. Fat Girl has a to-do list almost as big as her beautiful body. It goes something like this: Don't wonk the math section this next (and last) time you take the ACT, keep Burke happy, meet one thousand senior-related deadlines, play practice, and, oh yeah, the biggest one of all—finish college and scholarship applications.

Now we can get to the point. Why am I printing my manifesto in the school newspaper?

Pop quiz! No, don't panic. It's multiple choice:

A. I'm running for homecoming queen.
B. I want you to testify for me when I go postal on some stick-figure supermodel or that freak pedaling his exercise machines on late-night infomercials.
C. I want the world to get a clue about life as a Fat Girl, from a Fat Girl's perspective.
D. I want to win the National Feature Award, for "outstanding journalism

promoting the public well-being," a scholarship to the journalism program of my choice. My family doesn't have much dough, so that's the *only* way I'm taking the big ride to higher education. Otherwise it's work a job and take a few classes at a time. I want the scholarship!

E. All of the above.

F. None of the above.

G. Don't you wish you knew.

H. Hint: It's not A.

I. Hint, hint: It might be B. Depends on the night—and the supermodel.

J. Hint, hint, hint: C's a really good bet. But then again, so is D. In fact, D's major.

I'll give you reports on what Fat Girl has been up to, and I'll answer the questions you send to fatgirlscholarship@gmail.com. Write to Fat Girl and send her to college!

Come on. You know you want to do it.

CHAPTER
ONE

I have two must-achieve-or-die goals this year.

The first do-or-die is probably the easiest: Write the best Fat Girl feature series ever, expose the politics and social injustices of being a fat female in today's world, and win the National Feature Award to ensure my collegiate funding.

The second do-or-die, related to the first, is earning admission to Northwestern University. I would, of course, accept the University of North Carolina–Chapel Hill or one of the other amazing journalism/mass com programs in the country, but I'd rather be at Northwestern. As for the entrance application, Fat Girl plans to win them over, freak them out, or both. No matter what, I'll bring my fatness to the table as an issue, instead of as an auto-reject stamped across my application.

A third task, not a do-or-die, and probably the hardest, is surviving the absurd number of deadlines pitched at my head, all because I'm a senior.

For openers, there are deadlines for class papers and

assignments, deadlines for ordering our special senior edition yearbook, deadlines registering for the last-gasp ACT, deadlines for registering for the way-past-last-gasp ACT, deadlines for signing up for homecoming committees, deadlines set by those homecoming committees, deadlines for buying homecoming game and dance tickets, deadlines for filing intent to graduate, deadlines for ordering graduation invitations, deadlines for cap and gown measurements, deadlines for ordering class rings, deadlines for Senior Shoot, deadlines for senior pics, deadlines for early college applications, and deadlines for regular college applications.

And all of those deadlines happen *before friggin' Christmas*.

It's insane. But I'm a senior. Insanity must become my mantra.

Never mind the whole grades-still-count-until-Christmas thing.

Or the fact that my advanced biology and calculus grades are so not in the bag.

English IV and theater I could do in my sleep, and the rest is journalism. Piece of Fat Girl cake there, except for the midnight cram-the-paper-together sessions, then speeding it one hour south across the state line to get it printed at a cut-rate little print shop.

I'll be getting to do the paper run again this year, since I didn't make editor-in-chief. Nope. Of course not. The good-looking guy got that role. Heath Montel. His family's known for being old-money rich. His mother's on the school board, and he's always been immune to the standards the rest of us have to meet. Oh, and he's not fat.

Neither is our journalism sponsor. No real surprises there. I think Ms. Dax really just likes to watch Heath bend over the drafting tables.

As people go, though, Heath's not so bad, even for a rich, handsome type. He's just...a little weird. Kind of a loner. And I've done the paper with him so long it's like working with my own shadow. At least I snagged feature editor, which looks reasonably good on my NC–Chapel Hill application and gives me a full–bore shot at the NFA.

Know what Heath said about my first Fat Girl feature?

Good work, Jamie. But maybe you shouldn't have started so strong. That'll be hard to top.

No, seriously. He said that.

All he needed was a cigar, tweed pants, and sus-penders, and Heath would have looked just like some 1950s version of Perry White from the *Superman* comics.

Okay, he's more than a little weird. He's hugely weird.

Editor–in–chief might be swelling Heath's pretty head, too, but I absolutely do not have time to worry about him, or about the fan mail and hate mail and question mail beginning to pour in after Fat Girl's first big rant. I barely have time to check on my best friends Freddie and NoNo, breathe, pee between classes, and stick to the senior obligations schedule I lovingly drafted for Burke and me.

. . .

"Burke!" I shove my way down Building Two's crowded hall at my lunch period, keeping my eyes fixed on the broad shoulders and thick dreads marking Burke at his locker.

Did he just flinch?

Oh, not good.

I slow down. Two scrawny freshmen bounce off my right arm, glance at me stricken with total fear, and flee into the crowd before I can grab either of them by their braided brown hair.

"Burke?" A little closer now, and he's definitely flinching. *Damn* it. What's wrong? Did he fail another earth science quiz? Because if he did, his average will suck and he won't be eligible to play next Friday and . . .

It seems like half the two thousand students at Garwood High are trying to cram into Building Two's hall, all at the same time. Wall-to-wall backpacks, blue jeans, chattering, hollering, hair gel, and sweat. Somebody has on bubblegum lip gloss, too. Gag. Bubblegum lip gloss would be illegal if I ran the world.

When I reach Burke, he turns to face me, but he only looks at me for two seconds before he hangs his head.

Big trouble.

His dark eyes, they usually sparkle. Today, they look like flat black plates.

I put my hand on his arm and squeeze. "What's wrong?"

He says nothing.

"Burke?" I scoot closer and try to look up at him.

This makes him grin, but the grin slides away. I have to push up on my toes to give him a kiss on his smooth, sexy cheek. Can't do more in the hallway, even though I'm Fat Girl, and I'm a senior. Our school's liberalism doesn't extend to sucking face in public. Garwood has a zero tolerance policy on all things sex, sexual, or even remotely physical between males and females. The way the ban's written, though, two lesbians or two gay guys could go at it naked and, technically, they wouldn't be breaking any rules at all. Nobody's tried that yet, but I've been offering to pay Freddie to give it a go.

"Come *on*." I bump Burke with my belly, glance around for teachers, then snuggle up to him. His arm drapes around my shoulder, and I love how heavy and possessive it feels. "It can't be *that* bad." Then, yelling over the squealing, screeching, teeming masses, "Right? Tell me it's not that bad."

"I'm grounded," Burke yells back.

Every single muscle in my body goes tight.

I didn't hear that. Can't be. Not possible.

Before I can say anything, Burke hangs his big head all over again, then bangs it against his already dented red locker.

I stare at him, feeling something like inferno mixed with ice storm. "No. Way."

Jersey Hatch doesn't know why
his best friend hates him.

He doesn't know how to keep random words
from flying out of his mouth.

And he doesn't know why he tried to shoot his own head off.

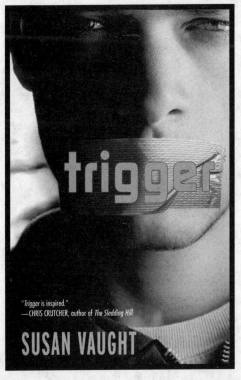

"*Trigger* is inspired."
—CHRIS CRUTCHER, author of *The Sledding Hill*

SUSAN VAUGHT

★ "Both engrossing and excruciating. . . . An original and meaningful
work that provokes thought about action, consequence,
redemption, and renewal." —*Booklist*, starred review

www.susanvaught.com
www.bloomsburyteens.com

BLOOMSBURY

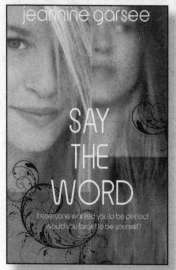